BREAKI RUM CLUB

An Ezekiel Novel

D Malone McMillan

ISBN:
ISBN 978-1-7320062-0-1 (paperback)
ISBN 978-1-7320062-1-8 (epub ebook)
ISBN 978-1-7320062-2-5 (epub mobi/kindle)

To my immortality: Gabriel, Andrew, Addison, Emma Grace, Davis, and a player(s) to be named later. Perhaps someday your parents will see fit to allow you to read your Papi's drivel.

"There were giants in the earth in those days; and also after that, when the sons of God came in unto the daughters of men, and they bear children to them…

Genesis 6:4

"And it came to pass when the children of men had multiplied, that in those days were born unto them beautiful and comely daughters.
And the Angels, the children of the heaven, saw and lusted after them and said to one another: Come, let us choose us wives from among the children of men to beget us children."

Enoch 6:1 and 2

PROLOGUE

This is the moving, true story of an African-American, transgendered teenager who, through unyielding grit, overcame crushing odds, discrimination, corporate greed, and corruption, flat-earthers, climate change deniers, and fascist republicans, to single-handedly reverse global warming, resolve income inequality, abolish childhood obesity, and shatter the glass ceiling, all while providing loving care to an elderly, aids-stricken Klansman, despite the Grand Wizard's daily racial and homophobic rants. Nah. This is none of that shit. This is the ending of the beginning of my story. Sit for a spell. Mine is a funny story, albeit one that, quite frankly, should scare the hell out of you.

Most people of my advanced age look back on their life like distinct chapters from a well-worn book. Some chapters a bit more exciting, some a bit painful, others just long and uneventful, yet still a singular book written in a linear fashion. Unique chapters punctuate periods of one's life, often giving the surreal, disquieting feeling one's very life story is dissociated from oneself. Maybe it's just me, but it is almost as if someone else lived those memories; or perhaps they are false memories planted by a mischievous garden gnome, or, then again…merely dreams. Perhaps our life book is a familiar story based on a real life but not just one's own personal history.

Here is where I am the exception, the anomaly if you will. My story is not a singular, linear book. It is not a trilogy, a series, or even the life's work of a prolific writer. My story would strangle the stacks of the most cavernous of stone-walled Carnegie. I assume the infinite stories filling my head to belong in the fiction section. An outcome, no doubt, due to a defect of birth. The creation of a poorly-wired brain or conceivably a series of unintended falls or intended shakes at a tender age. Hobo, my ethereal vagrant and sporadic, uninvited confederate, gives assurance my stories are of the non-fiction variety. Then again, I am at a complete loss to explain Hobo and am uncertain if he himself is not a product of my propensity to combine copious amounts of dark liquor with high quality pharmaceutical drugs. An unintended consequence of my futile strategy to keep the mischievous gnomes, Cherubs and devils that haunt me at bay and my tentative grasp on reality, at least partially, intact.

Of a somewhat more disquieting nature, my stories are not linear. Each individual story tends to fold upon itself in time, intersecting on occasion with other stories while running parallel, perpendicular, or any of the other infinite, tangential angles in between. There is no order and it can be maddening for me and the ever-narrowing circle of those unfortunate enough to give a damn about me.

Like most others, my stories remain implausibly autobiographical in nature. And like others, when telling our story, we tend to lean toward a favorable bias of the main character... ourselves. I would like to say I am unbiased. That would be my first lie. I will promise at least a half-ass attempt to keep the favorable bias to the barest of minimum. Off we go.

Hi, my name is Ezekiel, Zeke for short. I am the grandson of sharecroppers and the son of a house painter. Dad was a bit of a religious zealot. A bit much like in the sense Charles Manson was bit of a homicidal nut. I dropped my stones in the shadow of a Missionary Baptist church in the late sixties. Jesus, Milk of Magnesia, and Castor oil were the cure-alls of my generation. Wholly useless remedies for my malady. Shrinks, not that they would have helped, were off the table for many reasons. Today if I darkened the door of a learned shrink, he/she/it might diagnose me as a bipolar with schizophrenic tendencies. I felt shit hard, real hard, generally on the down side. Darkness was my frequent companion. Mom, she called me moody. Dad called me a snotty-nosed little sissy and set about to toughen me up. When Dad caught me balling, without the benefit of obvious compound fractures or free-flowing arterial wounds, he would punish me by having me wear one of my older sister's dresses.

Once I teared up at a half-squashed kitten in the macadam road just up the hill from our asbestos-shingled house. Dad pulled our Ford pickup over onto the narrow shoulder of the road surface, halfway into the ditch. He motioned for me to get out of the truck. I stumbled out, landing one converse into the putrid water laying still at the bottom of the ditch. Dad produced a shovel from the rusty bed of the truck and held it out toward me. Shaking in anticipation, I reluctantly took the offered weapon.

The kitten lay writhing in pain in the dust of the road, it's matted fur stuck in the partially melted tar. In all fairness to Dad, the kitten was a lost cause. Killing the miserable creature was a gift. But hell, I was eight years old. A tender achievement for a heartless executioner. Dad impatiently motioned for me to swing the shovel. The kitten looked at me, pleading. Sweat poured down my closely shorn head and into my eyes. I was determined not to cry but the sweat burned my eyes. Swiping my forearm across my forehead to clear the sweat, I heard the all too familiar sound of Dad sliding his belt through his starched work pants. Whispering, "I'm sorry," I brought the shovel down hard against the kitten's tiny head.

Against my feeble objections, we left the kitten in the middle of the road. "Got not time for that silliness. Vultures gotta eat, too." Somehow this indignity felt more wrong than anything.

Dad's life lesson failed to toughen me up suitably and, as such, he intensified his campaign. Playing sandlot baseball, my friends and I found a litter of baby rats in the empty lot across from our house. Their mama was nowhere to be found. I stole some milk from our fridge to feed them and Dad, curious, covertly followed me over.

He howled in disgust upon seeing the rats. "Damn it to Jesus, I have raised a pussy." Pussy was a new word for me. I wasn't sure what it meant, but based on context clues, I assumed it was an undesirable thing, along with God's eternal damnation, shit and hell. Dad rarely cussed and never took our Lord and Savior's name in vain. This was not a good omen.

Dad gathered the baby rats and placed each in turn on a fire ant hill. My friends all scurried home. He held my head in his rough hands and forced me watch them die slowly, writhing in agonizing pain, kicking with the toe of his paint-splattered boots any of the poor, wretched creatures that escaped the hill back onto it.

The summer nights in South Georgia were warm and humid. Sweat pooled in my belly button as I waited for Dad to fall asleep. I weren't gonna abandon those wretched baby rats to the vultures like I had the kitten. Guilt was more powerful than the fear of my Dad. Slipping out the window, careful to make no noise, I ran across the street to the empty lot. There I gathered the creatures' bodies, swollen and bloated, into a paper lunch sack and hurried back to a corner in our backyard under an old native, pine tree. With a stick, I scraped out seven small holes in the loamy soil between the roots. I buried each of the creatures in their own tiny grave, placing a thin sheet of toilet paper over each one as a tiny shroud before filling the graves with the fresh earth. I hurried to retrieve some marble tile salvaged from a rubble pile at a nearby construction site and stowed beneath our frame house. Stealth was critical. Dad would beat me for sure if he found me. There were only six pieces of marble. As such, I placed a small marble marker on six of the graves. I adorned the seventh grave with my prized arrowhead I fished from the pocket of my cut-off jean shorts.

Kneeling, I prayed to Jesus to give the baby creatures a good home. I was more than a bit confused if animals went to heaven. I asked my Sunday school teacher. He said it was a silly question and didn't offer an answer. Even at eight, I was pretty sure my teacher didn't have a real clue. God wasn't just a mystery to us children. Adults pretended to know God, but they didn't. I did know animals deserved a darn site better than they got and deserved entry into them pearly gates more than most humans. It was an early test of my faith. Why my

God, an all-powerful and just God, did not intervene on them rats' behalf? They were babies and never had done anyone no harm. It broke my heart to think there was someone that could end evil and suffering and just chose not to.

Still so, I believed in God. Well, a creator for sure. Just not exactly the omniscient, all-powerful, just God my Dad praised with extended arm. Never could get my arms around that dude like he could. The whole suffering of innocents bit. Who knew baby rats could teach such a powerful lesson. I drink a lot now trying to keep my demons, Cherubs, and garden gnomes at bay. I see shit I don't want to see. But now, just a few pages in, and I am repeating myself. It's not all bad, the dreams, that is. I just can't tell what belongs in this world or another.

Time, you see, I have come to believe, is the conscript of us mere mortals. A lame invention to measure something, quite frankly, unmeasurable. A quantity without beginning or end...just a now. Think of time as another religion. A set of agreed upon lies that helps us sleep at night by giving definition, if only a false one, to concepts beyond our grasp. We glide through this life, self-assured we are the grand masters of our universe, yet blissfully bathed in a giant cesspool of ignorance. With each new scientific discovery, we reveal only greater helpings of our infinite pool of ignorance. Each step forward amounts to thousands of steps backwards; consequently, the flat-earthers of only a few centuries past were relative geniuses to modern day scientists, at least to their breath of ignorance.

Oh, shit! I promised you a funny story. And then...

New York City; January 2017: *Barack Obama, the former President of the United States will be sworn in as Secretary General of the United Nations this afternoon. Obama is seen by the global community as the ideal candidate to unite our planet under one world order. Obama's appointment of O'Grady as vice-president and Obama's subsequent presidential abdication, elevating O'Grady to the presidency prior to being confirmed by the Senate, has left the American political leadership system in major disarray at an inopportune time.*

Congress continues to refuse confirmation of a new Supreme Court Justice until it completes an investigation of Justice Scalia's mysterious death, leaving the court deadlocked with eight justices. The President-Elect, Hillary Clinton, was indicted shortly before Election Day for money laundering, not registering as a foreign agent and accessory to murder of three of her own staffers. President O'Grady has refused to vacate the office until after Clinton's case is cleared.

GOP Senate Majority Leader Senator Manny Rodrigues from New Mexico called the situation a, "Mexican Standoff." Thousands of black-clad, white college students have surrounded his office on the Hill calling for Rodrigues' resignation over the inflammatory racist remarks.

Alongside Global News

CHAPTER ONE

Waldo was restless and started licking Sue's face. It was after 8 am and he needed to pee. Wiener dogs have small bladders. Sue reached over to nudge her common law husband Brad only to discover he was not in bed. She lit a smuggled Canadian cigarette before trudging into the living area. American cigarettes were a prized passion among the smoking community in San Pedro. Canadian cigs came in a close second. Belizean smokes fell outside the ranking.

Brad was lying face down on the tile floor in the living room, adjacent to a pool of vomit tainted with blood and chunks of undigested corn. Then again, does corn ever really digest? He was unconscious and, based on the swelling and discoloration of his face, comatose was not an undesired state. We really should have taken him to the island's clinic the previous evening. I feigned

1

sleep from the comfort of the recliner that I was sharing with our asymmetrical rescue dog Jaws. Settlement as to who rescued who remains hotly contested.

Jaws cautiously stepped off the recliner, making certain to stomp on my privates, and stretched. Downward facing dog, he farted and ambled to the front door. Even Black Labs have urgent morning bladders. One of the downsides of dog ownership is toilets existing out of doors...if you are lucky.

"One of you rat bastards is waking the hell up and walking the hell down with me." Sue cursed a lot. She was crazy smart, yet insisted in salting every sentence with damn, shit, hell, piss, or fuck. The whole vulgarity is the crutch of the ignorant rule didn't apply to Sue. She was the fabled exception that proved the rule. Sue, like my wife Rose, was a small woman with a large mouth. The kind of woman that get their male escorts in frequent fisticuffs. Fortunately, I am an old man. And you can't win a fight with an old man...unless you are another old fart. And I had a fair shot of winning that fight or, at least, out-running another old dude. We old farts are not known for our speed, endurance, or ability to maintain an erection. Then again, us old guys rarely fight. It hurts way too much the next day, week, month. Pfizer, thankfully, has improved our capacity on the latter recreational activity.

Brad was not so fortunate, if being old has its fortunes. Brad was certainly more a lover than a fighter. Tall and thin with a quick wit, he loved to experience life at its fullest. He was open, friendly, and generally well-liked. His adage was to "live fast and die young" ensuring he would make a pretty corpse. Smart money placed their bets with Brad realizing his melancholic objective.

Sue and Brad shared a four-story walk up in downtown San Pedro. The building was on Front Street and sat above a series of small bars, tchotchke shops, grocery marts, and liquors stores. The back of the apartment overlooked the town's colorful walled cemetery that peculiarly fronted the beach, populating prime real estate with those holding little appreciation of the stunning view. San Pedro's breathing populace during season was half tourist, one-fourth locals, and one-fourth expats. Expats were mostly Canadian or American, Brad and Sue were the former, Rose and I the latter.

Lola's was one of the small bars positioned under their apartment building. It was a small sports bar catering to expats. Next to Lola's was a larger bar, popular with some of the more colorful of the village's locals and the occasional inebriated, ill-informed tourist or the well-informed, drunken ones looking to get laid or score some stank weed. The previous evening, Lola's had been packed with a crowd watching the Sweet 16 basketball tournament on the big screen sets that lined the bar's walls. It was tourist season and both bars were packed, creating a dangerous brew of the three distinct demographics in the resultant crowd spilling into the narrow street.

Brad sauntered up to the mahogany bar to order Fireball shots. He wedged himself between two female tourists. You knew he was getting drunk when he switched to imported liquor. Stay local and you could live cheaply in San Pedro. And that meant several varieties of pretty good Rum or the local Belikin brew. Four nicely tanned and shapely cheeks enticingly peeked out from the minuscule thong bottoms. With every season, the suits shrank, and the breasts grew. Time is a cruel judge. Future generations will make judgment based solely on their generation's whimsical fancies of truth, of right and of wrong, and the ubiquitous selfie will stand as enduring evidence to our actions. The pendulum always turns.

3

The tourist chicks wore matching sandals and tight-fitting t-shirts. The bikini tops had been surrendered for cosmetic purpose and, based on the pleasant presentation, both shared the same talented plastic surgeon. Context clues further suggested it was chilly. It was not. The shirts were cropped, displaying matching tramp stamps: a bulldog pissing on a gator. The contextual clues at hand suggested they were mother and daughter but not one of a conventional relationship. Brad was in no hurry.

Golf carts lined the narrow road outside. The roads had all been recently paved with concrete pavers but very few cars were on the island. Deuce, a native to the island, was occupied with providing cursory, unsolicited cleaning of the parked carts. He was a lanky man with an unnaturally erect posture. His head and face were partially covered with random tuffs of wiry white hair. He was the island version of the city windshield cleaner in traffic. He seemed harmless enough and was well-known to Sue.

Deuce was the founding member of what Sue had coined The Breakfast Rum Club. If he or any member of the club was awake he was in a drunken state. It was in their unwritten bylaws. Deuce had a single eye the color of the Caribbean Sea. The second eye was missing, and he made no attempt to cover the scarred-over socket. In sum, his appearance was somewhat ethereal.

"The Pineal Gland," Deuce said to me without looking up. Oddly, his voice carried effortlessly over the mayhem of the bar. I guess I had been staring. The entirety of the width of the bar front was open to the street.

I thought, "WTF" but made no attempt to be heard over the din of the bar. I then immediately thought "WTF" is wrong with me for thinking in textual language.

"Your third eye, Zeke," Deuce again responded without looking up from his task at hand.

4

I slid my stool back and walked out to the street to attempt a normal conversation. Deuce held out his hand and smiled. He had perfect, brilliantly white, movie star teeth. They shown against his blackness, casting a shadow behind their target. He didn't ask verbally for a tip, but it was the universal gesture. I gave him $5 BZ half again translated to U.S. currency.

"What about my third eye?" I asked.

He smiled broadly and moved on to the next cart. "Mr. Zeke, I may not be school educated like you Americans, but I am pretty sure most of us be having two eyes." He lifted his head up and smiled again, displaying his empty socket. "There are exceptions, but they generally be for one eyeball, not three."

He finished with the second cart and held his hand out again. I fished into my pocket for another bill. I only had a ten. I hesitated. Deuce added helpfully, "That'll do just fine."

Sue walked out and embraced Deuce. His face lit up. She was a nonjudgmental woman and generous with her tips and snarky retorts. It was smart to have friends on the street. Not that that was the purpose behind her generosity. The entirety of The Breakfast Club looked out for Sue. She could walk freely alone in the dead of night knowing someone had an eye out for her wellbeing. Singular and inebriated, perhaps, but an eye nonetheless. I walked back inside. I couldn't afford this conversation.

"Where in the hell did you go?" Rose asked as I squeezed in beside her on the bench. Brad was still at the bar and Rose was fending off the drunk tourists solo.

"Chatting with the founder of the Breakfast Rum Club," I answered just as Kentucky scored the winning goal in double overtime against Duke. The crowd roared, drowning out my response. There was a contingent of drunken fans of both teams at Lola's.

"What?" Rose asked.

I cupped my ear and shrugged.

"Did you manage to order my tomato soup and grilled cheese?" Rose shouted above the noise. Lola's was peculiarly well-known for this classic kid's lunch meal. Toddlers, old people and drunks tend to lean to similar behavioral characteristics.

I shook my head no and Rose stood. She was a bit irritated with me. A not uncommon state. She had wanted to go home earlier. Rose taught at a local elementary school on the island. She was the only one of us that had a job and a schedule. We drunks erroneously believe we are a blast to be around but those of a more sober state tend to disagree. At this point, Rose strongly disagreed. Rose grabbed my arm to stop me and fished the golf cart's keys out of her backpack, pointed at Brad still at the bar, and said "You need to do something about that before Sue sees him. Later. Take a cab, asshole." The "asshole" was unspoken but well communicated.

A growing pyramid of shot glasses stood in front of Brad and the mother-daughter duo. Both of his hands were currently occupying choice real estate on each of their bums, gently squeezing as if testing the ripeness of a peach. "No bueno," I said to no one.

"That son of a bitch better not be buying." Sue joined me at the table before I had time to intervene. Sue was not the type to display jealously but I had a feeling this was going to be a bad night for Brad.

Without prelude, rapid blasts in the street echoed off the storefront walls. Sue and I clicked glasses. San Pedro is a great place to visit and not a bad place to live. It is prudent to be home before midnight and never, ever visit San Pedrito on the other side of the airport's runway. With strict gun laws and the early hour, we calculated firecrackers, not gunshots. We calculated wrong.

Dozens of people from the street and the neighboring bar started pouring into Lola's, overcrowding what was already beyond its Fire Marshall quota of people. I make myself giggle at times. No Fire Marshal. People kept pouring in. A volatile mixture of locals, hookers, and independent pharmaceutical reps squeezed into every available inch of floor space, knocking tables over and spilling drinks. I stood on the bench to get a glimpse of the street. Dozens of serious looking GSU officers stood with assault rifles pointed toward several figures prone in the sandy street.

"GSU?" Sue asked. I nodded yes. "No bueno," Sue added.

The local San Pedro police are a friendly, honest, well-meaning sort. Pretty much leave tourists and locals to their own devices, turning a blind eye to most petty crime and, on occasion, choosing to be conveniently inept at solving crimes involving locals. San Pedro is a small island with a population of about 13,000 people. Take out the expats, and it leaves less than 9,000 locals. The police, as such, are pretty much kin to or are friends with every single local, never more than two degrees of separation. Not judging. This shit happens in the U.S., as well.

Now, the GSU, The Gang Suppression Unit, these guys are run by the state and are from the mainland. They are bad asses and to be toyed with only at one's own peril. Uncle Pedro cannot save your ass from their brand of policing. Crazy ass McAfee can attest to the no-nonsense policing of the GSU.

The local drug and sex entrepreneurs tried to blend with the expat/tourist crowd of Lola's to avoid being swept up in whatever madness the GSU was conducting. A plus-size hooker in a petite size dress bellied up to the bar beside Brad and his two new best friends. She, in the process, knocked Brad's shot glass pyramid to the ground, shattering several of the glasses. The glass ricocheted off the concrete floor and sliced the daughter's foot. Blood ran freely from the flesh wound.

"Bitch," She screamed.

"Whore," the hooker ironically retorted.

Then shit got real. The mom took a poorly conceived and ill-executed swing. Alcohol falsely encourages white girls they are on an even plane with ladies of color in the dancing, carnal, and fighting sciences. The hooker ducked. Brad did not. Chaos ensued. Sue and I headed for the exit. "What about Brad?" I offered as we were safely in the street.

"Let his new girlfriends take care of him."

The GSU officers confronted with the crowd pouring out of Lola's roughly pushed us to the far side of the street. I stumbled over one of their suspects and face-planted by the prone, shirtless figure. On his arm was a familiar, burnt-in tattoo of remarkable detail. It was a Panther Paw. The logo of the New Black Panthers. I knew this guy. He was Khalid Muhammad.

∞∞∞∞

There is no disgrace in surrender or so I, along with the French, tell ourselves to protect our self-esteem. Sue stood poised impatiently at the door with one hand on her hip, Waldo in her other arm, and Jaws at her feet nervously prancing. His version of the pee-pee dance. Sue was priming to release a stream of expletives to inspire one of us to get moving. Brad was not an option. With a blinding headache, I reluctantly surrendered to my inevitable fate and stumbled down the eighty-seven flights to the ground floor of her four-story apartment building with Sue and the assembled beasts. Perhaps I exaggerate; it is my nature. Thanks, Mom.

Stale cigarette smoke, urine, and cheap rum smells announced the presence of the Breakfast Rum Club. It was a bit chilly, damp, and windy and the BRC had moved their meeting from inside the confines of the picturesque cemetery to the graffiti decorated stairwell. "Morning, boys."

"Morning, Miss Sue," Deuce responded to Sue. He gave me an almost imperceptible head nod which I returned in kind. The other club members likewise nodded and continued drinking rot gut rum from the bottle without offering to share. I was okay with that. Other than Deuce, the four of them together could not assemble a solitary ration of teeth.

"Where's Tarbaby?" Sue asked.

Deuce nodded toward the graveyard. "In the yard wit' his girl."

Ambergris Caye is coral island elevated from the seas by scant few centimeters. About 500 meters offshore is the second longest living barrier reef in the world. Without said reef, the island would be an underwater feature of the mainland. Consequently, there is precious little fresh water on the island, but the salt water table is just a few feet below the sand. The local departed are entombed above ground in concrete block crypts. Many of the tombs were painted in bright Caribbean colors, giving the cemetery an anomalous festive atmosphere. Some of the tombs remain empty or partially occupied while others have been vandalized over time, exposing their skeletal guest to the favorable tropical view. The damaged tombs have been repurposed as convenient horizontal shelters for the Club to engage in the more carnal of their instinctual urges with a modicum of privacy, if not decorum. It's more than a bit disquieting to stroll the yard beholding two sets of opposing feet writhing in awkward unison with attending feral groaning.

9

Tarbaby's girl came out of the gate from the yard folding a $10 BZ. Tarbaby rented his love by the quarter hour. She smiled warmly at me. I shivered a bit. "Somebody walk on yo' grave, handsome?" She asked, running her long-painted nails across my stubble. She greeted Deuce sensually, "Morning, Deuce." Deuce nodded. "Where is that tall hunk of a man of yours?" She asked Sue.

Sue gave her a ten and the apartment key. "He be upstairs, honey. Go make his morning a special one."

I gasped. Deuce laughed. Waldo peed. Jaws farted.

We strolled over to the market across from Lola's to get me a soda. As we entered, Linus walked out.

Linus and his partner Lucy were midgets. Don't judge me. It's their word, not mine. I seriously doubted the Peanuts pairing's real names were Linus and Lucy, but they were the ones offered. The two had worked for Sony as code writers in the ground-breaking video game, The Garden of Eve. Yes, Eve, not Eden. The world building game let a creator create a world of their own making or step into history at any point in time. Most of the game's characters had free will but the creator could influence their actions. The game used actual social pages, web sites, and other real-world apps to interface with the creator. The game had been a huge hit for Sony but had not been without its controversies. The game blurred reality. People had been murdered, divorced, beaten, and robbed for things that had only happened within the virtual confines of the Garden.

After finishing the code, they both retired and purchased Lola's from an American expat. I had known them for only a few years, but somehow it felt I had known them since they were children. Many a night you would see one or both behind the bar. Like Sue, they were crazy smart and liked to party. "Morning,

Sue," Linus greeted. I got the nod. Everyone loved Sue and tolerated me.

"Morning, little man," Sue rubbed his head. He would have nut-shotted me had I tried.

"Uhhh..." Linus struggled getting his sentence started with Sue, "Hate to bother you."

"But I can see you still plan to," Sue finished. Why did everyone like her so much, I thought? She could really be a royal bitch at times.

"Brad..."

"What did that mother fucker do?"

"More like what did he not do?" Linus replied, rubbing his finger and thumb together in the universal sign for dinero.

"I knew it. That bastard was buying those sluts drinks. "I'm gonna stab his ass in the eyeball. No, too quick." She thought for a moment, "Columbian neck tie." I flashed back to the hooker she had given the keys and sent up to see Brad thinking she might have already accomplished the task of ending Brad's life. "Cuanto questa?" Sue asked Linus.

"Uhhh...Let's just round out at an even thousand."

"Belize?" Sue asked. The BZ dollar was tied to the U.S. dollar, two to one.

Linus shook his head no. "U.S."

"Mother fucker. Behead and Columbian neck tie his scrawny ass."

I foolishly injected "I think you have established that point already." There is a smart-ass that lives inside me. It should rest more often. Sue shot me an evil eye. I pondered the logistics of beheading and placing a tire around his neck absent his recently displaced head and subsequently setting it on fire. Seemed a bit complicated and overdone.

Pushing a rusted old beater bike with a mangy dog

in its basket, Tarbaby rolled up to us. I deflected. "Oh, look at the cute puppy." It was anything but cute. "What's his name?" I asked, rubbing the mutt behind the ears.

Sue replied, "Dinner, dumb-ass."

CHAPTER TWO

"Straight as an arrow, I'm telling you."

"Your point, little man?" I asked Linus

"My point, fat man..." We really were good friends, "... God does not draw in straight lines."

Separating Mexico from Belize on the Caye is a narrow, shallow waterway; The Boca Bacular Chico. Some, including Linus, have speculated the waterway was dug by the Mayans a few hundred years BC as a convenient way to move goods through the jungle. The Mayans traded in salt, fish, and coconuts. It is still a wildly popular trade route but for drugs, guns, and humans.

"It ain't that straight and who the hell makes you an expert on God's drawing style?" Linus pulled his button-down shirt back to reveal a t-shirt. 'I am the God of Eve.' Lucy and Linus had written the God portion of the code for Garden of Eve.

I shrugged "So what. How does that make you an expert on the real God?"

Deuce interjected, "Suppose he is."

"Linus? That a statement of fact, a question, probability, or a possibility?" I wasn't sure if Deuce was delusional and suggesting Linus was God or just an expert on the celestial being. Currently being of sober mind, I was going with expert.

"That little shit couldn't play God if he slept in a Holiday Inn Express every night." Lucy joined us from the back of Lola's. Lucy was going with an alternate answer. It was coming up on noon. She moved to the front, opening the overhead door and securing it with the help of Deuce. Linus shot her a bird.

"Ah, young love. I only hope Rose and I can enjoy the same love you two little shits have for each other." They both gave me the single digit salute.

"That's disgusting, but speaking of…" Linus said "… where is your lovely wife?"

I looked at my wrist for my nonexistent watch. "At work… somebody gotta pay the bills." Didn't want to think about it. Rose had ignored my text and calls all morning. I was in the proverbial doghouse. I hoped Jaws would share. Now I was being the delusional one.

Tossing a butt into the street, my sister Ruth strolled through the doorway. Her marriage to Mormon Mike had been suspended over the holidays in Utah. A devout Mormon, his parents even more-so struggled with accepting my feral sister. Predictably, the long-deferred, Mormon wedding ceremony had proven disastrous. Ruth chose the road never travelled. She followed us to Belize, leaving her kids behind with Mom, and Mike back in Utah to explain his poor life choices to the church elders. Mike was currently in Mormon time out. The fate of the marriage was yet undecided but leaning strongly toward dissolution. The midgets had given her a job as the day cook. They were my little Cherubs. "You're late," Lucy noted.

Ruth looked at her wrist, also lacking a watch, scanned the room absent any paying customers, shrugged. "It's still daylight out. And these losers never tip." I resented that remark. I mean, it was true, but Ruth was staying at our condo for free, at least when she was not out all night on the town. The girl was over fifty, looked thirty, and acted twenty.

Lucy punched me in the arm. Linus tossed an apron toward Ruth. Ruth disappeared into the kitchen, leaving the apron on the sandy floor.

"She'll sober up in a couple hours," I promised feebly. It was noon. I ordered a beer. I was a drunk but, if nothing else, I was not a member of the Breakfast Rum Club as of yet...small victories. Diverting the subject away from Ruth I asked, "So tell me again how it is you believe the Mayans dug the river?"

"Canal. It's a canal."

"Pretty sure that myth has been disproved. What do the scientists call it?"

"Settled science," Deuce offered. "Every generation we get another batch of settled science that unsettles the last generation's. The entire notion of settled science is a giant oxymoron. Every solitary new discovery leads us to dozens of new mysteries. The more we know, the more ignorant we realize we are...or, at least, the authentic ones among us."

"Exactly," Linus exclaimed, pushing a double shot of rum to Deuce. Deuce stared at the glass for moment. And with undue reverence, it was cheap rum after all, choked it back in a single practiced fluid motion.

"Nectar of the Gods." Deuce continued after softly replacing the shot glass on the Mahogany bar top. "If these brilliant, over-educated assholes really had a micron of an idea how insignificant they are...we are... they would shit their cotton panties. We aren't even the flea on the dog's tail."

"Do I even know you?" Linus asked. "Where in the hell did you go to school?"

"School be for snot-nosed rich chilrin."

Linus looked at me, noticing Deuce had reverted to his homeless street person vernacular. It appeared at times Deuce was playing a part. I shrugged, and Linus continued his interrogation as Sue walked into the bar with Waldo and Jaws lapping at her sandaled feet.

"Where in the hell do you live?"

Deuce nodded toward the graveyard. Sue deadpanned, "Senorita Rodriquez Drive, Lot 7, San Pedro Memorial." Deuce shrugged.

Jaws' wet nose rummaged my pants pocket in search of a treat, and, finding none, he scampered to the kitchen to locate Ruth, a more malleable target. "How the hell the Mayans pull that engineering feat off with sticks and stones?" I asked, immediately hearing myself and regretting the obvious stupidity of the question.

"You see the ruins around here? How did they pull off a twenty-story pyramid?"

You really couldn't walk a mile or two without seeing some signs of the Mayan culture. Belize sits just below Mexico's Yucatan Peninsula. This area has been lousy with Mayans for over ten thousand years. Ambergris Caye was a coral island and even much of the mainland was largely flat. Yet there were raised mounds in every direction. Beneath those mounds was the remnants of a great culture that had mysteriously collapsed. I nodded my head in agreement, "Yeah, okay. I don't get that, either. None of it makes sense how they built this shit with the tools and engineering skills they had at hand...but you made your point."

Motioning for another drink, Deuce piped in, "What it is makes you think they only had sticks and stones?"

"Science, asshole."

"Science your religion, Zeke?"

I nodded no. Sue replied, "Yes. And my religion hasn't killed anyone this week."

Deuce turned his empty socket on Sue, "So this planet your God tells us is a couple billion years old. Right?'

Sue threw up her hand. "I ain't got no time for this." She walked back into the kitchen. Over the doorway was a candid sign that read "Pequeno Cocina." It was a tiny kitchen. Jaws was a big, clumsy dog. It must be getting crowded back there. Sue had a backstory I wasn't familiar with. She was late thirties and crazy smart but made a point to avoid engaging in almost any intellectual conversation, offering only brief, insightful comments before disengaging the conversation. She had left Canada to come to San Pedro sans visible employment. Her computer skills were off the chart and her knowledge of the financial markets and international banking system far exceeded mine. Otherwise, I knew little about the woman. She was, like most in my life, a bit of an enigma, but an attractive, interesting sort with a large, unbalanced chip on her shoulder. Like many expats on the island, she was running from something, had something to hide, or some quirky blend of both.

Deuce sat silently waiting for a response. Not sure if he realized Sue had left the room. And shit, I didn't know the answer. I attended South Georgia public schools, but I nodded yes, assuming the question was more of the rhetorical variety.

"And even in our small slice of recorded history...a few thousand years...we have seen civilizations, The

Mayans, Egyptians, the Romans...come and go."

Deuce looked at me for affirmation for which I gave him in the form of lifted glass. I kinda heard of all those guys before. He repeated his rum ritual before continuing, "What kind of stupid are you to think in all those millions of years prior to our record of history there weren't other civilizations, other great empires that have also crumbled beneath the weight of humanity? Maybe even more advanced. But what do I know?"

Pretty sure Deuce, the homeless guy that cleaned golf carts for rum money and resided alongside Senorita Rodriguez skeletal remains, just called me stupid.

"And Sue's nascent religion, science, would end up killing us all, again, if given enough time." Deuce motioned for another drink.

"If?" I asked. "We on the clock?"

"This look like the free clinic for drunks?" Linus asked, thankfully ending our one-sided debate.

Deuce paused and looked around. "Yeah, kind of does." Deuce pulled out a soggy $20 BZ note and left it on the bar. He stood at attention, saluted Linus, said "Thank you for your service," and left.

"That is one weird ass dude," I noted.

"Pot, kettle, black." Lucy offered.

Holding up Deuce's $20, I ordered another beer. Lucy snatched the bill and grabbed me a beer.

The mouthwatering aroma of fresh, fried snapper wafted through the bar, overpowering the stale odor of spilt beer, cigarettes, urine, and Brad's dried blood and gray matter. Sue appeared from the kitchen, skillfully balancing two large platters of the deep fried, beer-battered fish, and another of conch fritters all the while artfully navigating the joint dogged efforts of Jaws and Waldo to dislodge her tasty load to a lesser, more suitable, altitude. Health food of the sea enhanced with the hot oil of slaughtered pig. Nature's bounty. Yum.

Successfully placing the platters on the bar, Sue bellowed, pointing out to the street, "Look, Zeke. I see your Jesus."

There was remarkable likeness to the bearded fellow I saw depicted all over the museums and church alters in Florence, but I was pretty certain, for a variety of reasons, this was not that guy. "Not even close. Jesus doesn't wear glasses." It was perversely the singular physical feature that did not fit the popular depiction of the Son of God.

"He's in disguise, dumb-ass. Don't you read? Celebrities can't stroll around in public without getting swamped by the paparazzi."

"You mean the glasses? That is a weak ass disguise for an all-powerful God."

Sue was a devout atheist. She had supreme faith in the lack of existence of an all-powerful, all just God. This was one intellectual argument she was prepared to engage in. "Hey asshole, it was good enough for Superman."

"What do you have against God, anyway?" Linus asked. Linus believed without God or at least the belief in a supreme being of some sort, civilization would have been improbable. Humans are wired to be self-centered and greedy. At our base, humans will kill to get what they want at the expense of all others. The absence of God equaled anarchy. Organized communities with agriculture, skilled military, and the arts, according to Linus' theory, are impossible without the belief in God.

Sue argued God was anarchy. She started listing her arguments, "One. More people have been slaughtered, tortured, and raped in His name than for any other reason. And that hit keeps on playing." Sadly, she had a point, but she was not finished. "Two. Science. Not a fucking shred of physical evidence of this dude." I abandoned the fried fish, taking my beer to a remote table in order to put distance between Sue and myself on the ever-increasing likelihood of a heavenly jolt of retribution. "Three," she continued, "suffering of innocents. Explain to me how an all just God allows innocents to suffer." "Four..."

Linus shushed Sue as the sound of shuffling sandaled feet signaled the onslaught of lunch rush. The fried snapper had done its job and several groups of tourists entered Lola's. Every seat at the bar was soon occupied as well as most of the tables.

Despite the threat from the Zika virus and the worldwide political turmoil, the Americans and Canadians had flooded San Pedro this season. There was not a condo or hotel room available on the island. Rumor had it the same was to be said for most of Belize and Central America. It was as if gravity had finally overwhelmed the northern hemisphere and pulled the entirety of its population south. Business for the midgets was good...maybe too good.

"Holy shit," Linus commented on the growing crowd that was quickly filling every niche in the small bar.

Lucy headed for the kitchen to help Ruth. Linus picked up the apron from the floor and held it up in front of Sue with his outreached T-Rex arms. She stared at the apron, frozen with indecision.

"Little help?" Linus asked, his palms upturned.

I giggled at the irony. Linus shot me an eat shit look without the normal trace of underlying humor.

Time slowed for a moment as if paused by an unseen remote. Choreographed dust particles danced in the sunlight reflected off the rows of scrubbed beer mugs. The din of the crowd faded to a low, undiscernible murmur. Deuce orchestrated an unobstructed path, making his way from the street through the crowd, impervious to the time warp as if he himself had slowed time.

He took the offered apron from Sue and, lifting her ponytail out of the way, he gently placed it over her head. With an uncharacteristic grace, Deuce affixed the tie with a delicate bow before he gently patted Sue on the bum and directed the full power of his one-eyed gaze toward me. He spoke clearly, absent any trace of island dialect and, without sound, "You cannot pause to consider the infinite perilous outcomes of each seemingly inconsequential decision you face each day, Zeke. You suffer a paralysis of indecision, and son, you do not wear it well."

Shattering glass broke the spell. The dust particles fell back into ordered chaos. Noise from the thirsty patrons filled the bar with the sounds of drunken commerce. Sue swept up the broken glass and began taking orders from the patrons. Deuce assumed a position behind the bar. I left in hasty retreat in search of more normal climes. I had seen this movie. It never ended well.

El Paso, Texas; March 2017: *President Abbott hammered the symbolic last nail into the Republic of Texas border wall today. After only six months, the new Republic completed construction of over 2,500 miles of walls around its border. Hundreds of thousands of Americans and Central Americans have applied for Republic citizenship since Texas secured its independence from the U.S. Abbott praised the Republic's citizens and his government for their hard work and ingenuity. Abbott stated the Republic would welcome all hard-working, educated applicants of any race or religion for citizenship but sternly warned the Republic of Texas is not a welfare state nor a criminal asylum. "Obey our laws and work hard and you are free to enjoy the bountiful fruits of our community. Don't, and you and your entire family will be harshly punished and expelled from Eden. Do not mistake The Republic of Texas for the corrupt, inept, politically correct, United States."*

A Republic State Department official estimates his office has a backlog of over fifty million applicants for citizenship for the Republic.

Alongside Global News

CHAPTER THREE

Tarbaby pushed his beater bike down the active runway carrying Dinner, alive and well, still comfortably traveling in style in the bike's basket. Both tires were dry-rotted and flat beyond repair, the wheels rusted and warped, scrubbing against the forks. Closely on his heels, a feral dog gave playful chase, barking at Dinner and snapping aggressively at Tarbaby's shoeless feet. A couple of bare-chested boys, roasted dark by the tropical sun, joined the motley parade, pestering Tarbaby for spare change for which no doubt he had none. An old woman tossed the foul contents of a chamber pot over the rail of her wooden shack that lined the runway just a couple feet beyond the low-slung wall. A smartly uniformed officer gave uninspired chase in a beater golf cart trying to clear the runway of the living flotsam with only marginal results. The sounds of the single engine of a Tropic Air flight gave ample notice and all dogs and humans wisely made their way to the edge of the runway, giving adequate space for the asphalt's intended purpose. Deuce spit over the fence, hitting the edge of the potholed asphalt tarmac and ordered another double shot of rum.

The Runway Bar is aptly named, paralleling the island's, well, runway. In all fairness, the bar sits at the far end and if a plane has yet to lose speed by this point in its travels, a bad day was to be had by many. Dogs, cats, people, golf carts, bicycles, hookers, drug dealers…all utilized the runway as a convenient crossing point and short cut into San Pedrito on the far side; the area of San Pedro best left to the natives or those fancying a shortened lifespan with a violent, anonymous ending. Like most bars on the Caye, it's open air, mostly dirt floor, and thatched with imported palm fronds. The development of the area had greatly depleted the availability of fronds for thatching. As a handy aside, importation of fronds made for cover of importation of more lucrative cargo from Honduras and Guatemala. The sand gnats were busy, and I asked for some insecticide. Deuce spat on his hand and offered. I declined.

Rose worked at the school just a few hundred meters down the cobbled road. Sue and Brad were meeting us there shortly to finalize plans for our sailing trip to the big ass Blue Hole and to meet the Captain. Rose would join us after she discharged her young, surprisingly eager, charges. Deuce just seemed to show up places uninvited. He reminded me much of an old friend, also a vagrant.

"You know Hobo?" I asked.

"You be thinking all of us homeless people be knowing each other? Like there be some big ole bum club. You a racist mofo, cracker?" Deuce smiled and completed his rum ritual, ordering another and motioning the bartender to put it on my tab.

I had learned in dealing with my friend Hobo not to argue with crazy. It is always a losing proposition. I had come to accept, perhaps even embrace, my position in life as the lodestone for crazy. Crazy always seemed to find its way to me. "So, what the hell was that magic you pulled at Lola's?'

"Magic, my ass, boy. I was just practicing me some of Sue's religion."

"She is an atheist, Deuce."

"Nah, man. She worships at the altar of science," Deuce laughed and looked down the runway toward the shack that served as the terminal.

I shrugged and finished my beer, swatted a gnat, and motioned for another. Deuce continued. "You overeducated white boys see the world in straight lines. Your creator...he did not use a straight edge. Everything be in curves and odd angles and waves and shit. Nothing be linear..." His rum shot appeared. He paused for his ritual before continuing "...including time."

"Look like trouble done found its way to our slice of heaven," Deuce pointed his glass at the passengers disembarking the small plane. Five large black man wearing all black with matching berets were waiting by the cargo door of the plane. The porter was pulling out heavy black canvas bags. "Those there men...are not unfamiliar with violence," Deuce added, unnecessarily.

I glanced at them, avoiding eye contact, and recognized the uniform of the Black Panthers. "Yeah, that can't be good." I had seen their leader pinned on the street by the GSU just a couple nights prior. It didn't take much to figure out why they were here.

"Them boys still pretty pissed your king didn't cede them Hotlanta, ain't they?"

"Expect so." It had only been a few crazy months since rumors of Atlanta being ceded to the Black

Panthers in order to create a sovereign Black Nation within the U.S. boundary had surfaced. It seemed like ages ago. Cooler heads had more or less prevailed, or so I assumed.

Shadows lengthened across the runway as the painted sky turned countless shades of soft pastels, making even the rusted tin-roofed shanties look majestic in the waning light of this day. "Another day ended, Deuce."

"And beginning," said Deuce, "and not just another, every."

"You speaking crazy shit now, Cyclops."

"My bitches," Sue yelled across the bar. She always made an entrance, a bit vulgar and unimaginative, but loud. It was her thing. Brad stopped at the edge of the shelter to finish his smoke. It was not civil to smoke weed inside the bar. Brad was a courteous soul.

"Let me borrow your mirror?" Deuce asked Sue.

"Old man. I look like a woman that carry a mirror?"

Leaned against the bar were two familiar, not unattractive sorts with identical Georgia Bulldog tramp stamps. The shapely matching tits and asses looked familiar. Like whale tails, each human female ass is unique to the trained eye. There were volumes of documented research available on the subject from the likes of the famous American researchers Flynt and Heffner. Sue, like most of the female of the species, less skilled in ass identification techniques, did recognize the distinctive tattoo. "Hold that. I'll get you a mirror, Deuce. Got something in your eye?" Sue asked.

Deuce scoffed.

Sue walked between the mother-daughter duo, firmly clutching a singular bare cheek on each ass. "Well hello, ladies." Brad walked by, quickly recognizing impending disaster and sensibly, and covertly moved on. Sue knew the bartender well at the Strip. To be honest, Sue knew all the bartenders on the island. "These beautiful ladies from Ohio…"

The daughter corrected Sue, "Georgia."

"Where the fuck ever." Sue addressed the duo before continuing her conversation with the bartender, "… have generously offered to pick up our bar tab tonight." She clamped down on the cheeks to punctuate her sentence as an order, not a request. The ladies started to protest but wisely thought better of it. Crazy is a powerful weapon when wielded by the experienced user. "I bet you or your hot little mama have a compact in that big ass fake Louie of yours."

Mama pulled out a bejeweled compact with a Bulldog logo on it and handed it over to Sue. Sue kissed her full on the lips, lingering to what purpose I shall not speculate, and ordered us another round before bringing the mirror to Deuce.

"I have seen this little trick, Deuce." Hobo demonstrated his theory that multiple realities could occupy the same space concurrently by using a mirror. It was a somewhat convincing parlor trick. I didn't need to see it again.

"I, on the other hand, have not," Sue noted. The bartender delivered our drinks. Sue raised her Panty Ripper to the Georgia duo in mock thanks for the round. "Keep 'em coming, honey." She blew a kiss, accentuated with a salty wink.

Deuce proceeded to demonstrate. He held the mirror up in front of Sue. "What do you see, Miss Sue?"

"A crazy, one-eyed man holding a mirror all up in my pretty face."

Deuce lowered the mirror and stared at Sue with his empty socket before continuing. Sue cooperated.

"An NFL football team's logo…"

"Is it really a team if they've only made the playoffs twice in a couple of decades?" I asked. My timing was poor. Rose had slipped in without anyone noticing. The Bills were her team. She took sports a bit too seriously and, like most Bills fans, was bitter, quick to anger, and in the company of other Bill's fans, demonstrated inappropriate and often life-threatening behavior. I was rewarded for my insensitivity with a smack to the back of my head. Brad laughed. Deuce frowned. Rose motioned for Sue to continue.

"...two bitches trying to escape." Sue turned and scurried up to the mom and daughter duo. "Early evening, ladies. Leaving so soon?"

They nodded yes. Mom added, "We paid your bar tab, bitch." The "bitch" was silent but clearly communicated.

"Frigging awesome. Thanks so much. Let me walk you to your golf cart so you can be on your way back to Ohio."

"Georgia," the daughter corrected again. Perhaps not the brightest bulb in the Peach State.

Sue paused. "Damn girl, do I look like I really give a shit where you are from?" She smiled broadly at the two of them continuing toward the golf cart. "The crazies hang out round here at night...right?" In a swift motion, Sue produced a box cutter and slit two of the tires. "Damn, you ladies got a flat. Hell, looks like two flats! Might as well come back in and be hospitable while you wait on Island Express AAA. I can send Brad over to pet your pretty little asses if you like."

Sue escorted the ladies to the bar and ordered us another round. "Might want to grab their credit card. Them Ohio bitches are known to run." She helpfully informed the bartender as she walked back to Deuce.

The daughter mumbled, "Georgia."

"Damn woman, what the hell be wrong with you?" Deuce inquired.

"The blade?" Sue asked.

Deuce eyed her with surprise, "Be a damned fool not to have one. You like herding cats. Over here, over yonder, fucking attention span of a two-year-old. Can you sit your skinny ass down?"

Sue sat. "Okay, Okay...Loser's logo, the whores, Tarbaby, and some fat, bald guy."

"Fuck you."

"I love you, too, Zeke, but Rose is right there," Sue whispered, kissing me on the top of my head.

"Gross, woman. I know where you put those lips."

Deuce frowned from the continued interruption. A drunk attempting to explain a critical concept to a bunch of drunks. Tall order. Holding the mirror steady, Deuce instructed Sue to move to an adjacent barstool. "Now what you see, woman?"

Sue described a slightly different scene in the mirror. Deuce snapped the mirror closed, "Voila!"

"Voila, my ass. That is one lame ass magic trick. You been drinking since breakfast, Deuce?"

"I never stop drinking, Sue." A true statement no doubt, but Deuce never appeared drunk. Perhaps this was his greatest magic trick.

"So, what is all the voila shit?" Sue asked.

"You a smart girl." It was a statement, not a question. Sue shrugged and sipped on her third Panty Ripper. "The surface of the mirror reflected different scenes concurrently. That means all at the same time." Sue shot him a bird. Deuce continued, "If you moved to that stool over yonder, you would see a third, that one a fourth, that one a fifth..."

"Third, fourth, fifth what old man?"

"Scene, Sue. Scene."

"And so?" Sue asked, genuinely confused.

"A solitary surface is capable of reflecting an infinite number of images at the same time based on the perspective of the viewer." Deuce had dropped the street vernacular.

Sue shrugged again. Deuce continued "Maybe time exists only as a tool for man to understand his world. Everything is happening at the same time and nothing at all is happening. Yesterday, tomorrow, and now are really just versions of now."

"Now the rum is talking."

"While I appreciate Deuce's theater, some of us have work yet to do tonight. Where the hell is our boat captain?" Rose interrupted.

Deuce stood and smartly saluted. "At your service, madam."

"You are shitting me, right?"

"Never, my Rose. And let me introduce my first mate, the honorable Tarbaby." Tarbaby had slipped in unnoticed and was at the bar, copping an unsolicited feel from the mother-daughter duo. Deuce motioned him over. Tarbaby attempted a bow but stumbled, righting himself with the table. Dinner came over to check on his new BFF.

"And the other stooge? There are three of you, right?" I asked.

"Correct. She couldn't make it tonight, but I believe you're familiar with her cooking."

"Don't tell me…" Rose spoke up. Deuce started to speak "No, I mean don't tell me."

Deuce nodded yes to Rose and whispered in a loud voice, "It's your sister, Zeke." I just stood there trying not to make eye contact with Rose. Ruth's culinary skills were limited, her ability to drink considerable, and her propensity for mayhem legendary. Deuce added to ensure my comprehension, "Ruth."

"Got it, Deuce."

We had chartered a 35-foot catamaran with four cabins. A third couple had chartered an empty cabin to offset the cost. Deuce and Tarbaby would sleep in the crew quarters, affectionately denoted the coffin. There was only one exit. Should the boat capsize, it could prove a difficult escape. Perhaps affectionate is a poor word choice. Ruth would likely sleep under the stars naked, even though the fourth cabin had been reserved for the cook.

"So, pray tell me kind sir, who else will be joining us?"

"The Brunel's from Jacksonville," Deuce replied, smiling broadly.

Dubai; April 2017: *President O'Grady arrived today in Belgium to meet with key members of The Green Climate Fund established by the Paris Climate Agreement. In a shocking announcement, O'Grady pledged $100 trillion over five years to the fund and a ban on all carbon fuel utilization in the U.S. by 2025. The funds would serve as reparation to the Brotherhood of Islam who now control some seventy percent of the world's oil reserves.*

Speaker O'Ryan called the move "...nothing short of treasonous. Transferring wealth to the profiteers of global warming seems at best, ironic, and, at worst, criminal." O' Ryan further warned the U.S. energy companies could not make the transition to non-carbon fuels in that short of time at any cost.

Secretary Obama stated, "This is a good...<dramatic pause, smirk>...first step...<dramatic pause, smirk>...toward...<dramatic pause, smirk>...global unity...<dramatic pause, smirk> and a sustainable environment."

Alongside Global News

CHAPTER FOUR

"You piss on me and I will drown your mangy ass," I vowed to Tripod, anxiously pacing a three-legged tango on board the boat. The foul little bastard was a serial pisser. Piss him off and he pissed on you. It was his thing.

Hobo frowned and admonished, "Language, Ezekiel. Vulgarity..."

"...is the crutch of the ignorant," I interrupted. This was not our first rodeo. Hobo was uncharacteristically clean-shaven and shorn. His nearly bald head was smooth and lily white along with his face below the beard line. It was a stark contrast to the leathery remainder of his exposed skin. He was wearing nothing but a pink ladies' thong and a generous smile. I once accused him of shopping from the unattended beach towels of lady bathers.

"Good to see you, old friend. Welcome aboard."

Hobo embraced me with a giant hug that lasted an uncomfortable minute. Hobo punctuated his malodorous embrace with two air kisses. He moved to Rose; she extended a hand to which Hobo ignored and moved in for a hug. Rose twisted sideways to avoid a full frontal. She was practiced at the maneuver, thanks in no small part to a creepy uncle and early onset puberty. She had an aunt who claimed she was an A cup at birth. There are pictures, countless, to support the claim. Yesterday's innocent, proud grandparent is today's pedophile. One should take care to judge without the benefit of historical context.

Jaws paced anxiously on the dock, whimpering mournfully, almost as if saying "please." Hobo knelt on all fours, coaxing him to walk the plank adjoining the dock. Tripod sat beside Hobo and turned his head to the side and whimpered pleadingly. Jaws was a rescue. Not unlike many such creatures, there was much credible debate on who rescued whom. However, he, Jaws, had been found drowning in a vat of chemicals in an industrial site on Jacksonville's Northside. Gang headquarters for Jacksonville. Being a Lab mix, he was bred for water and loves it, but is deathly frightened of anything without a gradual beach entry. "You got this, buddy," Hobo instructed Jaws.

"Get your fat, hairy ass in the boat," I yelled at Jaws, "Act like you got some damn balls."

"Too soon," Rose deadpanned. Rose rarely squandered an opportunity to deliver an emasculating, editorial comment. It was her thing. With beauty, one must tolerate crazy.

Hobo stood. "Show some respect, Ezekiel. These majestic animals are the only true living beings left on your planet." He added air quotes around living.

It was his nature to speak in nonsensical riddles. I,

having learned to not engage in a logical conversation with an illogical person, wisely let the comment stand. He did not.

"Only dogs widely survived the great water purge."

"Flood? Dogs survived the flood? And which flood do you speak of, Katrina, Sandy, Floyd, Harvey?" I was violating my own tenet to not debate with crazy.

Hobo scoffed. "The Flood. It is only natural dogs show a healthy respect for the power of water. They watched helplessly as water destroyed every living land-based thing on this planet."

"You forgot the Ark." Hobo looked puzzled. I added, "You know that Noah fellow and the whole two by two thing."

"Oh, yeah. Your Bible story."

"Duh."

"Like most myths, there is a kernel of truth in that story, Ezekiel."

"My Dad would argue more than a kernel, Homeless Bob." That wasn't Hobo's name. Over the years, he had given me so many different names, I settled on Homeless Bob and shortened it to Hobo. It had stuck.

"And your Dad would be correct. There are universal myths...'" Hobo dramatically added air quotes around myths, "... in almost every religion, every culture. A creation myth, an end of time myth, and a flood myth. There are some 500 ancient texts, many predating your Bible, that reference a great flood that destroyed the entire world. The story varies from text to text, but most speak of a great Ark that served as a depository for the animal kingdom."

"And Noah and his family?"

"Many of the recorded stories, Ezekiel, do in fact include a single, righteous family that was spared." Hobo grabbed the cell from my hand. "Remember, dear Ezekiel, everything is relative. One often judges history from today's perspective, mistakenly coloring the past with a modern palate."

I shook my head, "Ingles, por favor?"

Hobo looked confused, "Ezekiel are you already drunk? That was English." I started to explain my sarcasm, but he continued, "Imagine for a moment you were charged with describing this communication device to let's say…a cave man." Hobo sat on a bench, crossed his legs, and placed his hand on his chin. "Okay, go."

"Fuck off."

"Ignorance, Ezekiel." Hobo shook his head in disappointment. "It would require an impossible cognitive leap to accurately describe this device…" Hobo waved my cell in my face, "…to someone that had yet to even discover radio, telegraph, or arguably, even the written word."

Rose chimed in, "You two losers bore the living hell out of me. Where is that sister of yours with some booze?" Rose left in search of a bottle of vodka and a more entertaining conversation. A great deal of patience was required, of which Rose possessed precious little, to deal with the quirky intricacies of my relationship with Hobo and, even more so, to handle Ruth on her best days. These were not her best days.

"I'll make it easier for you, friend," Hobo continued. "Fast forward a few dozen millennia to the 1700's. Describe your cell phone to an early American." Hobo resumed his mock interested student pose on the bench.

"Native or invader?"

"Dealer's choice."

"Okay, I will play your little game. Native: Really loud drums and smoky fires that can draw pictures or words fast as you can think them."

"A little racist, but okay."

I started to argue the racist slur. I struggle mightily

understanding how a nonjudgmental statement of fact can be considered racist. But it's a new world of political correctness. Damn millennials and their participation trophies.

"Invader: letters and drawings delivered by a flock of exceptionally speedy pigeons. Do I get points for using the politically correct term of 'invaders' for early European explorers?"

"Well done, Ezekiel. You must use the language of the time to describe an object beyond the cognitive grasp of a group of ignorant people. Noah's Ark, Ezekiel's Wheel, Ark of the Covenant, pillar of light... all of these accounts perhaps describe technology beyond the vocabulary or understanding of the writer or reader of the period. Even the story of the virgin birth a few decades ago seemed unto itself a miracle. Now just about any major hospital in the states can pull off a test tube fertilization and ultimately birth without the benefit of either party ever having achieved carnal knowledge."

"Pretty sure there is a shortage on God sperm."

"One should not mock, Ezekiel, what one is too ignorant to understand." Hobo continued. "Let's examine your Bible Myth. Just how large was that Ark of Noah's?"

"I have slept since I last attended Sunday School. And I never knew the length of a cubit."

"Your best guess, then."

"The size of a half-dozen school buses."

"Yeah...no. Roughly, assuming a cubit to be twenty inches in length," Hobo pointed to his elbow tracing a line to the tip of his middle finger "Cubit. The Ark of your Noah was over 500 feet long." Hobo held his hands out wide, falling a bit short of 500 feet, but I got his visual. "Think almost two football fields long. The boat was eighty feet wide...half a football field. And fifty feet high…" He mixed his similes. "That's a five-story building. The Ark of Noah could hold closer to a hundred school buses…on each of the five floors."

He paused to let the mammoth size sink in. "One big-ass boat. I get it. What's your point?"

"So, your Noah fellow, some 600-years-old by the time he started construction, and his three sons…" Hobo held up his thumb and two fingers to further illustrate the paucity of available manpower, "…constructed an actual colossal wooden boat with primitive hand tools and no experience in boat building? And, even if they pulled this off…yet still, could this massive wooden boat be capable of withstanding the forces of a great flood?"

I shrugged. "So the good book says."

"And even still, two of every land species along with sufficient food and water could be stored within its walls?"

"Seems like water would not be an issue."

This time Hobo shrugged in defeat. I heard him, though. I wasn't a caveman, after all.

Rose returned, exasperated, sans alcohol. "Can't find another soul. Worse yet, no booze."

I looked at Jaws, still whimpering and pacing on the dock. He is a 125-pound dog. I really did not want to carry him over the plank against his will. Leaving him was not a viable option unless I abandoned Rose, as well. Those two were attached at the hip.

"An icy cold beverage, sir and madam?"

I turned to see Deuce, barefoot, holding a plastic platter with two plastic flutes of champagne and a small bowl of dark liquid. He was dressed in all white with Captain Epaulets on his shoulder and hat, also suitable for a naval officer of high rank. His clothes were clean and neatly pressed. Clean shaven, he offered Rose a flute with neatly clipped nails. "What the fuck, Deuce?"

"Ezekiel!" Hobo shouted.

"What?" It was going to be a long trip if Hobo was going to assume the role of my mother the entire time.

Placing the bowl of dark liquid on the deck, Deuce retreated to the interior. Island music flowed out from inside. Jaws sprinted across the plank and lapped up the dark liquid. "Jack," Rose speculated. It was his favorite indulgence. He had many, as his girth would attest.

Hobo resumed his all fours position, placing his face in close proximity to Jaws. He was warmly greeted by a flurry of face-licking. Hobo returned the favor, licking Jaws on the nose. Jaws extended his paw to stop the madness. Hobo shook it.

"These creatures gave us comfort on the trip over and now they serve mortals as companions and guides to the hereafter."

"Us who?"

Deuce answered, "Our intimates" as he carried a second platter with a similar set up to the first, but the bowl was filled with milk instead of Jack.

"Intimates? Your drawers?" I asked.

Jaws entertained himself, chasing Tripod around the perimeter of the deck. Tripod was of indeterminate breed, likely some mix of terrier and was, as the name suggested, missing one leg. He had adapted well to his handicap and was deceptively quick. Perhaps quick is a relative term. Jaws was built for comfort, not speed.

"Our ancestors." Deuce pointed at himself and Hobo. "But in a tangential manner, yours, as well."

"So, you do know each other?" I smiled broadly.

"But of course," Deuce answered.

"There is a club of old homeless dudes." They laughed. I did not.

"My bitches," Sue announced her arrival in typical, if not original, fashion.

Hobo frowned. Deuce handed Sue the plastic champagne flute, bowing elegantly from the waist. "Where's that lovely man of yours?" he asked in a French-Canadian Mountie accent.

"Brad?" Sue asked, her face characteristically screwed up in contempt. She was a very animated woman. Facial translation; Brad's doghouse period had yet to expire. Deuce displayed the faintest of knowing smile and nodded. "Schlepping my shit," Sue answered.

"It's three nights, Sue. How much luggage can one tiny woman need?"

"A lady needs her fucking options." Sue gulped the champagne and reached for the second glass. Deuce placed the bowl of milk on the deck and lovingly removed Waldo from Sue's newly-acquired, oversized, fake Louie.

Hobo dropped to the deck and exchanged tongue pleasantries with Waldo. His nearly bare ass was in the air, wagging his invisible tail, mimicking Waldo's excitement. Sue smacked his bum, "And who is this fine piece of ass?"

Hobo stood and bowed at the waist. "Please, madam. I beg you not to refer to me as such." Sue stared blankly at Hobo.

Hobo continued, "A fine piece of tail, butt, bum, hiney…all perfectly adequate descriptions of my sexually desirable physique."

I made the introductions. Had to love Sue. She was unfazed by my ethereal friend. After all, she was accustomed to the nonsensical frivolity of the Breakfast Rum Club. Not much could shock her. Standing barely over five feet, Hobo's lithe body weighed less than Jaws. His red hair was shorn tightly, but a faint red glow was evident. It was his eyes; crystal blue, piercing, alive… ethereal.

Brad struggled down the dock, dragging two hockey duffels behind him with a third inelegantly affixed to his back which was bent by the evident weight. Deuce whistled and Tarbaby's head popped out from below deck, a blunt in his mouth, food crumbs in his scraggily beard. Deuce frowned and motioned for Tarbaby to assist Brad.

Finally, all aboard, we got underway. Deuce made a striking figure at the boat's helm. Tarbaby was similarly attired in white but absent the attended formal effect by a colossal margin. His shirttail was half-tucked in, his uniform wrinkled and stained from sources best left anonymous. His pant legs were rolled up haphazardly to just below the knee, exposing the tell-tale scars of at least a brief career in the cane fields. He had shaved at some point but with poor effect, leaving as much stubble as he removed, giving the appearance of a cheap black and white copy of a Jackson Pollock. He did prove an able-bodied sailor as the trip progressed.

"Where the hell is your missing crew member?" I asked Deuce

Deuce frowned and focused his missing eye socket to below deck. "Your sister has not proven a reliable hand."

"Keel haul her ass," I suggested. I was growing weary of my guilt by association. I deflected, "And where is the Misses," I inquired of Hobo.

Hobo smiled broadly. He knew I was curious as to who would be playing the fictional role of Ms. Brunel in this version of reality. "Don't you worry. She will find you."

∞∞∞∞

Ships are not known for their spacious cabins. And this was no ship. Yet still, the cabin boasted a full size sleeping platform and its own efficient, if not effective, private shower and shitter combo. Before the trip was over, I had secretly pledged to track down and torture the sick fuck who designed it. The combo is the equivalent of collocating a sewage and recreational facility. Oh wait…Deuce helpfully communicated the described chamber of horrors was known as a "head." I'm no sailor, but I am certain I preferred a different variety of head. Rose was ambivalent on the subject at best. Also given the male dominance of the sailing world, I rather expected my preference and the sailing world's term for bathroom are not totally unrelated. Just saying. We stowed our luggage in the meager space provided and made our way back to the deck.

Deuce gave the assembled a short safety/welcome/ instructional briefing. Sunscreen, hydration, life vest, beer cooler. Not wanting to spend time unstopping the head, he gave careful, detailed instructions on the proper usage of the marine head, admonishing the ladies to flush only body waste, placing all paper products in the trash bin. Even Rose giggled. Why is bathroom humor even a thing?

Hobo, technically a guest on the trip, pitched in and assisted Tarbaby and Deuce in getting us "under way", also known as leaving the dock. Sailors, not unlike most professions, develop their own language that often use familiar words and phrases in an unfamiliar manner. With an inordinate amount of time at their disposal, sailors tend to have a massive, specialized vocabulary.

Ruth was still AWOL. The late afternoon sun was to our starboard, casting long shadows of the mast into seas, alternating in vibrant hues of blue and green. Starboard is, for us mere land mortals, to the right, facing forward. A light breeze filled the sheets and Deuce killed the engines and disengaged the boat's

GPS. He set a course using an antique brass compass mounted above the wheel.

"You need I grab a knotted rope and check for speed?" I asked. Deuce focused his singular eye forward to the horizon.

We moved to the stern (I was rapidly learning sailing jargon) of the boat and sat on the port hull steps leading to the water. We let our feet drag in the slow-moving water and watched a pod of dolphins frolic in the boat's wake. A pair of frigate birds blocked the waning sun, casting an ominous shadow on the sea.

Brad and Sue occupied the starboard hull steps, smoking cigarettes while blatantly ignoring each other's existence. A large plank floated by, nicking Brad's toe. It startled him, and he yelped, dropping his cigarette onto his stomach. He yelped again. I added, for comedic relief, "Damn sea plankton." Sue and Rose gave me a courtesy chuckle. Brad did not.

Wearing the tiniest of white thongs, Ruth emerged with a beer in hand, scooching me over to the side to make room for herself on the bottom step. She placed her colorful toes in the water and laid her head back on to Rose's lap with her eyes closed. At nearly fifty, without the benefit of surgery, exercise, or healthy a lifestyle, she was a remarkable beauty. Her skin, frequently interrupted by tattoos, was otherwise smooth and flawless. Her body was lean and muscular, much like a trained athlete, not a lazy drunk on a weed inspired, junk food cleanse. God had blessed her with a remarkable set of genes. Perhaps she had commandeered my ration.

Rose pinched Ruth's nose shut. I took her beer and finished it off in one gulp. She cracked an eye. "Leave me alone, assholes."

"You do understand the economics of our relationship?"

Ruth cracked the other eye open. "What does that even mean?"

"We are the clients, the guests, the paying customers. I believe you are the cook, deck hand, dish washer, toilet cleaner, and waitress."

"Unless you fuck me, feed me, or finance me, leave me the hell alone."

"Duh...two out of three, dear."

"I forget..." A sly smile crossed her face, "...Which two?"

"Gross."

Ruth grabbed the beer bottle out of my hand and turned it up, frowning when she realized it was empty. She held the empty out to Rose, indicting she required another.

"Yeah. Let me know how that works out for you."

I may have mentioned Belize is home to the second longest barrier reef. It runs pretty much the entire length of the country, paralleling the shore. Our waypoint for the evening was just off the coast of Belize City. We were sailing inside the reef. The ride would be smooth if the weather held. Unfortunately, at Deuce's insistence, we were not using the engine and, as such, making only four to seven knots.

Ruth stood and removed her top, leaving her naked but for a tiny, triangular patch masking only the precise entry point to slot B. Brad's eyes grew the size of saucepans. Before I had time to utter protest, Ruth gracefully dove into the still blue water with barely a splash. A line followed, snaking out toward her. Ruth grabbed the line effortlessly and let the boat tow her for several minutes.

Deuce leaned over the stern, propping his elbows on the rail and called out, "It's a fair swim back to the island." He produced a knife in his left hand and kinked the line with his free hand. "Tide still heading in." He lifted his long, leathery finger in the air. "Favorable wind. You ain't old yet. On the other hand, you ain't no spring chicken, either. You smoke a lot, drink a lot more, and haven't exercised in a vertical position at least since, hell, well, ever." Deuce paused for a moment, waiting for a reply.

Ruth raised a solitary finger.

"Lot of boat traffic right here. Your best bet is gonna be flag down another boat. Tits are still nice. Lot of tats, though," Deuce mused. "Some guys are turned off by that. Me personally, not a fan. Still some horny old fisherman will likely pick you up, use you as bait...maybe fuck you." Deuce mumbled, "Sadly, not sure which your crazy ass would enjoy more." Deuce cut the line.

Quickly, the boat distanced itself from Ruth. Deuce smiled broadly and waved. Ruth waved back but with only two fingers. She was a stubborn, prideful woman. I wouldn't say she had a death wish but death sure as hell held nothing on her. She lived life on the razor's edge without benefit of a net. The boat suddenly slowed as the main sail noisily slithered its way down the mast. The dogs congregated in the zephyr on the equipment deck looking on in anxious anticipation.

Exercising a perfect swan dive from atop the boat, Hobo swam toward Ruth. Tripod jumped from the zephyr and began his three-legged dog paddle after his best friend. Ruth began swimming in the direction of shore. Hobo fastened a roll of duct tape to his head. He rightly anticipated a struggle and swam to the conflict armed for battle.

Hobo was a Renaissance man. There was little, at least of the good works in the world, he was not proficient at. He was an insufferable twit at times, but

45

at his soul, there was only good. Incapable of lying, he was a master at hedging and equivocation. His outward appearance was bizarre and no doubt his personal hygiene was wanting. Yet, on the whole, he was the most remarkable being I had ever encountered. Of his history, I knew very little. Ruth knew him better than I did. I once feared Hobo's knowledge of Ruth was of the Biblical variety. But she volunteered little regarding her relationship with Hobo and him even less.

In short time, Ruth was gagged and bound. Hobo was practiced at hogtying and rescuing my sister against her will. Kidnapping, if you will, but for a good cause. Hobo hand-fashioned a tow rope with the duct tape and attached the rope to Ruth's gag. Swimming a practiced side stroke, he made good time back to the boat, now dead still in the water. Tripod swam parallel to Ruth, keeping a suspicious eye on her. Brad assisted Tripod with the lookout, keeping a close eye on Ruth's exposed perky twins breaking the water like a submarine conn tower.

"Enjoy your swim?" I asked

Ruth grunted. Rose rolled her eyes. Tripod peed. Jaws farted. Brad enthusiastically clapped. Sue likewise punched Brad with enthusiasm.

Deuce sliced the duct tape from her wrist, handed her the knife, and retreated into the boat. He returned with a towel and a pressed white uniform. He placed the uniform on the bench and held a towel, waiting for her to shower off. Rose held the hose as Ruth stood, sliding her bottoms down her legs. Ruth was heavily tattooed and pierced. She wore her story on her body as armor. Wordlessly, she toweled off and dressed in the uniform provided, sans any undergarments. She tied her long, raven hair in a neat ponytail using a thin slice of the duct tape.

"Souvenir?" I asked.

Conflict resolution, the thought suddenly occurred to me. I had seen this all wrong. Hobo's appearance always signaled the onset of chaos in my life. I thought he brought the chaos or was the origin of it. For certain, his presence short-circuited my defense mechanisms for demon containment. Yet, perhaps he did not usher in chaos but, in fact, chaos ushered in Hobo.

Proportioning guilt is a long-held tradition of our legal system. Justice being blind combined with the unquestionable and steadfast honor of the practitioners of law almost always found the most guilt in those with deepest of pockets. (Yet, likely least responsible of all the parties engaged in the argument.) We train, incongruously on purpose, some of our brightest kids to lie for a living. To argue the side, not of justice, but of pocketbook girth. Sadly, our culture embraces this oxymoronic practice. All empires crumble. Clearly, we got next. And there I go again, with marginally tangential political commentary, at best.

"Well turn the damn engine on," Ruth yelled at Deuce.

Deuce continued his muttering regarding the senseless, inconsiderate delay created by Ruth's "shenanigans." He assigned her the majority of the blame for our slow progress. Annoying as it was, it really had but taken no more than a few minutes. On the whole, he was just aggravated with having Ruth as a reluctant crew member. Then again, we were all a bit aggravated as to her presence as a crew member. Never the less, Ruth had a legit argument; the winds were somewhat favorable but not trailing. The fault was only marginally hers.

"Storm's brewing," Hobo said quietly.

"I see that, Captain Obvious."

"Deuce is the captain." Hobo's grasp on sarcasm was

limited. Hobo shook his head no and pointed off to the horizon where a row of ominous clouds had formed.

Deuce vanished down below, leaving Tarbaby at the helm. At some point, we should have been concerned that our fate was in the hands of the Breakfast Rum Club's unsteady hands. I pinched myself. It hurt.

"You are just gonna leave a mark, Ezekiel." Hobo shook his head and scoffed.

I shrugged. It was an imperfect method of clarifying my reality. Yet it was the only tactic available. Deuce returned, decked out in storm gear. He looked like a 1970's Madison Avenue ad firm's interpretation of a seafaring angler: Big yellow hat, raincoat, and boots. He had even added a pipe.

Deuce instructed Tarbaby to prepare the boat for the storm. To my dismay, he did not order the hatches battened. I wondered where his flair for the dramatic had gone. Come to think of it, I don't recall hearing any words articulated.

Dishes crashed to the floor. Books and board games tipped off the shelf onto the sofa, spilling small parts across the deck. The boat rocked violently, slamming head first into waves that were not welcome on the inside of the reef. The wind tore at the main sail, causing the cat to break contact with the water on the windward side. We huddled inside the cabin, pinched against the wall of the leeward side. The dogs lay at our feet. The smell of wet dog permeated the cabin. Although likely, the smell was just as probable from Tarbaby, not the dogs. Deuce's head was invisible in the darkening rain. His bright yellow slicker billowed in the wind.

Tarbaby lit a joint. Rose rolled her eyes. I asked, "Shouldn't you be outside helping?"

"Hell no. Can't swim." He motioned to Ruth and shot-gunned the joint into her mouth.

"Gross," Rose needlessly commented.

"Awesome. Middle of the perfect storm and a deranged captain is at the helm and his crew is getting stoned."

"Hyperbole much?" Ruth asked. "Relax. Hobo is outside."

"Yeah, that. The nut is likely playing king of the world at the bow."

Ruth exhaled and nodded, "Yeah, likely"

"I always thought it would be in a plane," Rose said calmly.

Sue asked, "What in a plane?"

"Meet her maker," I replied. Rose was deathly frightened of air travel. I had the scars to prove it.

The sliding glass of the cabin slid open, the wind died, and the rain stopped. The light from the full moon silhouetted Hobo's naked body. His hair was long and curly. His beard full and unkempt. "Oh, but you already have."

Rose kissed my lips softly, gently nudging me awake. My head lay comfortably in her lap and we both were on the cargo netting strung in the front of the boat between the cat's two hulls. It was dark out with no moon and the stars shown brilliantly. Tens of thousands of small pinpoints of lights shimmering in the night sky unpolluted by heavy industry or the illumination of civilization. This was the majestic night sky of which the Mayans gazed.

The boat rocked gently in the surf. The sail was down and only the running lights of the boat were illuminated.

"When did I fall asleep?" I asked.

"Shortly after your bat-shit crazy sister got back on board."

"Right here, Rose."

Ruth lay fully naked on the adjacent net under the stars. I was thankful for the limited lighting. I noticed to her side a clean shorn Hobo likewise sans clothing, his pale skin glowing in the dark.

"You awake, sleeping beauty?" Hobo asked me, rhetorically. He continued, "How is that pinching trick working out for you?"

I ignored the bait and pointed in the sky. "That is a strange cloud."

Sue and Brad were sitting on top of the cabin with the dogs. She replied, "It's the Milky Way, dumb-ass."

I started to argue but Hobo added, "Forgive him, Sue. South Georgia public schools and a long history of prescription drug and alcohol abuse."

I raised all four fingers on my free hand and waved them in the air but did not otherwise comment. It would be funny if it were not true on all three accounts. Hobo was a lot of things, but he was rarely, strike that, never, wrong. Seemed improbable, though. I felt I could reach out and run my fingers though the Milky Way. Sue held her phone into the sky and pointed out a particularly bright star. "There is Mercury. You see it." It was more a statement than a question. She felt it self-evident.

Brad was otherwise occupied, straining in the dim light to see other, more non-celestial heavenly bodies and did not respond immediately. Sue poked him, "You dumb bastard, you aren't even looking." Jaws opened a long, mournful howl, staring into the heavens. Waldo and Tripod joined in, an octave or so higher. We all laid back, stared into the heavens, and listened to the pleading song of the canines.

"Damn, dudes, enough," I tried to interrupt the musical interlude. It was cool for the first half hour. Now it just grated on me like a dentist scraping tarter off my teeth. Felt like I was watching a chicken interlude on Family Guy.

"Show some respect, Ezekiel. The boys miss home."

"It's been a day. A bit early to be homesick."

Hobo pointed off into the sky at the brightest of celestial objects not in the planet arc. "There, Sue. What does your expensive gadget say about that star?"

Sue dutifully pointed her phone at the star. "Cool, bitches. That is Sirius, the Dog Star."

Hobo filled in, "It is the brightest star in the sky. Technically two stars but they appear as one from the perspective of your planet. The Egyptians marked the flooding of the Nile based on the star's helical rising."

"What the hell, man?"

Hobo stood and shook his head. The running lights dimmed, and we were in complete darkness; and for that, I was thankful. Hobo's naked body was only a silhouette against the sky, absent any disturbing detail. "Helical rising. The annual event on which the star is visible above the eastern horizon just before the sunrise."

Sue chimed in "You are all so fucking stupid."

"No. I get that. But you, my crazy ass friend, seem to be suggesting the Dog Star is their home. As in literal, not mythological, permanent residence."

Hobo shook his head slowly in the affirmative and added "... and mine."

"Then you are all most certainly going to be late for dinner." Jaws came to the edge of the net and licked my face. Jaws has an extensive vocabulary, mostly centered on food and naps. We had taken to spelling certain words in front of him, but even so, some hard consonants he associated correctly with the word.

"Dogs," Hobo continued, "...have been here several millennial dating back to the crash." Hobo said "crash" as if it should have meaning to me. It did not. "According to the Aztecs, dogs predate the present race of man."

"Present?"

Hobo ignored my question. "According to Indian legend, the King Yudisthira made a great pilgrimage to heaven. He brought with him an entourage, as kings and celebrities tend to do, and a dog. By the time he finished his epic journey, all his entourage, save his dog, had perished. The gatekeeper to heaven refused admission to the King's faithful dog. Yudisthira replied he would as soon go to hell as enter a place that did not allow his dog. Turns out, this was the gatekeeper's test of Yudisthira's worth. In fact, the dog was himself a God."

"Your point?"

"Dogs are represented in ancient recorded history in almost every culture as important family members, guides, companions, and even themselves deities. Mayans, for instance, thought dogs were guides to help negotiate the watery expanse of the afterlife and upon arrival at the gates of paradise to assist in any last-minute challenges to entry."

"Your history lesson would be so much all the more comprehensible if you were only wearing britches," I offered.

"My nudity offend you?"

"Yeah, kind of does. And while we are on subject, Ruth, can you at least cover your genitals." Ruth stood. The running lights came back on. Brad gasped. Sue punched. Hobo giggled hysterically like a little girl.

"Pipe down," came the order from Deuce, his head emerging from a porthole in the galley.

"What? Do we look like a teenage slumber party?'

"You seemed disappointed I failed to previously use the nautical order 'baton down the hatches.'"

Tarbaby stumbled toward the bow of the cat, a blunt in one hand, a Belkin Stout in the other, before tumbling face first onto the cargo netting, losing the beer to the deep. To his credit, he saved the blunt. Ruth reached for the blunt and took a long pull before gracefully diving into the dark abyss. Hobo tossed a line.

"Your crew…Captain, my Captain," I paused, "be three sheets to the wind."

CHAPTER FIVE

"Watchers."

With exaggerated caution, I cracked an eye from beneath my hat, deliberately scanning my limited field of vision. I saw no one. Repeating the process with the second eye, I scanned my remaining forward perimeter with the equivalent outcome. Pastel shades painted the still darkened sky, signaling our star's looming arrival. The sheet flapped gently in the morning breeze, accompanied by the faint tap of the stainless rigging against the mast and the soothing sound of the twin hulls slicing through the Caribbean Sea. Frigate birds circled overhead in anticipation of a charitable meal. The heady aroma of coffee wafted in the heavy morning air cloaking the all too familiar musky scent peculiar to Hobo.

Hobo's faceless voice continued in a soft, measured cadence as the boat gently rocked in rhythm with his words. "That is what the son of men called us...Watchers. We were not Gods. Not even creators. Stuck on this tiny spinning rock only by accident. Gabriel tasked us to help your fledgling world. But it all went so terribly wrong."

The sail snapped as the wind freshened. I closed my eyes and continued laying perfectly still. Hobo had rarely offered a genesis story. Sure, he had stories, but this one seemed different, flavored with the exotic taste of naked honesty. This was not a tale seasoned with his usual ambiguity, obfuscation, evasion, and equivocation. I urged him with my silence to continue.

"The serpent corrupted...," he added, before he was interrupted.

"You like it black?" Deuce nudged me with his giant, well-manicured, bare foot. A peculiar indulgence for a man electing domicile in a scenic boneyard. I tilted my head up, squinting into the morning sun.

"Coffee?" I asked.

"No, your cock. You like your cock black?" Deuce grinned.

I ignored him and glanced behind me to find no one there. I sat and took the offered coffee. Deuce extended his bony finger toward the south. "That's Goff's Caye. We will be there in an about an hour. Breakfast in thirty. Ruth is cooking. Might want to eat a little sumpin' 'fore then." He patted me on the leg before standing.

I sipped the dark coffee. There was a faint hint of rum. Deuce smiled. "Nectar of the Gods."

"Where is Hobo?" I asked.

"No mi siglo para miralo."

"English."

Deuce pointed to the starboard side of the boat and returned to the cabin. I watched Hobo for a few minutes as he swam Indian laps, his lily white ass reflecting the first light of morning, around our slow moving cat.

Goff's Caye is small spit of a coral island, not much more than an acre in size, a dozen miles off the coast of Belize City. It sits on the edge of the barrier reef close to the English Channel. Aside from a brightly painted picnic pavilion and a primitive two-hole privy, there are no structures on the island. A shallow dock extends over the water suitable for the tenders of the giant cruise ships to dispatch their plump, sun-kissed charges on its exotic, sandy shores. Fortunately, the island was absent gift shop, titty bar, casino, motorized wheelchairs, or endless buffet. Consequently, it was not favored by many of the cruise passengers and remained unspoiled. The portal beside me cranked open and Rose popped her disheveled head out. She wordlessly commandeered my coffee and sipped. She motioned toward the caye now clearly visible off our bow. "Goff's Caye." I noticed two sleek speed-boats tied up on the dock. I added, "And we have some wealthy company."

Rose took a second sip of what was once my spiked coffee. "Started your day early." Deuce appeared with a second cup and knelt to the deck to pass the cup to Rose. "Did you flavor this one, as well?"

Deuce smiled and winked his scarred, empty socket. A disquieting look, to say the least.

I pointed to the dock where several armed, uniformed men were now clearly visible. "Did you arrange a welcoming party?"

Deuce squinted and frowned. "I did not." He hustled back to the helm. The sail tumbled to the deck and the boat quickly slowed to a drift. Tarbaby dropped the anchor. We came to a dead stop some 500 meters off the island, still inside the reef in less than ten feet of water.

"Breakfast, bitches," Sue called from the aft deck. I

made mental note to work on expanding her colorful vocabulary with more conservative hues.

An ironed white linen cloth covered the table. Six porcelain plates were set with freshly polished silverware and cloth napkins. A crystal pitcher of mimosa sat as a centerpiece with fresh orange slices floating among the glistening cubes. Ruth appeared from the galley with a large serving bowl of scrambled eggs. She was dressed in her pressed whites, buttoned and tucked. Her hair was pulled back in a neat ponytail tied with a sliver of duct tape. Her face, without makeup, radiated in the morning light.

"So, doesn't your sister look nice this morning?" Rose asked.

"Shit." I knew the look. Moreover, the list, in its entirety, of potential carnal partners on board, was disconcerting. Strike that. Downright disturbing.

"Good morning, brother." Ruth served me a large scoopful of eggs. Bacon and sausage will be out in a moment." Tarbaby followed with the meat. He was strangely clean shaven and neatly dressed absent requisite mystery stains. "Isn't it a beautiful morning?"

Sue tilted her head, Rose laughed, Brad sighed, I gagged. "You got to be kidding me."

Deuce sat, held my hand and bowed his head. "Please bow your head for grace."

Awkwardly, we complied. This was not our customary ritual. Sue and Brad were straight up atheist, believing all available evidence suggested a chaotic genesis and religion to be a construct of the man to control the masses. Rose, Ruth, and I were spiritual but not in a conforming matter. Some less conforming than others. Hobo, still damp from his morning dip, wedged himself between Rose and myself, leaving me flanked with an insufferable twit to my left and the senior member of the Breakfast Rum Club to the right. Their hands were both dry and strong. Their grips firm. The air was remarkably still. Barely mid-morning, the sky darkened, and the stars shown brilliantly. Deuce's unspoken voice was clear. "The seventieth son of the seventieth son and final son of man. May we do your will. Amen." The dogs howled. I opened my eyes squinting into the light. Everyone, save Rose, was eating, oblivious to the midday celestial sighting,

"You good, Zeke? How many cups of Deuce's Ambrosia did you drink this morning?" Rose asked, suspicious of my characteristically odd behavior. I clearly amped up my peculiar a notch for her to take notice.

I looked at Deuce. He winked his empty socket. Hobo giggled. Brad passed a platter of French toast stuffed with cream cheese. Sue smiled. Jaws farted.

∞∞∞∞

The prevailing breeze had rotated the stern of the boat toward the island. Hobo squeezed his slender frame in beside me on the bottom step of the cat. Our feet dangled carelessly in the emerald water. "Look familiar?" He pointed to the two men in street clothing standing at the end of the dock, separated from the armed, angry looking minions just far enough to be out of earshot yet close enough to intervene should the occasion warrant. Theirs was an ostensible, nervous trust, their body language conveyed an alliance out of necessity, not one of friendship. Stalin and Hitler came to mind. I secretly pondered which monster was which. The tropical sun was up, now fully illuminating the suspicious scene with its harsh light shimmering off the innumerable shades of blue and green. The cat's anchor had slid on the sandy bottom and we drifted to no more than 200 meters off shore, earning the unwelcomed interest of the armed goons.

"No, not really." I strained, but my old eyes really could not make out the features of the two men in question at this distance. They could have been anyone.

Deuce flung Hobo a pair of binoculars. Hobo snatched them out of the air with one hand without taking his eyes off the unfolding scene. "Try these."

"Well, I be damned." I put the glasses down for a moment. "I thought he was spending his days in sand land."

"UAE. No need to be such a flaming racist, Ezekiel. And it would appear as he is not. Your president needs to complete his duty before the ninth planet returns once again." Hobo pointed to the dock. "And the other man?" He asked.

I ignored his request. "First off, he is the ex-president and current Secretary General of the United Nations. And one B, he was never 'my' president. Thank you. Secondly, what's Pluto got to do with this eccentricity?"

"Not the dwarf you have to worry about. It's Planet X, Wormwood, Nibiru, the Destroyer. She is seven times larger than Earth and, on this orbit, she comes close. So close, she will take up some two-thirds of the visible sky." He pointed again toward the dock. "Focus."

"Well, at least your Planet X just comes close and will not collide with Earth."

"Did you pay attention to anything in science class beside Cathy's panties?"

"In all fairness, it was a South Georgia public school, and they were exceptionally agreeable panties attached to a very lovely, young lass."

"A planet with a gravitational pull of seven times the size of Earth, traveling some 2,000 miles per second, passing even within 50,000 miles of Earth...what is it one might call such a scenario?" Hobo asked.

"This a test? You know I hate fucking tests." I was on vacation, not at camp poorly disguised as a science camp for fat kids.

"Language, old man, language. Your insistence to salt your vocabulary with coarse and vulgar terms is a vile insult to your ancient heritage." Hobo sighed and shook his head in disappointment before answering his own question. "Heralded by marked changes in climate, volcanic activity, earthquakes, I believe the term you are looking for is extinction event."

"To be clear, I wasn't looking for a term. But, yeah... that is a term I have heard in a few apocalyptic movies. Further, I am a coarse and vulgar man, Hobo. Feel free to exit the theater at your earliest convenience should I offend your delicate ears." I was getting annoyed at the forced morality Hobo asserted. I continued, "But aren't we a few hundred million-years-old. Where has your destroyer of planets been hiding out?"

"Some believe it's on a massive, elliptical orbit that brings it through your solar system every 360 years or so. The orbit rarely intersects so closely with Earth."

"But something that damn big...wouldn't it at some point come close enough to create a little havoc or at least get noticed?"

"Rose is spot on. You need to work on your listening skills."

"What listening skills?"

Hobo gave me his disappointed face. "Numerous ancient texts chronicle sighting of a massive celestial object and unexplained natural disasters timed to the event. Sea partings, walls crumbling, earthquakes... floods...to name a few you might have heard of. Now, can we please focus on the task at hand? Let's fix what is in our power to resolve and don't worry about that which is not within our power to control."

"You reading motivational tweets in your spare time?" I asked. Hobo frowned. I held the glasses up, studying the second man. "How the hell did he get out of jail so fast?" Khalid Muhammad of the Black Panthers was exchanging a rigid handshake with the Secretary General of the United Nations and former U.S. president. Unfortunately, a likely scenario for the Rose Garden. Yet, not a normal every day event for a small dock in a tiny island off the coast of an insignificant third world country in Central America. I continued to watch as the two boarded different boats, each followed by a contingent of the dangerous men. They sped off in opposing directions.

"Peculiar."

"Not so much." Hobo said. "Once you establish who he is, nothing he does will surprise you anymore."

"He being the former president of the U.S.?"

"An agent of the seed of the serpent" Hobo said, with an uncharacteristic dread in his voice. Hobo jumped up.

"What the hell, man. You can't say something like that about our former president and just jump and leave."

"Not your president...right?"

Hobo joined Tarbaby on the deck and assisted him in lowering the launch into the sea with Jaws and Waldo already securely aboard. It was carnival seating and the two wanted to ensure the most comfortable seats allowing for the best view. Rose provided tinted doggles and a bright orange life vest for Jaws. No doubt Rose had applied a liberal coat of SPF 50 sunscreen, as well. She was a helicopter mom.

The breeze stiffened, and waves crested the shallow dock. Hobo stepped back down to water level, tying the launch off at the steps. Tripod leapt off the deck, landing gracefully on the launch's undulating bow. He assumed a three-legged "I am the king of the world" pose. No one laughed. He seemed disappointed. I gave him an air high-five in appreciation for his comedic attempt. Tripod lost his tentative purchase on the damp deck and slipped into the water. Everyone laughed.

"You wanna give the Tripod a hand there, Ezekiel?" Sue asked.

"Oh, hell no." I had seen this movie. Tripod was pissed.

In a foolish effort to restore spousal privileges, Brad belly flopped into the water and eagerly lifted Tripod into the launch, receiving a golden shower of love for his efforts. It was Tripod's signature move. Tripod and Sue were intensely satisfied with the outcome.

"Your trouble, Ezekiel, is that you can't seem to grasp the immense elasticity of reality." Hobo whispered.

"What the hell does that even mean?" I had heard this line of shit from him before. I had grown tired and frustrated at his riddles. "Speak English...I know...you are speaking English." I yelled in frustration.

"Language, Ezekiel. Language," Hobo admonished me again.

Deuce leaned over the stern and asked, "You boys having a lovers' quarrel?"

"While I have great love for this son of man, we have no carnal knowledge of each other, Deuce," Hobo deadpanned.

"Good to know. An ancient pledge to Gabriel is none the less a pledge, I suppose. Even if it is ill-timed barn door closure." Deuce squinted into the sun, pondering before continuing, "Then, again, I believe that oath applied specifically to the female of the species."

"Regardless, Deuce, I have no carnal knowledge of Ezekiel," Hobo replied, nonplussed.

"What about Ezekiel's sister?" I thought I might as well ask. Hobo ignored me.

Deuce giggled and gave Hobo an out. "You mind giving Tarbaby a hand with the cooler? Zeke drinks a lot of beer."

"Pot, kettle, black," I said to Deuce.

"You really got to work on that racist attitude of yours, Ezekiel."

Deuce laughed, I sighed, Jaws farted.

"Where did Brad disappear to?" I asked. Deuce laughed and pointed toward the bow of the catamaran. His lips were affixed to a very large pink flamingo blow up raft. "Yeah, that is going take a while." His face was already pale and damp from the effort.

Sue added cheerfully, "...and there are two of those giant bitches." She took a long pull on her cigarette. "He really should give up smoking. Brad's lung capacity is for shit." Sue looked to Rose for affirmation; "You know what I mean." The girls shared an intimate giggle at my gender's expense.

"I represent that remark."

Rose smiled and kissed me on the cheek. "Yes, you do, honey."

"Ouch."

"You know I have a compressed air tank," Deuce noted.

"I do," Sue deadpanned.

"Can Zeke borrow it?" Rose giggled coquettishly.

Hobo maneuvered the launch to the shady side of the boat in order to keep the dogs cool. "This could take a bit."

"Nah, he will pass out shortly."

On cue, Brad heroically face-planted onto the cargo netting strung between the cat's twin hulls. The flamingo, half-inflated, folded over onto Brad, expelling its meager air pressure and giving the appearance of two exhausted lovers. I grabbed a beer. Deuce grabbed an air tank. While Deuce inflated the flamingos, one pink and one blue, a mating pair I could only assume, I nursed Brad back to consciousness.

"Still in Sue's doghouse?" I asked Brad.

Brad took a long pull, finishing the cold beer, "Under."

"What spousal commandment did you infringe?" Deuce asked, making quick work on inflating the floats.

Brad shrugged. I answered for him, "Played a little grab ass with a hot little mother-daughter duo and rung up a massive bar tab in said process."

Deuce squinted into the sun, rubbing his gray stubble. "Nah, Sue be a good woman. Comfortable in her own skin. What else you do, boy?"

Brad shrugged again. Ruth brought us all a beer. She had changed into her daring tiny white thong. Deuce raised an eyebrow. Ruth pecked him on his check innocently.

Deuce laughed and eyed Brad with his empty socket with a knowing look. "You didn't…"

Brad scrambled to his feet. "I think maybe you did." Brad walked off.

"Did what?" I asked.

"I think Brad gained Old Testament knowledge of Tarbaby's whore," Deuce speculated.

"Not that I condone said fornication. Or in the case of Tarbaby's cemetery whore, even understand its fleeting appeal." I shuddered to the visual. Sloppy seconds was never an attractive option, but I was reasonably certain Tarbaby was on the second or third page of the whore's well-worn dance card in the graveyard. She likely rented her love out in quarter hour increments. "In Brad's defense, Sue did send the

girl up to him and compensate her for said services...
in advance."

Deuce looked at me as if I was nuts. "Okay, I heard it."

Deuce threw his beer back and smiled broadly
while affixing lines to the giant floats. He tossed
the lines into the water and drug them to the stern. I
found the girls effortlessly treading water behind the
boat sipping mimosas. Ruth awkwardly climbed onto
the pink flamingo performing a disturbingly sensual
impromptu lap dance, providing an unencumbered
view of her intimate tats. Sue inelegantly mounted
the blue inflatable, sans the overt sexual performance.
Tarbaby secured the inflatables lines to the launch as
we all climbed aboard, save Hobo.

∞∞∞∞

Seven lumps of coal cast an irregular shadow across
the dock. Coal. The long dead remains of dinosaurs cast
to the ground by some streaking meteor, comet, or, if
Hobo was correct, massive planet. The gravity of which
shattered Earth's protective ice ring, creating some
massive flood subsequently chronicled by virtually
every ancient civilization. Stuff of fairy tales, I know.
Science scoffs.

"Who smuggles coal?" I pondered. It had been
rendered worthless by our previous president. An
energy source that gave life to so much of this civilization
now demonized by the politically correct, man-bunned,
hipster, socialist crowd. It is so easy to be a liberal. It is
the apparent moral high ground. Save the planet, feed the
poor, greed is bad, rich people are evil, all religions (save
Christianity) though misguided are peaceful, everyone
is a winner, you can be anything you want to be, do what
you want, sexuality is fluid, there are no consequences.

Problem is, this is the stuff of unicorns, pots of golds, fairy tales, white men that can jump, and trashed white girls that can dance. Let's get real. With massive amounts of data, infinite funding, and the world's finest computing resources, the weatherman still presents THIS afternoon's weather forecast as a percent chance of an event. And betting against the weatherman is typically the smart money. Yet still, it is settled science the Earth is getting warmer and man is singularly to blame. The entire concept of settled science is simply absurd. Generation after generation, we mock our ancestors for their ignorance as we promulgate a new flurry of certainties that trample on the last generation's set of settled science. Our ideas, our shared truths, will be held just as barbaric to future generations. Facts are rarely facts. Truth, I hear, is not subject to the whimsical fancies of the masses regardless of level of educational attainment or degree of consensus. Predisposed bias, self-interest, and the entire collection of human flaws sways almost all data collection and analysis. Yet, we blindly insist we base our decisions and findings on this false god of data. Facts over perception, we delude ourselves.

During the nascent years of the computer revolution, a professor urged his charges to always consider "garbage in is garbage out." He continued, "The written word conveys more weight than that of the spoken, the typewritten more than that of the written, and the green bar printout more that the typed." I said nascent years. He added, "Yet it is often the truth lies in the reciprocal order." His lessons largely discarded by the pride and arrogance of the overeducated, overconfident jesters that run our government's institutions, our corporations, and most disturbingly, the hallowed halls of higher learning. Pseudo-knowledge is the false god of the Millennials. They anxiously await the extinction of the Boomers and their archaic ideas where Millennials can reestablish the dream of the utopian one free world of love, peace, and justice we Boomers destroyed. Good luck with that.

"Political rants aside, why are there seven lumps of coal on a remote coral island off the coast of a tiny, nascent country?"

"A gift," Deuce answered my unspoken question. "Your president, former president," he corrected himself, "gifted the lumps to Khalid Muhammad, his naïve ally. And not just coal, Zeke, sea coal."

"A distinction without a difference."

"Perhaps. Sea coal washed up on the shores of ancient Peru. Some suggest it was used for heating, smelting, and cremation."

"Cremation? The Incans cremated their dead?"

"Only the ones they preferred not visit the afterlife."

"Makes no sense. Does Belize even have any coal deposits?"

"Unlikely," Deuce added, "But I think it more a misguided symbolic gesture and a gesture not appreciated by Khalid. Carbon was the building block of your world. And coal is pretty much a chunk of concentrated carbon. If one wanted an Earth creation mulligan, one might begin with carbon."

"That seems like a stretch, and why seven lumps?"

"Cathy Carter in your Sunday School class, as well? Everything of note is divisible by seven."

"First, no. She was a left-handed Catholic...a Lutheran. Secondly, have you ever heard of the Baker Act?" I paid attention when Rose was studying for the Bar. "Family members can get you tossed in the loony bin without your consent." I smiled a malicious smile.

"Don't mock, Ezekiel. You wear your fake disbelief

on your sleeve and it is unappealing. Embrace what you know to be true."

"That you and your butt buddy Hobo are bat-shit crazy?"

"The very fact that bats shit implies nothing but order. Eat, poop, mate, sleep. It is what you animals do."

"That the Readers Digest abridged version of mankind? I think Tarbaby is the only sane one among you assholes."

"We might need to add drink to Tarbaby's list," Deuce replied with a sly grin.

"Ahhh. A sense of humor. Perhaps you are a human after all. And whom might want said creation do over?"

"America: Land of the serpent."

"A little help?" Tarbaby interrupted our conversation struggling to lift the beer-laden cooler onto the dock.

I knelt down and grabbed the handle to the cooler. It was heavy. Thicker and consequently heavier, the local brew is bottled in reusable bottles. I took solace in there was enough beer to last the afternoon on the Caye.

"Need a break." Tarbaby dropped his side of the cooler onto the dock, lifted the lid, and extracted a beer, opening it with his front tooth.

"That explains a lot," I motioned to his missing teeth before grabbing a beer from the cooler. I sat and used the opener conveniently located on the bottom of my sandals. Everyone else had made it on shore. Brad and Rose were putting on snorkel gear. Ruth, sans top, was on the swan float tied to a proximate palm. Sue occupied the adjacent swan tethered in turn to Ruth's inflatable.

Sue yelled, "While I am still young and beautiful."

Deuce walked by carrying additional provisions, stooped down and grabbed a beer for Sue. "Why the hell Ruth not helping?" I asked.

"Your sister. You tell me why."

"Hell if know. I'm just happy she has her hoo-hah marginally covered."

Three beers later, we managed to get the cooler to the covered picnic area. I wandered off with two beers in hand toward the back corner of the island sheltered by a small cluster of trees. Mangroves, actually, but they had grown peculiarly high. On the west side was a narrow opening in the mangroves. I cautiously peeked my head in, prepared for a random jaguar to pounce through the opening. The probability of said event was low but the consequences high. A campfire still glowing with remnants of coal, coconut hulls, and burnt palm fronds was at the opening's center. Coral chunks surrounded the fire pit. A spit supported by mangrove branches held a small, tin kettle filled with a dark, aromatic liquid. A felled palm lay conveniently close to the fire pit. In the trees, several planks of washed up driftwood from the carcasses of ill-fated boats had been lashed together to make a small sleeping platform. A tattered piece of blue tarp covered the sleeping platform, the corners gently flapping in the breeze. The mangroves were dense above it. Between the tarp and the mangroves, the area was sheltered from a small storm. A large storm would flood the entire island. A pink plastic chair hung from another sturdy branch by two frayed hemp ropes, forming a make shift swing. A second platform was visible from the sleeping platform higher in the mangrove above the tarp. A blue plastic barrel with mosquito netting lashed to the top collected rainwater from the tarp and sat at the rear of the clearance.

I climbed to the highest platform and located a dry bag stowed underneath. I grabbed the bag and sat on the platform. In each direction, there was a small opening in the mangrove. Approach vectors in all directions could be monitored from this location. I opened the bag. Waterproof matches, a sat phone, and a handful of MREs poured out onto the platform. In my irrational haste to return the items, I knocked most of the contents off onto the sand.

"Need a hand riffling through my belongings, Ezekiel?"

I peeked through the mangrove leaves searching for the source of the familiar voice. In the dim light at the bottom, I saw a vision. "Mrs. Brunel, I presume?" Petite with pale skin despite the tropical sun, she had her long blond curls pulled back into a ponytail. Her blue eyes radiated like her invented husband Hobo's. She wore pink booty shorts and a heavenly smile. She had the body of a gymnast, small, yet powerful. Every muscle, every delicate curve, was flawlessly delineated. In every way, Aja was a vision. A not so subtle clue that God was a man or a lesbian. She nodded. Aja was a vision of few words. She motioned for me to come down. I scampered down the mangrove. Aja wrapped her arms around me, kissing me on the check, pressing her not unattractive bare breast against my chest. Overall, not an unpleasant moment.

Rose is a woman with intense mystical instincts. She walked through the narrow opening, clearing her throat. I turned sidewise in a futile attempt to hide the evidence of my guilt. Aja moved to embrace Rose. Rose stuck out her hand. "It is so good to see you..." Rose looked down surveying my vision, "...all of you...again, Aja." Aja smiled. Rose smiled back at Aja with one eye while glaring at me with the other. A unique, disquieting talent. It was not the first time I had been busted appreciating the demonstration of God's delicate handiwork on Aja.

"Did you say again?" I asked Rose. "You have met Aja?"

"The stupid act ain't gonna play, Ezekiel. She is the

little tart that fell in your lap at Cirque de Soleil that was shacking up with your crazy buddy Hobo in the Windstream."

I raised my eyebrows, wrinkling my ever-expanding forehead. Reality, Hobo explains, is elastic and runs in parallel waves. This, at times, seems unique to me as no one else plays along with my perplexing narratives. The previous meeting with Aja, I thought, was in one of those parallel waves. I pinched myself, concluding this was that wave, or that was this one, or yet another wave with intersecting points in time.

Aja laughed and turned to Rose. "Want a tour of my place? Ezekiel has already made himself at home." I blushed. Rose flashed. Aja jumped into the tree, making the platform in two graceful steps.

"You live here?' Rose asked.

"Nah. Just been hanging out watching for the past few days."

"Watching what? The Jesus and frigate birds? This place makes Gilligan's island look like a two-star Cancun resort during spring break."

"Serpents." Aja deadpanned.

CHAPTER SIX

The mast cast a long, ominous shadow into the sea. The cat bounced in the water, straining against the anchor line. Deuce struggled against the wind to bring the launch alongside the cat. Brad, leaping across the void, misjudged the waves and slipped into the sea. The current pushed him under the launch, effectively executing a self-inflicted keelhaul. Sue shrugged and jumped aboard effortlessly.

I was a dozen or so beers in, a bit sunburnt and brain fried from the conversation with Aja. I had expended half my time probing her for additional information that I did not receive and the other half willing myself not to ogle her bare breast. She did not seem to object to or even notice my attention or discomfort, but Rose held one eye on me at all times to ensure should my eye wander south and linger, there would be consequences: silent, swift, severe.

I searched out our cabin and jumped into the head. To date, I had showered outside on the aft deck and pissed overboard, avoiding the cramped head for all hygienic duties, save one, or, should I say, number two? There was currently a queue waiting for the outdoor shower. The ladies felt the need to shower, shampoo, shave, and condition, despite Deuce's stern warning on the limitations of fresh water. I was eager to get in between the luxurious ten-thread count Belizean faux cotton sheets for a little down time reflection prior to dinner and a second round of competitive drinking. After banging around for ten minutes in the tight confines of the hurt locker searching for the shower, I discovered a furtive bracket toward the low ceiling. It appeared to be in the prime location for a showerhead but, to my growing frustration, there was no showerhead attached nor piping leading to the bracket. I yelled upward through the open portal for help, but Brad had the music set at a level appropriate for a nursing home for retired eighties big-hair rockers. I could tell by the motion of the boat Deuce had us underway. No help was imminent. I was on my own to uncover the mystery of the missing head.

Frustrated, I hurled the liquid soap bottle at the mirror but instead found the faucet. There was a reason, despite the promise of my childhood dreams, I was not a major league pitcher. The faucet dislodged and hung by a flexible tube to the floor, solving the mystery of the missing showerhead and furtive bracket. The soap bottle, however, split, emptying its slippery contents on the fiberglass floor.

Problem solved, I thought. I attached the faucet to the bracket and turned on the water. It was inexplicably ice cold. I slid from side to side in the confined space on the soapy, tilting floor, finally getting my footing with the assistance of the trash bin contents recently reduced to a toxic mush coating the floor with an unattractive, yet lifesaving shit-tinged, coarse surface. "Frigging MacGyver," I said aloud, congratulating myself on the ingenious solution. I think I mentioned I had consumed a few beers.

We were heading to Half Moon Caye, which meant we would venture outside the protection of the reef into the Caribbean Sea. The marked increased rocking of the boat signaled Deuce had breached the protection of the reef. Seawater began pouring into the open porthole situated on the wall of the head, solving yet another mystery of why the openings were called portholes instead of windows or underway holes. I struggled, slipping on the mush, and fell face first onto the plastic toilet. My knee, nose, and forehead were bleeding liberally, attempting to one up each other in a macabre contest to bleed me out. Smart money was on my nose. I managed to close the porthole as the shower water finally heated up and began spraying steaming hot water up my ass. I let out a primal yell as I lashed at the showerhead, knocking it off the wall. The showerhead was now comfortably positioned to unleash its lethal steam directly onto my exposed genitals. I screamed again and fell forward into the mirror, cracking both the mirror and my skull. Moments later, the world got smaller as I sank to the floor which was rapidly filling with water from the drain clogged with toilet paper and trash can flotsam.

Tarbaby eventually discovered me and lifted me onto the bed naked, soaking wet, covered in mostly dried blood, toilet paper mush, and the remnants of the trash bin contents. The flood had covered our cabin in about two inches of pink water, soaking all our clothes and much of our electronics.

"Zeke, you are a bit of a mess." Tarbaby noted

quietly, as he went about cleaning up as best he could.

I gingerly felt my forehead. A 3-inch gash above my eye was still seeping blood. Pink toilet paper mush covered both knees. Peeling the mush off yielded sizeable gashes on both knees still seeping the limited remainder of my blood supply.

Rose popped her head down through the overhead portal. "Dinner is...what the hell, Ezekiel?" She dropped down through the portal onto the bed. I screamed in pain. Rose looked down at Tarbaby lifting our wet bags off the floor. "Be happy, be very happy you are critically injured, husband." I think she meant it.

Tarbaby and Hobo lifted me through the portal and splayed me out on the cargo netting. Rose hosed me off. The cold water shrunk what little dignity remained. The water also opened up the wound above my eye. Sue brought an ice compress and held it over my eye in what I thought a genuine and, in her case, rare, act of kindness. "I hope you're a grower...sure as hell not a shower." Rose, in a similarly rare moment of compassion, tossed a towel over my junk.

Salt water splashed over the bow from the force of the waves. The salt water on my open wounds was not pleasant. Deuce dropped the sail, slowing the boat's forward motion, and came to inspect my wounds with a flashlight held in his teeth. "Gonna need some stiches," he pronounced.

"And a blood transfusion," Sue helpfully added.

I relentlessly mocked Rose for preparing for little emergencies that never materialized. Sewing kit, first aid supplies, hunting knife, spare undies, 380 semi-automatic, flashlight, water, super glue, spare magazine...all part of her gear. Outside the spare drawers, all unused items. Consequently, I forgave her current enthusiasm. Like the broke clock, this was her moment to be right. Hobo and

Tarbaby carried me to the rear deck dining table. Rose brought out the suture kit, swabbed my head thoroughly with the enclosed antibiotic wipes and began to thread the needle. My level of dread was severe. Her level of inappropriate excitement, palatable. I was ambiguous as to her level of sobriety, but it likely exceeded mine.

"You ever done this, Rose?" Deuce inquired.

"Hell no, but I watched a YouTube video once."

Deuce shook his head. "Once. Okay then...good to go." Deuce turned around and started heading back inside.

"Where you going?" I feebly asked. At the moment, he irrationally seemed the only sane one on the boat.

"To get some killer weed to keep me from vomiting watching this shit show."

Rose, indifferent, shrugged and began. I squealed and jumped. Sue laughed. Brad puked. Jaws farted. Hobo grabbed Rose's hands and said, "Weed first."

Deuce handed me a lit pipe, and, without encouragement, I took several deep breaths before dropping the pipe to my side. Deuce had good weed connections. Hobo took Rose's hands and guided her stitch by stitch with closing the wound above my eye. All said and done, I felt no pain, only a bizarre detachment as she executed the procedure, gaining more confidence with each stitch. Next, without Hobo's assistance, she stitched up both knees and expertly scrubbed and bandaged my miscellaneous scratches and cuts.

Sue leaned over, nodded approval of Rose's needlework before lifting the cloth covering my junk. She giggled. "That little thing will never get old."

∞∞∞∞

Surveying his bedchamber, the prince lay awake, surrounded by pillows and blankets, impatiently awaiting minstrels and well-bosomed maidens to greet him with merry song and infinite nourishment. Annoyed at the delay, Jaws greeted me with an accusatory sideways glance before farting and licking his phantom balls. Jaws had an air of entitlement and was mystified at the world's failure to satisfy his lofty expectations. He was the optimum millennial, demanding the fruits of hard labor, sans the labor.

Tarbaby had swabbed the floors, replaced the sheets, drained the bathroom and hung our wet clothes across the cat rigging to dry in the Caribbean breeze. Jaws, still damp and sandy from his frolic on the caye, restored chaos to Tarbaby's order.

The day's near lethal level brew of beer, weed, pain, and sun had worked it's magic. I fell instantly asleep atop the damp, sandy sheets, snuggled up against Jaws. His farts and heavy snoring were music to my ears. Rose cursed under her breath, stripped her damp and bloody bikini, and stepped into the boat's tiny hurt locker to shower. She denies possessing normal bodily functions. Her full, sensual lips woke me as she kissed Jaws. He farted, kicked me in the balls, and stepped over me to wedge between the wall and me.

"Gross," Rose exclaimed.

"Yeah, he stinks."

"I was talking about you. You're bloody as hell and stink like shit."

I felt my forehead. Blood was oozing out. Caked blood had congealed with sand and generously spotted the sheets. Yet, even so, there was no way in hell I was returning to the watery torture chamber to shower.

"I'll sleep on the netting." Rose slammed the cabin door. Seemingly, I had joined Brad in the spousal doghouse. Jaws planted his massive paws in my gut to gain suitable height and shimmied out of the porthole above the bed in search of better company. I rolled over into a pool of damp, sticky blood. "Shit," I mumbled.

∞∞∞∞

Reggae music filtered into the cabin along with sounds of laughter and the smell of weed. The boat slowed and shifted direction. I braved the hurt locker and showered without incident before heading top side to survey the frivolity and hopefully locate the nearest doghouse exit. Moonlight danced off the water, and eerie shadows swayed in time on the beach like ghostly lovers. A solitary, dim light illuminated a wooden dock that appeared to be Deuce's intended target. Deuce succumbed to technology, fired up the engine, and lowered the sail from his spot at the helm. Hobo jumped off the bow as the cat gently slid by, securing the line as the boat gently bumped the dock. Tarbaby secured the stern.

"You are alive," Deuce noted, although, from the tone of his voice, this may have been a question rather than a statement.

I nodded. "Appears as such. You are pretty good at this captain shit."

Deuce tipped his hat and smiled. "Where are we?" I asked.

"Half Moon Caye."

"People live here?"

"Live? A few. Caretakers mostly."

The island was dark, lit, poetically, only by the half-moon. Hobo switched off the dock light and Deuce killed the boat lights. The stars leapt from the sky like tiny pinpricks of light on a dark canvas. The Milky Way seemed impossibly close, blazing a blurry swatch across the middle of the sky. Mars burnt a flickering bright orange and Venus dotted the sky adjacent to the moon. We gazed into the sky with an uncharacteristic awe. This was not a philosophical crowd. At the sizable risk of being corny, it was a transcendent moment. We were in reverence of something that we saw every night but never really saw.

"Beautiful, is it not?" Hobo asked rhetorically. The answer was self-evident.

I nodded in agreement.

"Gotta get home soon."

"Just where the hell might that be again?" I asked Hobo. "East Saint Louis?"

Hobo pointed into the sky at the brightest star. He was consistent with this fable.

"Beer me, bitches," Sue yelled from the bow of the boat. A chorus of dissimilar orders with analogous meaning rang out. Everyone was lying face up on the net, gazing into the night sky. I grabbed a handful of beers and headed to the bow. Deuce switched on the cat's underwater lights, providing a bit of additional illumination without spoiling the celestial view.

I handed out the beers. Sue just stared at me without accepting the brew. "Got an opener, dick weed?"

I tagged Tarbaby in. He opened the beer with his good tooth. Sue frowned but accepted the beer, wiping it off with the edge of my t-shirt. I surrendered the shirt for said purpose and assumed a position by Rose. She snuggled up tight against me, more to keep warm than as a romantic gesture, I sensed. I took what I could get. I laid face down, staring into the clear, illuminated water full of life. A family of menacing Barracudas lay motionless, staring back with malevolent eyes. A large loggerhead turtle surfaced briefly for air before returning to the bottom to continue his perpetual snack of sea salad. An eight-foot nurse shark swam by disturbing the sand, revealing a couple of juvenile rays. Parrotfish, sergeant majors, blowfish, ribbon and a host of other colorful tropical fish danced beneath me in a choreographed display of the beauty and horror of life. Predators prey. It is their nature. The Cuda lashed out with implausible speed, taking a parrotfish in a single flash of motion.

"Damn skitters," Rose yelled.

Sue slapped Brad hard across the face. "Damn, missed him." She slapped Brad again.

Deuce laughed. Hobo produced a citronella candle as a battalion of mosquitos arrived to reinforce the vanguard. Paradise had its pitfalls. Aja shared a bottle of insect repellant. She offered it to me.

I laid quietly, admiring the show. "No thanks."

"You'll get eaten."

"No, he won't. He is immune to skitters," Rose explained.

Sue starred at my back, "Mother fucker's a tiny-dicked vampire. Skitters ain't even landing on him, much less biting the bloodsucker. Professional courtesy?"

Rose giggled. "He chased the mosquito fogger through the neighborhood as kid every night. He sucked in enough DDT to alter his genetic makeup."

"Bullshit." Sue exclaimed. "Ain't even you dumb-ass rednecks that stupid."

"Truth," I mumbled, confident I had just called myself dumber than a dumb-ass redneck. "Right about dusk every evening in the summer, we would climb the hill at the entrance to our neighborhood. Soon as the skitter truck made the turn down our street, we raced blindly into the toxic fog down the uneven road trying to stay in the fogger's slipstream. Winner was the last kid still in the fog. I won a lot."

"Seems pretty dangerous for a bunch of kids." Sue noted, not believing my story.

"Seems stupid." Rose noted. "But..." she whispered "... he is from the south."

"I represent that remark." Stupid or not, I was damn proud of my heritage. "At least us rednecks don't intentionally fall down mountains strapped to a pair of thin, parallel sticks."

Jaws gingerly jumped up on the dock, leading Tripod and Waldo for a brisk, exploratory stroll on to the sandy beach.

"My tiny baby is so cute," Rose said, admiring Jaws' backside as he sashayed down the dock.

"The only thing tiny about your boy is his legs," Sue accurately noted.

Ruth spewed her beer. "Jaws has the legs of a ballerina." Ruth took another gulp of beer before adding "And the body of an offensive lineman."

Rose gave her a harsh look as everyone else smartly stifled their laughter. Rose did not cotton to anyone making fun of her child. Giving me shit was perfectly acceptable, if not encouraged. Criticism of her baby, warranted or not, would draw live fire from her dark eyes.

Ruth raised an index finger. "Your boy is a fat ass. Deal with it, Rose."

Gauntlet dropped, Rose returned fire, "And you are a lazy whore.'

Tarbaby smiled, "She ain't lazy."

Ruth smiled, "Ahhh, so sweet, Tarbaby. The defender of my honor."

I shook my head. Rose started to argue that was not high praise. I whispered, "Technically, honey you should have said she is 'lazy' and a 'whore.'"

"Truth," Rose nodded.

June 2017: *Secretary General of the UN Obama announced the relocation of the UN headquarters to Brussels today in a news conference. "The U.S. <dramatic pause, smirk> has far <dramatic pause, smirk> too long <dramatic pause, smirk> abdicated <dramatic pause, sip of 'water', smirk> its duty to lead. Consequently <dramatic pause, smirk>, until the U.S. <dramatic pause, smirk> recognizes its duty <dramatic pause, smirk> to the African community <dramatic pause, smirk> for a safe, and sovereign space <dramatic pause, smirk> within its borders, the U.S. <dramatic pause, smirk> will lose <dramatic pause, gesturing to be seated, smirk> its seat on the UN Security Council. This represents <dramatic pause, smirk> another step <dramatic pause, smirk> in a new World Order <dramatic pause, smirk> led by men <dramatic pause> and women <smirk> with vision."*

To facilitate the headquarters relocation from New York to Brussels, Obama announced a $1.2 billion assessment to be paid by the United States.

Alongside Global News

CHAPTER SEVEN

Ancient star light faded from the sky supplanted with a full palette of fresher pastels blooming just beneath the horizon. The wind was dead calm, and the ocean stood flat, shimmering a widening array of blinding colors, reflecting the artist's ethereal talents. I pulled myself up to a sitting position, finding myself alone on the bow. The aroma of coffee filled the air and the sound of running water signaled the presence of others stirring about. I stumbled toward the galley to grab a cup spotting Hobo showering naked on the stern. Hobo grinned broadly and mouthed a silent good morning. I shook my head. I had seen this man naked more times than Rose as of late. I grabbed a cup and shortly Hobo joined me in the galley with a towel around his waist. "Let's explore." It was more of a command than a request.

We walked down the dock and crossed quickly to the opposite side of the island. The Caye, shaped like a half moon, was less than a hundred yards wide. This area was mostly cleared of undergrowth, dotted with palm trees, a few makeshift shacks, and a couple of official looking wooden buildings with rusted tin roofs sprouting long, thin, radio antennas; overall giving the appearance of an upside-down cockroach. Iguanas the size of Jaws lingered on top of the coral while a herd of crabs scattered at our feet, scampering between fallen coconuts for cover from the invading hordes.

The sun breeched the horizon in a spectacle of searing light shimmering off the sand and sea, casting long shadows interrupted with slashes of vivid colors. Hobo guided me to the far side of the island and we sat at the edge of the water on a collection of old stones and bricks cast into the sea by some largely forgotten hurricane. A rusted beam lead to the remains of an old lighthouse partially submerged in the sea. Chaos always wins.

Hobo gingerly placed a chunk of coal on the rusted iron beam with a strange sort of reverence. "Know what this is?"

"Coal," I responded. My grandmother burnt coal in the fireplace. It was the family's only source of heat. On a cold afternoon, I would watch a single piece burn for hours while my mom joined her mom and my aunts around a large wooden form, sewing small scraps of material together to fashion a colorful patchwork quilt from scrap fabric. Then again, to be fair, she didn't have a television. I could watch the coal burn or listen to a bunch of old women complain about growing old and old men.

"Not just coal, sea coal."

"A distinction without a difference."

Hobo ignored me and continued, "Carbon, in its

most natural form, along with quicksilver, are your world's most precious resources."

"Not it's people?" I mocked. Hobo tilted his head and his brow furrowed. I clarified, "Our world's most precious resource... people, right...you meant to say people."

"Humans don't even crack the top ten. Gluttony, avarice, pride, lust, sloth, envy, wrath. Humankind once had the capacity for greatness. Now, most of humankind is reduced to mindless robots with, at best, the illusion of free will."

I shook my head. Again, do not argue or reason with crazy. "Okay, what about diamonds and gold?"

"They have their uses, but you humans so overvalue plentiful, largely decorative, resources."

"Talk about plentiful. There is a shit ton of coal in the ground. And our last president pretty much rendered it less than worthless."

"But did he?" Hobo asked.

"You paying attention to the news, Hobo? The president made it illegal to use the material in all fifty states. Almost every coal company in the world has gone, or is going, bankrupt."

"First off, there are only forty-nine states. Texas is its own Republic." Hobo corrected me.

It was a hard habit to break. Texas was thriving since its secession. A flood of American immigrants was attempting to seek asylum in the newly formed Republic. Real estate values in the Republic had exploded and economic growth was double digits.

"The question is, are you even listening to yourself? The media is just the public relations arm of the rich and the ruling elite. Best to look to the right for the real story if the media is pointing left. DeBeers made a market in diamonds which are plentiful and, quite frankly, not all that important of a resource."

"Yeah, I watched the movie. First decent DeCrappo film before he began jetting around the world in a private plane preaching to us mere mortals about climate change."

Hobo ignored my comment and continued, "And gold has some unique and useful characteristics. However, the supply should logically outweigh the demand. Your people pay to have gold dug from the ground in massive quantities, return it underground in locked vaults and then pay armed and overfed men to watch over it. You cannot eat it or use it as fuel. Humans just hoard gold. At the end of the day, it's just another Beanie Baby racket."

"So, you are saying I wasted over ten grand collecting Beanie Babies. Ouch." I had not.

"And who do you think is buying those bankrupt mining companies, Ezekiel?'

"The Kingmaker, George Smith, or, so I read in the public relations forum."

"And what might you know about him that ties him to your former president?"

"First, 'George Smith', my ass." I added air quotes. "What a half-ass alias."

Hobo nodded and smiled. I continued, "Smith was one of the suits we accused of manipulating the 2008 election for Barry. But then I woke up."

"But did you?"

I started to answer but thought better of it. I have always struggled identifying one reality from another. Maybe, in fact, there were no realities, just some virtual world we all imagined we lived in.

"Where are your other suits?" Hobo asked.

I thought for a moment, "Sam, the Shah of Iran's nephew, is dead. Decapitated by the BOI for 'failing his mission' as I recall. Goldstein, the Jewish money guy, was murdered in Florence by a gay prostitute." For some inexplicable reason, that brought me a touch of inappropriate joy. "The union dudes, I don't know. Frio Loco...well, he is kind of sort of the president, until the election gets resolved, at least."

"Let me help with the math, Ezekiel. All your suits are dead, save two; Smith and Frio."

"Guess that solves the mystery of the puppet master's identity. How did Smith get to be God, anyway?"

Hobo grinned. "Sarcasm, right?"

I smiled. Hobo was not very good at recognizing sarcasm. "Well, at least he thinks he is God."

"Funny thing, Ezekiel, you are pretty close to the mark. Smith has a lot in common with you."

"How so?" I foolishly took the bait.

"Seventieth son of the seventieth son. He is the darkness. Pedigree of evil; most recent, it was cash stolen from the Jews."

"What was he, all of twelve during the Nazi Rule?"

"Nineteen by the end of the war, but you miss my point. His godfather confiscated millions from Jews with little George in tow. This money made it into George's hands. But that is just the beginning. Hitler did not happen overnight. Nazi Germany was a slow-moving disaster. Many rich Jews saw it coming and secretly moved their immense wealth into numbered Swiss accounts. Many of those accounts remain unclaimed." Hobo added air quotes around "unclaimed."

"Why is that? Surely some family member survived Hitler."

"Likely, but without the account number and password, the Swiss bankers never officially released the money."

"So, how does his this help our kingmaker?"

"Little George was Jewish. A detail he cleverly hid

while helping his godfather loot the Jews' money. After the war, he successfully played the victim, worming his way into a job with Credit Suisse. Long story short, he stole the money, hundreds of millions. Then there was the Nazi Gold."

"But didn't the U.S. Army recover all the Nazi Gold?" I asked. Toward the end of the war, the U.S. set up special units to recover looted art, currency, and gold.

"Some, maybe even most, but we are talking billions. The Nazi's were very efficient murderers and thieves. Smith spirited away over half a billion in gold."

"Nice little nest egg if you don't mind forgoing sleep. Wasn't some of that gold pried out of the mouths of Jews?"

Hobo nodded.

"That is one sick and twisted bastard."

"Yes, his kind is indeed twisted." Hobo paused, staring off at the horizon. "But it wasn't a nest egg. It was his starter capital. Smith used his wealth and inside connections to manipulate markets, currencies, and political parties to expand his wealth and influence to unimaginable levels. Coal…" Hobo lifted the coal from the beam, "… is simply his next game. Drive down coal prices by hyping environmental concerns."

I finished Hobo's thought, "And buy up the coal and rail companies pennies on the dollar. Next, manipulate a gas and oil shortage and pocket massive profits."

"Sober you can be insightful, Ezekiel."

"Sober, you are insufferable, Hobo."

Sweat dripped from my face onto the rusted beam as our shade expired and the wind laid down. Hobo placed the coal into an inside pocket of his speedo making for a bizarre, asymmetrical codpiece. We headed back for the short stroll across the island to the leeward side.

"You know, Hobo, I can't seem to find the truth.

Everything I have learned, read, been told…hell, nearly all my beliefs keep falling apart with even a cursory inspection. As a society, we get a consensus on something and hold that consensus as fact."

Hobo smiled.

"And just when did we decide that consensus equaled the truth, Tuesday?"

"To paraphrase Napoleon," Hobo stood rigidly with his head tilted regally and placed his hands down his speedo, "history is just a pack of lies agreed upon."

"Not just history…everything. In the time before a digital footprint, our hero's fucked, farted, lied, and cheated just as much as today but with great anonymity."

"Coarse language aside, Ezekiel…" Hobo relaxed his pose and continued, "…sober Ezekiel is on a roll."

"We invite deception and fancy the story stained with the sex juices of adulterous whores and greed-driven kings. We desire passion, hope, and heroes and don't really give a rat's ass about the truth or consequences. A passionate, fictional story suits us better than the truth. We live in an age where the perception of the truth is far more important than the actual truth. And rather than correct the story, we mold our actions around a collective, false narrative."

We approached the dock. The boat lay quietly. "Not a creature is stirring," I noted to Hobo. He managed a courtesy smile. We sat at the edge of the dock shaded by a giant palm bent almost horizontal to the water by a century of tropical storms.

Hobo pointed to the palm, "Determination is a key element to success."

My toes touched the clear, blue water. A ray hiding in the sand flew away. A four-foot barracuda eyed my toes with too much attention. I lifted my feet out of the water and tucked them under my legs. I pointed out the 'cuda to Hobo; "They must be Brits." Before Hobo could ruin my clever joke, I added, "'Cause they have a shitty dental plan." Hobo shook his head, absent even a courtesy smile.

"Do we even know the truth anymore?" Hobo was rarely forthcoming. As of late, he spoke in sentences I could understand instead of riddles. I wisely took the opportunity to pick his mind in a rare moment of clarity. History, by its very nature, should be a static story. It's in the past, yet we revise it endlessly to suit the current popular narrative.

Hobo shook his head vertically. "Like you said, we color the past with today's palate."

"What? The great Hobo quoting little old me."

"If you drank a little less, it might happen more often. Man's version of recorded history is a pack of lies severely influenced by the politics of those that pen it. Yet, there is an unbiased version of recorded history that is available."

"Pray tell. Amazon Prime?"

"You mock..." Hobo began.

I interrupted, "What I don't understand. Which is a shit ton."

"Human DNA contains memories."

"Say what? Microscopic DNA seems like a small, inefficient memory storage system. One would think its capacity better served for more important tasks like, say, how to build a brain."

"Even you aren't that naive. In your lifetime, Ezekiel, memory, storage devices, have improved ten-thousand-fold. Your cell phone has more memory and computing capability than that of the entire space shuttle."

"Truth." I nodded. But to recover all memories of all our ancestors on tiny DNA strands seems improbable, and then there is the whole manner of accessing the data."

"Not all memories. The human brain doesn't even move all memories to an accessible long-term memory, just the important ones."

"So, you are suggesting my DNA has the important memories of all my ancestors?"

Hobo nodded yes. "More like the most powerful memories. Recalling the location of one's keys is important. Seeing ones grandparents nude in the sex act, less important but more powerful."

"Calling bullshit, Hobo."

"Fair enough. It is a cognitive leap. Take Rose, for instance. Remember your trip to Naples and Pompeii?"

I nodded and quietly replied, "yes."

"What did she say?"

"That she had been there before."

"Had she?"

"No."

"Yet, Rose recalled a detailed story about escaping from the eruption of Mt. Vesuvius. Care to explain?"

I whispered, "She is just little bit nuts."

"Like you, Ezekiel, the definition of crazy is one that does not conform to the norm, so yes, she is a bit nuts. Also, like you, she is in touch, frankly even more so than you, to additional senses not available to most."

I heard Rose was crazier than me. Hobo had something right. "So, what makes her special?"

"There are no coincidences, Ezekiel. Rose, even Jaws, is with you for a purpose."

A school of mullet aimlessly passed underneath. The barracuda slashed through the water effortlessly, slicing a mullet in half. A pair of rays mopped up the leftovers and, in a matter of seconds, there was no sign of the mullet murder. Perhaps chaos is order.

"Powerful memories are imprinted on DNA. Like

running from a natural disaster, public executions, riots, plagues, massacres...."

"And witnessing grandparental coitus," I added, helpfully.

Hobo continued as if I had not interrupted. "Billions of people, each with tens of thousands of imprinted events. The collection and indexing of those unfiltered events would reveal a true account of history."

"Seems a herculean task, at best."

"Calculating pi was once a herculean task, as well. Take the cognitive leap, Ezekiel. What was unthinkable to a caveman is now displayed in ancient history museums."

I nodded. We were quiet for a moment. The sun warmed my neck as it climbed above the island. Life stirred on the boat. Deuce nodded from the bow, a mug of rum-tainted coffee in his hand. Tarbaby's head stuck above the coffin as he pulled himself out while balancing a beer. He pissed over the side of the boat while waving at us and destroying the idyllic view with his stubby member. I knew my time with Hobo being forthcoming was very limited, so I pressed on.

"What makes Rose so special...other than the obvious physical traits?" I self-high-fived.

"She is a Watcher."

Deuce walked up behind us with two mugs of coffee, mine spiked with rum. He sat, his long legs extending into the water. I pointed out the barracuda, still silent in the water, observing the action just underneath us, apparently not sated by his recent sushi breakfast.

"Don't be filling the boy's head with too much," Deuce said to Hobo.

"Running out of time," Hobo said, gulping his coffee and pushing off into the water. He swam with a grace and ease of a dolphin, barely disturbing the water.

New York; June 2017: *George Smith, the wealthy political kingmaker, has reportedly been quietly purchasing the assets of U.S. rail companies and worldwide coal reserves. It is estimated, through numerous shell corporations, Smith owns almost eighty percent of the coal reserves worldwide and majority ownership in every major railroad company in the U.S. Given the recently announced ban on fossil fuels, Smith has acquired trillions in assets for pennies on the dollar. Joe Kernan of CNBC said this morning on Squawk Box, "Smith has either gone mad or knows something the rest of us do not." Kernan further stated he would bet the latter.*

Guest anchor Davis Waite, the Executive Vice President of Waite, Waite, and Waite Financial, the second largest commercial lender in the world, speculated, "Smith or his puppets may have orchestrated the collapse of the coal markets. Wait for the next shoe to drop and it will be too late. You have to anticipate Smith's moves or you lose."

Alongside Global News

CHAPTER EIGHT

"Boobies," Rose squealed, pointing over the railing. She had the sense of humor of a twelve-year-old boy. Brad eagerly looked in the direction of Rose's extended arm. He was sorely disappointed.

The viewing platform was on the western end of the Caye at the end of a surprisingly long walk through an eerily canopied jungle. The Caye presented as two distinct ecosystems. More likely, the western end of the island was simply the natural state. Man, even in scant numbers, introduces chaos disguised as order in an orderly world disguised as chaos. School bus sized iguanas lined the jungle path, threatened only by the appearance of my Go-Pro. Their agents had schooled them well. The mosquitos, on the other hand, were unencumbered by representation and, as such, fearless, plentiful, and only slightly smaller than the indigenous dinosaurs. My childhood DDT vaccination provided adequate protection from the skitters. The others were less fortunate. Brad's face was swollen from a combination of skitter bites and fierce skitter pseudo-swatting. Sue held a grudge.

"At least there are no skitters up here." I looked at Brad's face in the bright sunlight and grimaced. The viewing platform breeched the jungle canopy. There was scant breeze and the mid-day sun was brutal. The metal rails were scorching hot and even the heat from the wood planks was quickly working its way through the soles of my sandals. Rare Boobies or not, I was ready to make my way back through the spooky jungle to the relative safety of the catamaran and the sweet comfort of shade and a cold beer.

"Red-Footed Boobies," Hobo began. "Look, there is an all-white one." He excitedly pointed as everyone began to make their way off the platform. Hobo began shooting video with my Go-Pro. I really needed to get pockets with locks on them when around him. "The white ones are unique to this Caye." Still on the platform, Hobo raised his voice to our back and continued, "The birds derive their name from Spanish sailors." As we continued walking, I heard his quick steps running down the platform. "Anyone venture a guess as to why?" Hobo started to answer his own question as he caught up to us.

"Slow your roll, scrawny ginger." Sue responded. "Bobo is the Spanish word for stupid. As in, mi espousa es muy fucking bobo. Spit balling here, but those birds looked pretty damn stupid."

Hobo's smile briefly faded with Sue's coarse language but quickly returned. His brow furrowed, and he cocked his head at a curious angle before continuing, "Perhaps I have underestimated your intelligence..."

Hobo paused, studying Sue intently before continuing, "...and purpose."

Shortly after lunch, grilled snapper tacos, we set sail for the five-mile cruise to The Big Ass Blue Hole. Big Ass differentiated this hole from the hundreds of other less notable blue holes in the Caribbean. This hole so blessed by Cousteau a few decades passed when he was a thing and did a thing at this site figuratively putting this hole on the map. The hole was already literally on the map or, at least, the charts. Rose and I planned to do a shallow dive of the Hole to cross off a bucket list item. We dove regularly since we moved to Belize, but I was definitely a blue-sky, open water diver. Caves freaked me the hell out. Sharks were Rose's kryptonite. I had managed to fubar my sinuses diving and regularly bled from my nose at depth. Then there was the series of cuts, abrasions, and gashes that decorated my body from the cat shower folly. If there were sharks, my expectation was the current state of my body would assure a cozy meet and greet.

Rose went below to change. I cracked another beer. Deuce nodded his disapproval. "The Hole is not a dive to take lightly."

"We are just going to do forty to fifty feet, turn the hole green, and come up for another beer." Deuce looked perplexed. I clarified our intent. "Blue hole, yellow pee..." Deuce scoffed.

Rose returned in Batman pajamas replete with cape. It was her mom's thing to send all her youngin's matching jammies every Christmas. Last Christmas, it was a superhero theme. She gifted me size smedium Antman. Not sure what she was saying.

"You diving in that?" Deuce asked Rose.

"Yup. Where's our dive shit, boss man?" I asked.

Deuce squinted in disapproval, nodded, and left us to secure our dive gear, only to return with mask and flippers about twenty minutes later. "Tanks empty." He noted. "Had to use the last of them to inflate Sue's flamingos. Priorities. You get that, right?" Deuce shrugged, handing us the snorkel gear.

Deuce navigated the cat through a narrow cut in the reef that surrounded the Hole. The water turned dark blue as we entered the much deeper hole. From a depth of twenty feet on one side to over three hundred on the other. He anchored inside the hole on a sandy shelf close to the circular reef.

Tarbaby tossed the tethered inflatables overboard. Aja and Sue followed them; Aja executing a perfect swan dive from top the cat and Sue, a notable, if not stylish, belly flop. She was bright, not athletic. Rose and I entered the water from the cat's steps and began the short swim to the reef. A pair of massive eagle rays swam ten feet below us, casting an even larger shadow on the sandy bottom. I recorded the ray's majesty with my Go-Pro I had secreted from Hobo's possession.

The splendor of the moment was hastily shattered as I Hobo appeared just a few feet behind buck-naked, smiling broadly, and keeping up with the Rays. That video was headed for the edit room floor. Hobo motioned for me to follow. I took a deep breath and swam down twenty-five feet, close to where the rays had come to rest in the sand. I maintained a healthy respect for their barb. Thanks, Steve. Hobo had no body fat. God blessed my ancestors with remarkable caloric efficiency and an ability to store most consumed calories for later use as fat. A handy feature when meals were spaced days, sometimes weeks, apart. Not so much when only hours separated meals and scant minutes between beers. Consequently, with my girth, it was a struggle to stay at depth without weights. Hobo grabbed my swim trunks as I started to float upwards. I continued taping the rays until I needed air. I motioned for Hobo to let me go. However, he was mesmerized by the rays and did not notice. Having exhausted my last breath of air, I surrendered my swim trunks and surfaced quickly, the fresh air gloriously filling my lungs.

Rose surfaced beside me, pointing toward my mask. Puzzled, I attempted to remove my mask, but Rose grabbed my hand, shaking her head no. She removed her snorkel to explain, but there was no need, as the blood from nose reached eye level in my mask. I really did not have a choice but remove the mask or swim blindly back to the boat now some thirty meters away. It is amazing how much blood the human nose can expel in a short period. I turned the adjacent water pink. Rose shook her head and sprinted back to the boat. The pink mist attracted friends and before either of us could make it back, the water was full of sharks. Nurse, I was hoping, but without my mask, I could not see underwater. Rose climbed on board with her limbs, if not her beloved, injured husband intact. Aja and Sue remained on the inflatables, calmly watching the shit show with a detached curiosity not appropriate to the situation. I began to climb aboard before recalling my lack of britches. I sank back down in the water for cover, forgetting the water's remarkable clarity.

Aja smiled. Sue giggled. "Looks like a penis…only smaller. That shit never gets old."

Rose reached her hand down to pull me up. "You're gonna lose what little you got if you stay in the water."

"My dignity?" I asked

"Oh, hell no, that ship has long since sailed. Your dick." Rose pointed at the circling sharks. Get in the damn boat, husband." I did not.

∞∞∞∞

"I don't get it."

"Don't make me pull out another make up mirror."

"So, nothing is real?" I asked.

"Well that would depend on the definition of real," Hobo answered.

"Okay, Slick Willy. Please don't start again with the riddles."

Hobo sighed. "We have been down this road before, Ezekiel. You are ignorant and simply don't have the base of knowledge to understand the universe."

"Thanks."

"Not an insult. Just a fact. All of humankind are ignorant fools on their very best day. Most simply playing a preprogramed loop in a child's game with a healthy amount of free will tossed in for the sake of variety and drama."

"Kind of feels like an insult."

"What did your Shakespeare say? 'The world is a stage, and everyone is an actor.'"

"Walks like a duck, smells like a duck, looks like a duck...let's call it, a duck. My Shakespeare quotes are limited to "'Romeo, Romeo, where the fuck art thou?'"

Hobo sighed again and nodded his head in disapproval "Vulgarity is the crutch of the ignorant."

"Color me ignorant. I think you already did, along with seven billion other souls. Let's start with some basics. Does the sun come up every morning?"

Hobo smiled. "Think of your universe as a giant amusement park. Inside the park, there are certain physical laws that universally apply. The Earth rotates and orbits your star, along with nine other planets."

"Thought you said Pluto isn't a planet."

"It is not. You forget Planet X and that, my friend, is a critical oversight."

"Oh, yeah...Your zombie planet."

"Time..." Hobo continued "...or, what you call time, is what you really don't comprehend. You humans tend to think in linear terms. Time is anything but linear."

"So, it's circular?"

"A circle is still a line, only curved. Time is much more complicated. It is everything and it is nothing."

"Something is different now, Hobo."

"How so, Ezekiel?"

"Your appearance in my life, although shit tons of fun, usually heralds my demons."

"Quite so. It is different this visit. I don't need you this time to see the other realities."

"You mean, the ones I don't believe exist."

"Sure, you do. It's called denial."

"The river in Egypt?"

"For a man that is drowning, you have a warped since of humor."

"For a man that is living, you don't have a sense of humor at all." "Drowning?" I thought to myself. That flooded my senses with a memory long ago stored away. "Since this, by all appearances, is our last chat, perhaps now is a good time for you to explain Jonas."

Jonas was a missionary. I say was, as he is, most decidedly, a part of history. He spent his last hours floating in a bathtub in a mental hospital in central Georgia. Our paths, Jonas' and mine, crossed when I was a boy, struggling to sort out my dreams from the real world. Jonas was a Peruvian missionary that spoke at our church. He was an odd fellow, and, although we had never met, seemed to know me and see inside my head. He left Peru as the sole survivor of a mass murder-suicide. The accepted story suggests the womenfolk of the village bashed in the heads of the men folk and kids before drowning themselves in Lake Titicaca. It was somewhat fitting Jonas' life ended in a similar, if not more sterile, fashion.

Hobo paused before answering, lost, as if weighing his response against the odds of me living long enough to dispute his answer.

"Your boy Jonas went off the deep end."

Okay, that is some bullshit. "You suggesting Jonas killed all the men and kids and then convinced the women to drown themselves?"

"Not at all."

"Then what the hell are you suggesting?'

"Jonas was responsible for the slaughter, that much is certain."

"You are doing it again."

"Doing what exactly?'

"Equivocating."

"Jonas did not kill the villagers. He was responsible for their deaths. That is not equivocation."

"The very fucking definition."

"Language, Ezekiel. Jonas attracted evil to a village of innocents."

Jonas was a true believer and a righteous man. Of that, I was convinced. He had apparently taken his own life decades after witnessing a mass murder-suicide. Never had I thought he was somehow even indirectly responsible for those murders.

"My world is upside down. Why are you here? Are you going to Jonas on me as well?" I asked Hobo, silently.

"Some truth to that." Hobo smiled. "The upside-down part, at least. This time, you need me because we need you. The coal thing is pretty much a sideshow. You, my dear friend, are the modern-day Noah."

"So, I am to build an ark and collect the animals two by two."

"Sort of. And before the serpent has a chance to further corrupt."

"What makes me so special? I am not a godly man."

"You, my drowning friend, are the last true descendant of the son of man."

"As in the first man and woman, Adam and Eve?"

"First man...second woman. The first woman, Lilith, did not work out so well."

The water was warm and embracing as the light dimmed. There was no pain. Oddly, no fear. My last breath expelled, my lungs filled with water, and I closed my eyes as the bull shark took me deeper into the hole.

Hushed noises shrieked violently, welcoming my descent. Stifled sobs trembling from hearts shattered. Snowflakes blanketed the old stones heralding ancestors most long ago forgotten. A lone cardinal, bright red against the snow, made difficult flight to a bare branch. The sweet, innocent proclamation of a baby's boredom interrupted the deafening silence. Silk stockings slid gently beneath layers of dark skirted, fidgeting women, adding disquieting harmony. Lips cracked from the bitter cold gave mild comfort against pink cheeks too frigid to feel the warm embrace. The dark, haunting strains of taps pierced the loutish silence. The stiff measured salute of old soldiers' bodies softened by time formed a long, faint line, disappearing into the cold of winter's embrace. Familiar stones peeked beneath the blanket of snow. Pines laden with snow sagged dangerously above.

A crushing pain on my chest woke me as I expelled the entire watery contents of the Caribbean from my lungs. I was dazed and still near unconscious. My lungs seared with insufferable agony, pleading for a fresh pull of air untainted by seawater. Blood freely poured from my calf, dissipating in concentric pink swirls in the blue sea. Inexplicably calm, I thought, this can't be good, and lost consciousness.

Boston; July 2017: *Researchers at MIT have confirmed they have successfully implanted "memories" onto living human DNA. Dr. Litto claims currently they can implant the equivalent of ten MB of data into DNA. Dr. Litto believes this implanted data will be passed down to future generations. "We are on the cusp of something very exciting with global implication here at MIT. One can only imagine the possibilities."*
Alongside Global News

CHAPTER NINE

Deuce used a sat phone to call for help and sailed back to Half-Moon Caye to wait for the helicopter to arrive. In all fairness, my injury looked much worse than it was. The bull shark never really bit down. The bastard gently, well, gently as a bull shark capable, grabbed my calf. The subsequent, unscheduled, guided tour of the Hole was a bonus. Somewhere along the way, I dutifully replaced the air in my lungs with blood-tinged seawater. Not a recommended activity for the novice diver. Hobo, I am told, returned me to the surface and did the honors of reviving me. Not looking forward to that video.

The rescue helicopter was a Korean War, vintage observation chopper. A basket for transporting a patient was outside the helicopter, perilously affixed to the skid. The precarious positioning of the basket made for a great view as I attempted to direct my puke into the ocean, only to have it swirl in inglorious chunks in every direction, save the intended, by the down wash of the chopper's blades.

Unimpressed by the bloodied towel and puke encrusted clothing, the Guatemalan nurses removed the makeshift tourniquet. They call a bloody scene like mine Tuesday morning. The bad shit came in at night and on weekends. Universally, the world's poorest pile on heaps of misery to each other. The nurses made short work with the six thousand stiches in my leg, and the generous dose of Oxy made the experience, if not pleasurable, damn sure painless. The jagged wound would provide a great conversation starter. At some later point, I would concoct a clever, heroic lie to match the scar. The primary concern du jour was the red fluid being siphoned into my veins. Rose would never buy an "I got HIV from a toilet seat story" and I was not up to speed on third world country blood screening protocol.

With a bag full of prescription meds, the nurses dropped me off in the waiting room, still in my damp, blood-soaked bathing suit, attached to an IV of clear fluid. I was charged with literally holding the bag. I fished out a $20, spotted a bored teenager in the corner, and bribed him to grab me a six-pack of Belikin. In short order, he returned with a five pack of warm beer and no change. I counted myself lucky. After three beers, I dozed off again. When I awoke five hours later, I was in a cab headed for the airport with Rose and Hobo.

Belize International Airport is what one might expect of a third world airport...only smaller. Rose forgot my passport, which only marginally complicated matters. Rose later pointed out I forgot my passport. We were flying Tropic Air and aviation and security rules for them were more guidelines. Hobo snagged a luggage cart and carted me through the luggage door wedged between a massive pile of indistinguishable black bags. "Act as if you belong. I'll carry a clipboard," Hobo said. Rose, in possession of a valid passport, went through the front door.

∞∞∞∞

It had been nearly a month since my unscheduled helicopter tour of Coastal Belize. I commanded a great view of the pool from my condominium balcony. I propped up my tattered appendage on the adjacent chair. It truly was an impressive scar and a great conversation starter, as predicted. My heroic lie was still a work in progress, but crocodiles, machetes, and nude lipstick lesbians were certain to be featured. Rose handed me my third or fourth rum and diet of the afternoon as we settled in to watch the local kids frolic in the pool. It was Sunday, the unofficial caddy day at the pool. Locals were welcome to use the facilities. It made for gripping entertainment. The owners and the knowledgeable guests lined the adjacent balconies holding rum drinks and smoking cigars in anticipation of a great shit show. Today, they would not be disappointed.

DJ and his very large family were regulars. He held a Spanish passport. His official story was that of a retired banker from Barcelona. He really needed a more convincing back story and alias. He was just north of six feet and about 180 pounds, give or take. Not massive, but DJ was chiseled from stone without a trace of body fat. Think Greek God with less hair. His tattoo-free body was popular eye candy for the tourists. The locals mostly averted their eyes. DJ and his large brood were certainly top on my list to avoid on the island. His face smiled, but his eyes never did as they remained vigilant constantly, scanning the horizon for threats or hot chicks in skimpy bathing suits. One could never be certain of motive. The island grape vine pegged him as ex-Mustad. Right or wrong on his back story, the man reeked violent intent.

The Jews, rightfully so, held no small grudge against the Nazis and, to this day, ceaselessly hunted down the old, crippled remainder of the Nazi party and, as importantly, seven decades later, the stolen property they managed to smuggle out of Germany before Berlin fell to the Russians. Seventy years after the fall of the third Reich, there were not many living Nazis but there was significant, unrecovered property. Even some fabled missing Nazi gold.

Argentina was ground zero for the hunt for Nazis. Coincidently, DJ spent his "banking" career in Argentina, Brazil, and Columbia. Unsubstantiated rumor suggested he was searching for Nazis and their gold. Somewhere along the way, perhaps at birth, DJ's moral compass was corrupted, and the pursuit became a personal enrichment exercise. Allegedly, he found no gold, but he had found something just as valuable; information. Information he used to blackmail very rich westerners that wanted to keep the source of their wealth hidden.

The Cleaver family on roids in a still life comes to mind. Fit, tanned, and all well-groomed. However, life was no still picture. I expect they would drop their mom off at the vet to be put down on the way to dinner and an MMA match, should the occasion arise. DJ's wife was likewise tall and lean. She had long, raven hair and dark, piercing eyes. A bit more approachable than DJ, she had an air of confidence that only came with years of training and a smoking hot bod. There were four boys and two girls, ranging from about four to thirteen.

The kids were playing what could only be described

as no holds barred, kindergarten fight club. The youngest was a sneaky little bastard making up for his small stature with boldness, stealth, speed, and raw-naked brutality. He had perfected the rear-facing nut shot and he delivered them with inappropriate gusto. The girls, much smaller in size, had been trained to inflict maximum pain; bite, hair pull, gouge, and scratch. They would short the boys as a diversion tactic and jump on their backs. From this leveraged position, the girls would initiate maximum pain tactics as the boys attempted to retrieve their britches from around their ankles. The boys flailed about wildly as the girls bit them about the neck and ears while gouging at their eyes until the boys banged them off their backs against a convenient palm tree. There was blood. Mom and dad sipped vodka on the pool deck, interrupting the slaughter only if a child lay motionless for an extended period or, on the unique evidence of, arterial flow. There was no concussion protocol.

A group of older, unsupervised kids developed an adult version of Marco Polo. "Beer out of the cooler." "Tastes Great." "Less filling." Tagging required the partial removal of the person's swimwear. To initiate the game, the teenagers dove off the elevated bridge into four feet of water, providing the occasional knee slapper. Smart money stayed on the balconies on Sundays. Yet, some tourists were unaware of the unwritten rule and foolishly ventured out onto the pool deck. Nothing like watching a full-grown man take a rare nut shot from a four-year-old girl with curls and pigtails. There was literally no way of winning that fight. The teenagers, once bored with the classic pool game of Miller Lite, played snatch and run with the lady tourists' tops, placing the captured "flags" high atop the roof deck onto a neglected potted palm. Ruth fearlessly ventured out only to have her top snatched off before she could sit. She chased the teenager down and beat him senseless before abandoning her blood-soaked top to the now unconscious teenager and finding a vacant lounger near the bar.

The local stank weed, wooden carving, jewelry, and textile salesmen moved in like a pestilence once the security guards took a smoke break. Yeah, there were security guards. Now, one should not get the wrong idea. Sunday was ordered chaos. Any other day was a peaceful walk in the park, perhaps even so much as boring. The resort management smartly cultured a natural balance to limit chaos to a single day. And viewed from a safe distance, chaos was a beautiful thing to watch. I mean, who doesn't like a good nut shot. America's Funniest Home Videos show has had a good run featuring nut shots and cute pets doing stupid assorted shit despite a series of lame hosts.

Not that I am an advocate for kindergartener fight club, but American children are soft and spoiled. Hell, we even protect their feelings from getting injured, much less their precious bodies. Competitive sports are too stressful for our kids, perhaps even child abuse. Consequently, participation trophies and games played without scoreboards rule the day. Third world kids grow up street smart and hard. When there comes a battle, again, we will lose to the team that is prepared to fight, not the team that is terrified to keep score in a soccer match. We have raised a generation of snowflakes that are not prepared for the harsh world that awaits. All empires crumble. We got next.

Rose pointed out toward the dock, taking my gaze away from the last tourist to have her top ripped off. The surgically enhanced tourist sipped on her frozen drink, making no effort to cover herself. Her female companions giggled and loosened their tops in hope they might be tagged next.

"What, hon?" I asked. "I don't see anything but the dock."

"If you could take your eyes off her tits, you might find the absence of the guards suspicious?"

Rose is bit of a conspiracy theorist. She sees the bad scenario in every situation first. This time, she was right.

"What tits?"

Rose scoffed and rolled her eyes. "Please."

"Shit, where are the security guards?" I stood and leaned over the rail, trying to locate any of the resort's security staff.

"No guards," I noted "...but check the fellow at the bar. Look familiar?"

"What the hell is our Black Panther friend, Khalid Muhammad, doing here?" Rose asked. She continued, answering her own question, "Exactly." She then started pointing out several suspicious looking gardeners pushing covered wheelbarrows in the vicinity. "Those assholes look familiar?"

Unfortunately, they did. The "gardeners" were some of the same dudes that we saw at the airport runway bar and again in Goff's Caye. "Call 911?" I asked.

"Sarcasm. Not appropriate for the situation." Rose noted.

"Pot. Kettle. Black." Rose was the reigning queen of inappropriate comments.

As we watched, one of the "gardeners" reached below his covered wheelbarrow and began to lift an object in slow motion. Even before we could identify the object, DJ leapt off the deck, slicing the gardener's throat before his feet hit the ground. The other pseudo-gardeners pulled AK-47s out and started firing wildly in DJ's general direction. Bullets ricocheted off the condo's walls, spraying bits of concrete into the adjacent balconies. A few meek onlookers took cover behind the deceitful safety of the glass doors.

DJ's wife swept an adjacent gardener's legs, knocking him to the ground. His weapon spewed automatic fire onto the pool deck, scattering the teenagers huddled under the bridge. She quickly straddled the gardener, forcing the heel of her foot violently into his nose and then again onto his windpipe.

Topless tourists and wounded teenagers scurried about like cockroaches in first light looking for shelter as DJ's kids ran into the fray. The smallest girl wrapped herself around the ankle of the largest gardener biting forcefully into his calf. He reached back to club her off with the butt of his rifle. Her youngest brother delivered a well-aimed nut shot, bringing the gardener to his knees before he could deliver the blow. The girl struggled but lifted the fallen weapon, securing the butt of the rifle between her arm and side. She fingered the selection lever to semi and fired a single bullet into his crotch. His pants turned crimson as he assumed his final fetal position, mumbling for his auntie.

Another gardener was on the deck with his pants around his ankles and his shirt pulled over his head. The largest boy placed the rifle center mass and squeezed. The oldest girl rode another gardener's back, gouging at his eyes from her bucking mount. The gardener slung her off. One of the boys executed a sweeping roundhouse kick, landing on the gardener's ear. Enraged, he grabbed the boy by the nape of his neck and started beating his head on the pool deck while still straddling the girl. A fatal error. The girl recovered and began biting his genitals, refusing to let go. The mother ended his misery, eviscerating him with a filet knife. Khalid Muhammad sat silently at the bar, drinking his frozen drink. The remaining gardeners fled, carrying off their wounded. The mom gathered her kids and walked over to see DJ floating face down in the pool, now red with his blood.

"Shit," Rose said.

CHAPTER TEN

The police concluded their thorough inquiry in less than an hour, not fretting to disturb the idyllic vacation of the witnesses. At best, a cursory investigation. Little doubt the police were keen to both the identity of the perpetrators as well as motive or had been well-compensated not to care. The resort staff dutifully taped off the pool and began the arduous task of cleaning up blood, guts, and grey matter, along with sundry articles of discarded swimwear scattered about the deck and floating in ominous clumps in the pool-like flotsam from a Hollywood choreographed shipwreck. Unencumbered with the baggage of customary human emotion, Ruth remained on the deck, topless, casually sipping on a frozen drink. The pool bar stayed open for business and the guests, eager for gossip and tragedy selfies, quickly filled it to capacity. Perhaps Ruth's lack of baggage was ordinary. Commerce ruled the day. Bills to pay, customers to serve, Facebook posts to publish, empires to virtually build. The Garden of Eve servers would twist this episode in a thousand different ways to Sunday.

One should not judge. Belize is an impoverished country, not an ignorant one, and a bad TripAdvisor rating was devastating to business. The sun silently slipped below the horizon, cloaking the chaos, and I drifted off into a deep Oxy and rum slumber.

∞∞∞∞

When I woke, Hobo sat in Rose's spot. I looked at him and turned away. "What new hell?" I mumbled.

"Thought you might like to chat Ezekiel," Hobo explained his presence.

"Riddles or answers," I responded. I was in no mood for Hobo's bullshit.

"We are done with riddles."

"What just happened?" I asked.

Hobo shook his head slowly from side to side. "Perhaps I should ration your questions if they are all going to demonstrate this level of stupidity."

"Okay, asshole." I had a pretty good idea of what had just gone down at the pool. "Smith had the Panthers take out DJ."

"Good so far," Hobo smiled.

"But why?"

Hobo frowned, "I really should charge you for that question."

"Blackmail," I responded, answering my own question.

His smile returned. "I'll credit you the question."

"I understand Smith wanting DJ gone, but what

do the Panthers get in return? They seem less than loving allies."

"A big slice of George's coal stock and, more importantly, what they really want...a sovereign nation," Hobo answered.

"You mean Atlanta? That shipped has sailed. How can Smith give the Panthers Atlanta? Didn't Obama try and fail?"

"Should charge you again. Your world is inverted. Normal rules...they just don't apply. You people have an unelected sitting president from a drug cartel that has unilaterally extended his presidency beyond his term. A historic female president-elect, without the benefit of a moral compass, waits impatiently in the wings to assume her destined seat. An eight person, evenly split Supreme Court sits powerless to do anything but posture and nap. Meanwhile, your boy Smith with strings attached to both sides incites violent chaos as cover. A man with that kind of money has a lot of power. Your presidents are just puppets. Look to the puppet master."

"Smith?" I asked, knowing the answer.

"This was not just about taking DJ out. Smith is playing 3-D chess and you are still thinking soda pop top checkers. DJ is just very attractive bait."

"So what is Smith's end game?"

Hobo paused before answering, as if contemplating just how much of the plot to spoil. "To wipe out the last remaining son of man. That, Ezekiel, takes a lot of money. Smith needs oil prices to skyrocket to make his coal and rail stock play work."

"And giving the Panthers Atlanta will do that? And why not just give them Atlanta without killing DJ? Seems a stretch, dude."

"Chess, Ezekiel. Had George Smith gifted the Panthers Atlanta, it would have raised their suspicion level. He made them earn the prize. Killing DJ accomplished two goals for Smith."

"Still don't see it."

"The Panthers have a mutual defense treaty with the Brotherhood of Islam," Hobo added.

"That was just a meaningless stunt. The Panthers aren't a sovereign nation and the Brotherhood sovereign status is built literally on top of sand."

"You're not listening to yourself. Your president gives the Panthers Atlanta and, with it, sovereignty."

"Yup. Still not following."

"Let me recap for the mentally handicapped among us. Paris, Brussels, London, and Munich have Muslim mayors elected by Muslim majority populations. Virtually all of Europe has at least a strong Muslim minority in their respective statehouses. The Brotherhood holds directly what was once the countries of Iraq, Iran, BAE, Qatar, all the Stans, and Syria, and which, not coincidently, control nearly half of the world's oil reserves."

"Okay. Still, so what?"

"All the serpent needs is a match to light the fire."

"And said match is the Panthers?" I asked, still skeptical of Hobo's mad conspiracy theory.

"Still not seeing it?" Hobo asked.

I shook my head no and wrinkled my pre-wrinkled forehead in a moment of confusion. I was not seeing it, that much was certain. But by shaking my head no to a negative, was I communicating an affirmative? Double negatives drove me further nuts. I think the Spanish had it right. A double negative was merely a reinforcement of the prior negative, not a canceling thereof.

Hobo frowned, "Don't overthink this. Your country is in the midst of a constitutional crisis. An unelected president sits on the throne. There are only eight

Supreme Court justices split evenly down the middle. Texas seceded from the union." Hobo paused, searching my face for a sign of comprehension. I grabbed my drink. Hobo continued, "One might, consequently, speculate that ceding the largest city in the south to a militant black group would push this severely bipolar country of yours to the brink of their second civil war in less than 150 years."

"An Ancient Astronaut theorist suggests the U.S. is already at said brink of war." I loved that wild-haired freak.

Hobo nodded in the affirmative, which I under-stood as meaning he agreed. None of this confusion of forming negative questions in the English language. I made a mental note to suggest Hobo phrase his ques-tions to me in this matter in the future. He continued, "The Panther's invoke the mutual defense treaty. The Brotherhood of Islam packs a crude, Iranian nuke in a shipping container headed to New York. The U.S. popu-lous predictably unites against a foreign threat."

I interrupted, "The Iranians have a working nuke?"

"The North Koreans do, so a prudent man should assume."

"Then why the shipping container? Don't the North Koreans have ICBMs? And why not just say a North Korean nuke? And we know Pakistan has nukes. The BOI controls Pakistan. Why not use one of theirs?"

Hobo frowned. "A little bit of knowledge is far often more dangerous than complete ignorance. At least the ignorant has a broke clock chance of being correct."

"Facts are important, Hobo."

"If a piano falls on your head, how important is it to you if the piano was a Steinway or a Yamaha?"

"Pretty damn important," I noted. "Yamaha makes keyboards. Fighting chance, I might survive the accident. Hurt like a bitch and leave a mark, but definitely survivable. Steinway, on the other hand...we are talking cartoon pancake disaster."

Hobo took my drink from my hand. "There is a time to play the drunken fool. This is not it. Point being, irrespective of the manufacturer, delivery method, or, even quality of workmanship of the nuke, the very act of attempting to nuke the U.S. will unite the populous against its attacker. The U.S. in turn nukes The Brotherhood and its oil fields back to the Dark Ages where they arguably belong. Europe stands by, thumb firmly inserted in anal cavity, paralyzed with indecision. Oil prices skyrocket, dragging coal with it. Simple as one, two, three, right? At least, that is the likely scenario. But Smith is crafty. He may play his cards differently."

"But you are going to stop the assholes, right?"

"Why would I do that?" Hobo asked, genuinely confused.

"Because that is what you do. You're that Viracocha dude charged with wandering the Earth disguised as a vagrant to stop us mere ignorant, drunken mortals from destroying our world." Hobo looked at me with a mixture of confusion and disdain. I continued saying the same thing just using different phrases, falsely interpreting my word selection to be the root of the apparent communication problem, "Save the planet. Rescue mankind from itself...for the good of the force or some bullshit like that."

Hobo paused and tilted his head before responding, "That is just it, Ezekiel. It's not your world anymore...it is ours. Has been since the flood. And that same chaos that has nearly wiped you out a half-dozen times since the Garden is coming your way and, this time, it is truly an existential threat."

"But aren't you the big God antivirus? You fix shit

for the Gods in order for them to keep their virtual playground open for business." I am a skeptic at heart. Hell, I am a skeptic inside and out. For years now, I considered Hobo a semi-harmless lunatic and discounted his mystical antics to my all too frequent exploitation of pharmaceuticals and alcohol. Lately, given mounting evidence, I had to consider that either I had for years simply been in denial to Hobo's true nature or now I was the raving lunatic. The latter explanation being more believable, the former more plausible. "Ask me, all in all it seems you and your Gods are pretty fucked up."

Hobo paused and scratched his beard. "No Gods here," Hobo paused, "But yeah, I reckon' it is pretty fucked up."

I interrupted Hobo, smiling, "Language, Homeless Bob." I had never heard him curse. It was akin to hearing a five-year-old say "fuck "in a Sunday school class. Humiliating as hell to the parent of the kid, but indelicately hilarious to everyone else.

He continued, nonplused, "We came here on accident..." Hobo extended his arms to full length, "... to Earth and found pretty much an idyllic world. But some of us just couldn't keep our dicks in our pants. In all fairness, ten thousand years is a pretty long time. We literally screwed up your world, creating a race of half-breeds. Hybrids that are physically and mentally far superior to you sons of men but missing something vital we discovered in you we can't replicate."

"A rocking bod?" I asked, rubbing my beer belly for visual context.

Hobo looked at my stomach. His leathery forehead wrinkled, and the corners of his mouth turned down. Hobo's eyes narrowed, and an exceptional solitary tear crept slowly down his bearded face. He continued after a moment, "No, Ezekiel, you have something our race has never encountered. Something truly enigmatic. You have an eternal soul. You..." Hobo pointed at me, "The last living, pure, uncorrupted son of man are the sole survivor."

"I see what you did there." I said, trying to lighten the mood. I had never seen Hobo so disconsolate. Hobo ignored my pun and continued, "The last living, pure DNA tied to man. The untainted creation of the true God sits before me. Our only link to something much older and more advanced than ourselves. Something our race may even see as God. Something we hold sacred."

I looked down at my belly. I was not a pristine physical specimen. And, like most days at this time, I was already more than a little buzzed, despite Hobo cutting me off. "I am your link to God? That is just kind of sad."

Hobo glanced at me and shook his head in agreement. "You have squandered your talents. You're a lazy drunk with a bad attitude and a foul mouth. But you are all we have, and we have to get you through the gate." He paused, "...preferably alive."

"Thanks," I muttered, reaching for my drink. "I thoroughly enjoyed today's lyrical musings from my neighborhood lunatic." Although truthfully, which one of us was indeed the lunatic, was up for grabs. I took a long-measured gulp from my reacquired drink before setting it down. "So then..." I asked the $64,000 question, "...If I am the only remaining real person... what the hell does that make the other seven billion people on this rock?" I turned and looked up.

Brussels; March 2018: *President O'Grady pledged the entirety of the U.S. active Armed Forces to UN control. Only the National Guard and the Coast Guard would remain under American command. Speaker O'Ryan discounted the possibility of such a "treasonous abdication of duty" clearing Congress to "zero {explicative deleted} chance."*
Alongside Global News

CHAPTER ELEVEN

Sue and Brad returned from the sailing trip to find their well picked through belongings lining the street. The local police force had meticulously secured a court summons to a broken floor lamp, requiring them to answer for a "gross" littering violation. Seems the landlord had been approached by the Panthers with a better deal for their apartment. Breaking the lease with Brad and Sue seemed far less problematic and more lucrative than being disagreeable with men accustomed to violence. When presented with the feeble man's choice, gold or lead, gold is universally the prevalent selection. A sad statement on our world. Not judging, faced with the same decision, I, too, would likely surrender my integrity for a few more breaths of air and a Lamborghini Aventador.

Make no mistake, Belize is a third world country. Most everything has value to someone. Here, one man's trash is a hundred men's treasure. Consequently, the remains of Brad and Sue's belongings were slim and scattered about, like well-traveled tsunami flotsam. Silver lining was the eviction facilitated their move to new digs a bit closer to us. Sue put it best. "It's just shit." Brad was decidedly less positive. He had lost his favorite Raptor's jersey along with a half-pound of imported weed. He seemed pretty shook up about the loss of both, although I kind of secretly looked forward to the day Brad encountered the kid wearing his favored jersey. I made a mental note to make book with the Breakfast Rum Club on the outcome of his future encounter with the hooligans. The Breakfast Rum Club had scant physical assets to wager, but bragging rights were a fierce talisman among the club members and could be used for serious leverage for just about anything under the tropical sun. Never underestimate the value of loyalty and determination of a man with little to lose.

"Fuck," Sue shrieked, her sunny disposition darkened. "The little bastards took my favorite pink rabbit."

∞∞∞∞∞

Patterns of reflected light danced off the sea like a cubic zirconia in a pawn shop showcase, distorting my view of the Yolo dock. Yolo was a large, motorized catamaran... essentially a fiberglass platform for transporting drunk tourists to a couple snorkeling sites and party spots close to the dock. At a top speed of about six knots, it was the ultimate slow ride. Today was the chill cruise. Take it easy. Thanks, Marshall.

After a brief snorkeling interlude, the boat meanders to a massive, shallow area of the sea. It is no more than four feet deep with a sandy bottom.

The resultant effect is simply stunning. Crystal clear water, an unnatural aqua blue, spreads to the horizon in every direction. The only interruption is a distant stilt shack punctuating the horizon. Fishermen used the shacks to stand guard at night over their lobster traps during season and as a convenient location to meet up and take lunch and the occasional secret hook up with each other's respective spouses. The shacks were not luxurious but offered a striking view, and of more import, privacy. The fish smell, depending on circumstance and hygiene, could also be an asset. You could see and hear anyone coming for miles.

It was at Sue's request we planned to come on the trip. With Sue, a request was not so much a suggestion but a covert demand. With her penchant for revenge and her talent for electronic mischief, a request always best accepted.

Yolo was a tourist thing and we had passed that stage. Sue had Canadian friends coming down that wanted to party, and I quote, "Like it was 1999." Sue had an eclectic collection of friends, present company not being an exception, and the smoking gun evidence… the entirety of Breakfast Rum Club. Consequently, Sue's friends held at a minimum promise of an amusing day. My wounds were insufficiently healed to submerge in fish poop and tourist pee infested waters but hey, there would be ample cold beer and unscripted entertainment. In my own curmudgeonly way, I was looking forward to what adventure the day might bring.

Rose and I snuck out of the house, leaving Ruth blissfully sleeping off her previous night's drunk fest, tucked in between the crisp sheets on our bed. Ruth, my sister, was a dead ringer for Rose and, on more than one occasion, I had regrettably on chance, fondled lady parts that shared my same parental units. Ruth had to work at noon, but she would have called in sick and joined had she known about the trip. Some people lived to work. Others worked to live. Ruth worked because Rose would throw her tired ass out of the house otherwise. Even so, it was under stated protest.

Sue waved us over to meet her friends, a group of four men and three women. The men were all late thirties to mid-forties and peculiarly, looked vaguely familiar, but I could not place them offhand. Two of the women were a bit portly and displayed the common symptoms of an extended pregame. Something truly exceptional about tailgating the 9 am departure of an all-day booze cruise. Props, bitches. The third, rather attractive, woman presently lipped-locked to the tallest of the shirtless men was well-known to me.

"Feeling ill today, sister?" I inquired. Not sure how she had managed to slip out of bed, shower, dress, duck work, and still beat us here. Who was I kidding? She was wearing the same swimsuit she slept in. Ruth disengaged long enough to greet me with an impish smile.

"And aren't you married still…at least legally, if not in the eyes of the Mormon Church?"

"It's okay, brother. He's not into women…he's queer."

"I think they prefer gay," I mock whispered.

"Just who the hell you calling gay, old man?"

"I'm sorry, dude. Not judging." I really was not. Bone who and how you please as long as "it" is over eighteen, conscious (Cosby rule), and with consent. (Written, witnessed, and notarized by an officer of the court on university campuses.)

"Why the hell would you judge? Someone die and assign God duties to your fat ass?" He poked my belly. "You seem an unlikely choice for chief deity."

I am slow to rise to visible anger, but I was well on

my way. Say what you want, but don't lay hands on me. Suddenly, his demeanor changed, and he smiled broadly.

His friends patted my back. "He's busting your chops, man. Ignore him. He is just confused at times which team he prefers to dress for. Confusion makes him grumpy."

"I guess that explains his boner," I noted.

"Glad you noticed," he replied, releasing Ruth and moving to embrace me. Rose intervened. "This gorgeous man is married in the eyes of thine, Rose. You best back the hell off. If anybody gonna suck his dick it is gonna be me."

I lifted my eyebrows and was about to make a comment.

"Not gonna happen, old man."

A husband can dream.

The proprietor (for convenience sake, let's refer to him as Captain Ron) of Yolo made the requisite safety briefing: don't bleed, puke, or pee on the deck. Paper items: shit paper, tampons, and condoms to be discarded in the trash, not flushed. I raised my hand to ask where he procured paper condoms and to inquire as to the effectiveness of paper construction in, out, and about a wet worksite. Rose, reading my intentions, yanked my hand down. Rose was getting to be less fun in my old age. Misreading the intent of my potential inquiry, Captain Ron held up an oversize bottle of chlorine bleach as a visual aid, "Not to worry, sir." He pointed at me. "We own stock in Clorox." The guests rewarded him with a courtesy chuckle. The crew collectively rolled their eyes. His shtick registered midway between mildly annoying and mildly amusing, leaning hard to the former with age.

Continuing the "safety" briefing, Captain Ron waved in the general direction of the alleged stowed lifejackets, assuringtheywerebothavailableinappropriatequantities, intuitive in their operation, and semi-functional. Captain Ron moved on to the essential element of all tour safety briefings. The "safety" in the briefing was cursory at best, so titled as to command the attention of the inebriated and, otherwise distracted, guests. Captain Ron lifted an opaque plastic container clearly marked "TIP" in no less than three languages. Captain Ron carefully noted the locations of all three "propina" jars conveniently located on the vessel. Belize is an English-speaking country and Captain Ron was a Canadian (a quasi-English-speaking country). Tourists enjoyed the exotic Spanish flair most of the Caribbean and Central American countries offered and the tourist-centric businesses obliged with bits of vacation Spanglish. Captain Ron pointed to a horizontal fill line on the tip jar and assured us the safety of both our belongings and lives was in the crew's capable hands. Insert courtesy chuckle from guests accompanied by enthusiastic applause from the smiling crew. Crew introductions followed; the bartender receiving the only appreciable applause. Captain Ron disembarked the boat to no doubt bang the Yolo's receptionist and lovely girlfriend of today's captain. Ahhh…island life. I secretly pondered if he would use a paper condom.

Nine in the morning or not, it was open bar and most of the guests were on vacation. The bar's queue wee-wawed through the middle of the boat. Ruth's queer friend noted, "Hell…it's ten am somewhere," before chugging a shot of local coconut rum. I opted for beer. This was no Gilligan, but an all day excursion. Pace seemed prudent. Ruth vehemently disagreed with my assessment, volunteering as designated tequila shot girl, vigorously pedaling colorful test tubes filled with the bitter nectar of the agave as if commissioned by Captain Ron himself.

Remarkably, Ruth's top was not the first to go. An impromptu birthday party was declared for one of Sue's portly female friends. Surprisingly for a forty-year-old chubby, the tits were not disagreeable. At least, I thought, the exposed tits did not belong to my sister. Until they did. Sue's friends, both male and female, began a motorboat contest on the two topless women. Ruth's tits were too small and perky for proper motorboating, but I came to realize this was not a contest with an objective scoring structure.

"I thought you gay guys didn't like tits," I asked. There was a level of discordant energy and enthusiasm, suitable for a tween age heterosexual boy fantasy pastime, being executed by middle-aged gay men. Not judging. Just observing.

Ruth's queer friend asked, "You a redneck homophobe?"

It was unclear if that was a question or a statement, but I responded as if the former. "Possibly. If asking that question makes me one, I will proudly wear that label."

He laughed. "You got a lot of chain to yank, cracker. Its pussy we don't care for. That shit stanks."

My forehead wrinkled, and I started to speak. The irony, self-evident, seemed lost. Rose discreetly raised an eyebrow and shook her head no. "But it's a softball," I said to no one.

Rose, determined to silence me, changed tactics and shoved Brad overboard. Sue raised her glass to salute Rose. "Who had Brad first in the pool?"

Ruth produced her cellphone from the side of her bikini bottoms and, without looking, said, "Looks like Sue is our daily Bingo winner." One of the crew tossed out a line. The boat did not slow further. I looked at my watch. It was 9:30 am.

∞∞∞∞

Shortly, we moored at Hol Chan. It is a Belizean national park and treasure. A narrow cut in the reef filled with colorful tropical fish, giant snappers, man-sized groupers, and car-sized turtles. Eagle rays and nurse sharks made the occasional appearance but, for certain during season, the spot was jammed with colorfully adorned, pink-faced tourists. It was season. The Captain insisted the girls replace their discarded tops, national park and all. Oddly, for a tourist-based economy, Belize was a bit intolerant of nudity and homosexuality. Ruth complied but birthday girl face-planted on the deck. The queer thoughtfully covered her with a towel after an impassioned dry hump with drink in hand. Sue's friends pulled out their phones, documenting and posting the sexual assault on social media. Al Gore most be so damned proud of his invention.

Most of the crew doubled as snorkel guides in order to avoid damaging the tourism trade with bad Trip Advisor reviews. Being washed out to sea and slammed against the reef until you bled out and or drown was not, according to previous Trip Advisor travelers, worthy of a five-star tour. Who knew? "Other than drowning your mate, did you not enjoy the view?"

Surprisingly, Sue donned a life vest and jumped overboard. She typically snorkeled above water, peering into the sea with a drink in one hand and a cigarette in the other. That left me, the bartender, and the semi-conscious birthday girl on board. Fish, the bartender, rearranged the towel to cover an errant boob that had meandered out from under the towel, and brought me a Belikin. He grabbed a seat beside me.

"Break time?" I asked.

"No, man. I don't get a break when there are assholes that stay on board too drunk or scared to go snorkeling."

I raised my beer. "Salud. You rather I jump and leave

you alone with that?" I pointed to the birthday girl. She had pulled herself up to a sitting position and was rattling an empty glass, demonstrating her desire for a refill.

Fish rose to grab a drink. "I'll make you a deal, ma'am. You cover those boobs and I will bring you another drink."

Fish moved to the bar to make her a drink. Birthday girl made a resolute effort to replace her top and semi-succeeded by managing to get one of her boobs in the cup. I raised my drink in mock salute.

She rattled her drink toward me. "You bring me a drink. I'll suck your cock." Fish thoughtfully brought me her drink; rum punch sans rum. "I'll split my tip with you if you take her the drink and holster that right tit."

I looked to birthday girl, "How about Fish brings you a drink and you don't."

"I don't what?" She slurred, eyeing me in a woefully ineffective attempt to convey sensuality.

"Suck my dick," I replied.

She giggled coquettishly "Your loss, pretty eyes."

Fish leaned over, still holding her drink out to me; "They are kind of nice."

"Still not putting her tit back in. Sack up, Fish," I suggested.

Fish wavered, sighed, and moved toward birthday girl. She face-planted against the deck, spilling the ice from her empty, successfully covering her exposed breasts. Fish sipped the punch and asked, "So why you not snorkeling?"

I shifted in the seat and propped my left calf up. The stiches had been removed but the wound still seeped a less than attractive light green mucus. There was no mistaken the origin of my wound.

"A little love bite got you scared."

"That, the threat of gangrene, and Hepatitis A

through Z." The piss and puke ratio to seawater was high on an idle day and today was anything but idle.

"My dad told me about you."

"Your dad?" I asked.

"Well...stepdad. I think you know him as Tarbaby."

I nodded. He continued. "Trouble seems to follow you around. Don't bring any on my boat." He moved to get up.

"So, whose team do you play for?" I asked.

"I am straight," he replied.

"Not the question I asked." Hobo's gibberish was clearly influencing my belief system. I questioned the nature of my reality.

According to my understanding of Hobo, there were only a few teams, and, even fewer real players. Most of mankind stumbled through life with some measure of free will, ignorant to the forces that created and even manipulated their actions. Pawns, really. Then there was the Watchers. The good guys in white hats. Not really of this world. Human in appearance but with supernatural knowledge and skills. The Watchers employed a series of lesser beings. Dogs for one. Can't place the exact connection, but they seemed to be sentinels for the Watchers. Then there were Cherubs. I think supernatural beings, as well, but not as powerful as Watchers.

Cherubs typically came in tiny pairs and seemed to offer protection and guidance. The primary players of the opposing team were the Serpents. Serpents and Watchers were two different sides to the same coin. They were defined not by their genesis, but by their choices. I understood less of the Serpent hierarchy, but they too employed a cadre of devilish minions. Of major note was the slim remainder of the men I once called the Suits; most only pawns in the Serpent's game and since discarded, Kingmaker Smith and our current President O'Grady the only remainders.

Fish removed his shirt and walked off. On his back was a tattoo of pair of angel wings. He paused and turned. "We have to get you back home."

"So I hear."

Sue was first back aboard. A long string of snot stretched from her nose to the deck.

"Nice," I commented.

"I fucking hate the water." She grabbed my towel, wiping the snot off before throwing it back on me.

Next aboard was the queer. I really should ask his name, I guess, but he seemed to like queer well enough as a moniker. And, as he pointed out, who was I to judge? Shortly, the remainder climbed aboard, and Fish busied himself making the drunk tourists decidedly drunker.

Queer gripped a Belikin Stout in one hand and a fruity drink in another. It was a shade of blue not found in nature, garnished with an entire fruit bowl. I had to ask. "You drinking both?"

"Damn, cracker. You think all us queers go for fruity drinks?"

"Kind of."

"You homophobic mother fucker." He took a sip of the fruity drink and ate a spear of fruit. "The beer is for my girlfriend." He pointed to birthday girl lying prone on the deck, face down in a puddle of spittle. He shook her a couple times. "Girlfriend. Wake the hell up."

"Not sure sexual assault victim qualifies as girlfriend," I noted.

Queer turned to Sue, "This here cracker your friend?"

"Hell yeah!" Sue enthusiastically replied. "My job to keep an eye on him."

All safely aboard, the Captain started moving the boat. Ruth saw this as a license to remove her top.

Queer took a long, hard look at her tits. He grabbed Ruth's hand and twirled her, inspecting her many tattoos.

"Well, I'll be damned. It's you." he said to Ruth. "You got married here a few years back?"

Ruth nodded yes, disengaging from Queer. Marriage was a touchy subject with Ruth.

"And you had a strange friend…big guy, bald, truck stop graffiti all over his body, bleeding in several spots?"

"Ardy," Ruth answered. "How do you know my friend Ardy?"

"We saved his ass. Some demon dog was chasing him out to sea. We pulled him on our boat and he partied with us a couple days. It got weird. I think we dumped him at your wedding." Queer smiled, reminiscing.

"Classy move, asshole. You guys splashed half the wedding party."

"Damn…just half?"

A not unfamiliar rhythmic buzzing sound caught our attention simultaneously. "What the hell?" Ruth asked.

"Oh, hell no!" Sue yelled at birthday girl. "That was my favorite pink rabbit."

"You want I get it back?" Brad sheepishly asked.

I pondered how many pink rabbits must she have in order to have a favorite one.

Sue, in a rare moment, was speechless and responded by a subtle nod to the negative. Birthday girl returned to the pleasing task at hand.

"Damn. It ain't a party 'til the pink dildos come out, girlfriend. Spank that monkey, bitch."

Rose turned to me. "This…" she paused, rotating her head toward the chaos, a la Linda Blair, a little too much for comfort, "… shit show is an all-time low for you."

I raised my beer. Not certain as to why this shit

show was now my shit show, but I duly accepted responsibility.

Sue mumbled "And they were brand new batteries."

Brad, in a futile attempt to extricate himself from the dog house, offered to retrieve the batteries. Rose pushed him overboard for the second time today. Fish threw him a line.

The boat arrived at the party spot, a panoramic aqua blue sea, interrupted by a volleyball net and a distant stilt shack. Brad walked up to the swim ladder but was unable to grip the rail to pull himself aboard. His hands were weak from holding onto the line for dear life the last couple of miles. Fortunately, the boat was slow, the sea warm. Fish tossed him a beer. Brad opened it with his teeth. Sue threw a life vest in Brad's general direction.

"Thanks, hon. Could have used this a couple miles back."

Sue reached down to the deck and warily retrieved her now discarded rabbit. She threw it at Brad, spanking him in the face with the business end. "Yeah. I want the batteries. And you might want to slice your face off."

Fish announced lunch served: Pork ribs, BBQ chicken wings, Belizean rice, and coleslaw. Yolo's meals were prepared in a local's home kitchen and were exceptional, given the obstacles of a small kitchen, low budget, no on-board galley, and time. Amply inebriated, I forgot my injuries. Rose and I jumped in the water, joining Brad at the stern of the boat. Exceptional or not, I was not waiting in line, and the salt water, the alcohol whispered, would do the leg good. Fish encouraged us to grab lunch before the other drunks finished it off. The budget did not allow for American-sized servings.

"I'll drink my lunch," I said, holding my beer in the air for an unwarranted visual aid.

"That's what I am afraid of."

Rose climbed back on deck, dutifully waiting in line. She secured us a helping of coleslaw and a solitary chicken wing. I naturally complained regarding the paucity of food. Rose unsurprisingly threw the wing at me in the water. I fished it out of the sea and ate it. Rose shook her head. Brad asked for her slaw.

Rose was the first to dive in but only by a millisecond. The boat emptied into the sea with remarkable speed and without a notion of grace. Bodies landing on top of each other some still holding the remains of lunch. Puzzled, I asked Rose, "There a fire?"

"Worse, much worse," Rose pointed to the cat. Birthday girl was poised over the rail, hurling copious amounts of red, viscous fluid into the once pristine sea while simultaneously squirting dark liquid fecal manner onto the deck from the other end. We swam toward the stilt shack to escape the toxic waste. We paused a hundred yards out. Brad squealed. "Sharks."

Likely nurse sharks or not, I was a bit sensitive on the subject and I started swimming back to the cat. Rose grabbed my ankles.

"You nuts? Birthday girl's bloody puke and shit is all over the deck. Spit balling here, but I'm putting odds are exceptionally high on multiple STD-infused, bloody puke." Rose saw the terror in my eyes and pointed toward the stilt shack just a couple hundred meters away.

I arrived at the shack first, immediately pulling myself on to the cracked and splintered platform. Chivalry be damned. It wasn't like Rose needed help, she was an exceptional athlete. Rose was protecting me. She always had. She pulled herself up on the platform, water dripping off her taut body. Sometimes I forget just how beautiful she is. "Damn, you are hot." Rose smiled. I self-high-fived.

Brad was nowhere to be seen but we were not alone

on the shack. The smell of boiling lobster wafted from the uncovered window. "Joining me for lunch, Ezekiel?" A familiar voice asked.

"You got to be kidding me!" Rose looked at me, accusingly. I shrugged. "She better not be half-naked."

"Who is…" I started to respond as Aja ducked out of the shack. Fortunately for my physical well-being, Aja was modestly dressed in yoga pants and a long sleeve t-shirt with just a hint of sculpted abs peeking out above the pants. Not that I noticed. Even so, she possessed an ethereal beauty and it was difficult not to stare. Aja offered lobster and lukewarm, bagged water explaining no electricity. We accepted, extricating the tasty morsels with a shared pair of rusty pliers and eating with our fingers. It was worth the shark-infested swim. Even Rose's face softened.

"What are you doing in the middle of literally nowhere?" I asked Aja.

She smiled, squeezing some water from the bag, and dripping some on to her shirt. I reflexively followed the water drop to her breast. Rose rolled her eyes. I flinched. Aja laughed.

"Watching" she answered.

"You have lobster traps?"

"No." she answered.

"Killing me."

Aja pointed off to the western horizon. "There. Can you see it?"

I raised my hand to my brow and squinted into the bright sunlight. A boat was racing toward us. I nodded my head.

"This shack is situated on a major drug smuggling route for Los Zetas."

"You DEA now?"

"Hobo was right. You are not that bright." Rose

nodded her head, her mouth too full of lobster to verbally agree.

"Ouch," I responded, genuinely a bit hurt. "Wait a minute. Los Zetas? Isn't that the Mexican gang our president was rumored to be a part of?"

"Not a rumor. He was their CFO so to speak before taking over the gang and consolidating Los Zetas with the other major drug gangs in Mexico. Now the Panthers and the Brotherhood are partnering with Los Zetas."

"But still, why are you here?"

"We need the disc to get you home," Aja answered.

"By disc, you mean the golden disc the old crone gave me to deliver to Hobo and by home, you mean your home...not mine."

Aja smiled, "I do."

"Did Hobo lose it?"

"No. The Panthers stole the disc on behalf of Smith."

"But why?"

"To keep you from going home."

Atlanta; July 2018: *Andrew Dean, an amateur astronomer, reported sighting a previously undiscovered planet on an unusual elliptical orbit. NASA Scientists confirm Dean's sighting and believe the planet to be the legendary Planet X.*

Alongside Global News

CHAPTER TWELVE

Sue rolled up shortly after one pm, about an hour, give or take, after the appointed time. She had gone native, adopting island time, as was the universally accepted practice. Canadians by birth, after all, were born with a warped sense of measurement to begin with. As long as it was divisible by ten, it was acceptable practice and superior to all things American, except cigarettes. "You damn Americans roll a fine ass fag."

A dangerously thin local, coal black with tufts of gray plastered to the sides of his head and scattered randomly along his jaw line, struggled to push a rusted-out wheelbarrow through the coarse coral sand. An eclectic mix of discarded materials, duct tape, and bumper stickers held the wheelbarrow together. The stickers were emblazoned with the emerging nation's slogan "You Better Belize it." The last stretch of beach was up a slight hill and covered with thick sand leading up to our table at the pool bar. Large beads of perspiration covered his deeply grooved skin. His tattered clothes were soaked from the effort of his load. His legs bore the familiar scars of a sugar cane laborer. Security waved him off, pointing to the sign warning the persistent beach vendors to stay off the property.

"No, Sir, I no be selling these people my wares this fine day. I just be giving Miss Sue a ride to these here good folk." He set down his load and pointed in our direction.

The wheelbarrow was covered by a thin, colorful blanket sold on the island as souvenirs by the locals. They were mass produced in China by prepubescent girls, imported by the Lebanese family that mysteriously had the grocery market cornered, and subsequently peddled as handmade souvenirs to the local tourists by cute little kids with big eyes, crooked smiles, and aggressive sales pitches. Rose, perplexed, walked over and lifted the blanket. Neatly curled inside lay Sue, fast asleep. Rose poked her cautiously as if she was a treacherous animal.

Startled from her peaceful slumber, Sue jumped and screamed, "What the hell, Hambone?"

Hambone was the Ringo of the Breakfast Rum Club. He lived with his fourth wife on sober days when he could hold even a menial job. His wife diverted his paychecks most weeks and kept him sober, in line, and at home. Hambone, on the rare occasion, managed deceit and intercepted his check. For a few weeks thereafter, he spent his time at least as a token member of the Breakfast Rum Club, sleeping with the dearly departed and the currently depraved.

"I told you not to wake me again 'til we were there." Sue reached up and pulled the blanket back over the top of her never opening her eyes.

Rose poked her again. "Damn it, man," she seethed.

"Miss Sue, I be eternally sorry I woke you this morning raking the beach by your window. I didn't start 'til after ten and I was quiet like that church mouse you tol' me about."

"No hell you weren't! Humming that damn happy tune, Hambone. Why the hell you have to be so damn happy all the time? Is it too damn much for me to ask you to keep your happy shit to yourself?"

"No, ma'am, Miss Sue. I apologize for my transgressions."

"What in the hell you even got to be so damn happy about, Hambone?"

"Plenty, Miss Sue." Hambone looked genuinely puzzled. "I gots my health, my family, my dog, she be fine, and the hens, they be laying eggs. My wife, she got a job as a wet nurse and I gots an unopened handle of Caribbean Rum back at the house stowed away from my wife's pryin' eyes. Baby Jesus, he love me… "

"Shut the hell up and push. You are going to make me late."

Rose spoke up, "You were late a damn hour ago."

Sue poked her head out from under the blanket. Rose had her hand on her hips and her head cocked to one side. I was intimately familiar with this pose.

"Don't judge me, woman. The bastard woke me up. He owes my ass." Sue pointed an accusatory manicured finger at Hambone.

Hambone hung his head in shame and nodded in agreement. Rose continued to glare. I handed Hambone a beer and pointed toward a chair in the shade beside Linus and Lucy. We had known the midgets, their word, not mine, for four or five years now, but still didn't know their real names. They were freaky little shits, though.

"Just how drunk did you get last night, Sue?" Rose asked

"Ask your damn husband." Now the finger was pointed in my direction.

"Not like I pried that big mouth of yours open and poured the Panty Rippers down your throat," I offered a mild objection. I was more than a little intimidated by Sue.

Rose raised a well-manicured eyebrow in my direction. "It is one thing to go out the night before a major hurricane makes landfall and get hammered with your... your..." She nodded toward Sue, Lucy, and Linus, searching for a pleasant way to say freaky friends. She settled on "...buds. But can you avoid using the words Panty Ripper and Sue in the same sentence?"

"It's not like I ripped her panties..."

"You damn straight. I don't wear no damn panties."

I shushed Sue, "Not helping. And, Rose, we went to Lola's for a steak. Might be our last hot meal for a while."

"I'm a God damn vegan," Sue argued from the depths of the wheelbarrow.

"Since when?" Rose asked. Sue had been known to suck the meat off a chicken bone.

"Tuesday."

"Those are leather sandals on your feet, Sue."

"It's not like I give a fuck about animals. I just don't eat meat."

"Charming."

"I might eat Lucy's cats, though. She just goes on and on about her damned pussies. I just smile and nod while on the inside, a tiny little piece of me dies every time she says pussy."

I gave Sue my best 'shut the hell up' look. She had yet to spot Lucy's diminutive frame. Sue misinterpreted. "You know how I hate furry little pussies." Sue smiled broadly at her coarse pun.

"I do now." Lucy offered.

"That was Lucy, wasn't it?" Sue asked Rose.

Rose nodded yes.

"Not a clear path out of this one?"

Rose nodded no.

Sue pulled the blanket over her head. "Hambone. Home."

Hambone dutifully lifted the wheelbarrow but one look at Hambone suggested he was in no condition to roll an empty wheelbarrow the mile or so south to Sue's, much less one filled with the humiliated remains of Sue. Lucy motioned to Linus. The two secured the wheelbarrow from Hambone and rolled it down the dock a few yards before depositing the wheelbarrow and Sue into the sea. Hambone obediently got up and retrieved both Sue and his wheelbarrow, even worse for the wear, if that was somehow possible. Linus gave him $10 BZ for any damage to the wheelbarrow. He overpaid. Sue wiped her face on Linus's shirt and grabbed his beer before sitting wordlessly at our table.

"Aren't you and Brad staying over with us tonight?" They lived in a first-floor ocean front condo. Perhaps not the ideal domicile to ride out a major hurricane. She preferred a location closer to the town than our condo. The closer to town, the better the internet connection. Sue depended on the internet to do whatever the hell she did that kept her in supply of American cigarettes, tobacco, and marijuana.

"Oh, yeah." She turned to Hambone, flipping her hand in a dismissive gesture. "You can mosey on home now."

Rose asked Hambone, "Where are you and your family staying to ride out the storm?"

"At home."

Sue laughed. "Hambone, you live in a cardboard shack. You better be getting to a shelter."

Before I could intervene, Rose had invited Hambone and his family to stay with us. We had a well-built second floor condo with hurricane-rated windows. It was the right thing to do, but well-built or not, it was only about fifteen-hundred square feet. And I was unclear on the size of Hambone's family. Further clouding the picture is that Rose failed to clarify the meaning of family. As so, the size of the guest list remained uncertain.

Late afternoon, the wind stiffened. Brad showed up as the pool staff was dropping the pool furniture into the pool and closing off the windward side shutters to the bar. We had a table outside partially protected from the wind. Storms hold an inexplicable charm. And this one was a Disney worthy prince.

"Something evil this way comes." Linus tilted his beer eastward.

Lucy's brow furrowed deeply. "Don't you take on airs, you little shit. You would have flunked English Lit, save I wrote your damn papers."

Once you get to know Linus, you forget he is a short asshole. His personality looms large and his voice deep, much like Tyrion Lannister on Game of Thrones, except sexier, according to Linus. I was facing seaward and noticed everyone looking over my back. "What the hell? I asked and turned.

What the hell, indeed. In the States, nothing says you are about to be bitch-slapped by a major storm more than Jim Cantore from The Weather Channel parked in your driveway doing a live feed knee deep into a puddle and dramatically bracing into the wind, however feeble. But this was Belize. What the hell was Jim Cantore doing here?

"I hate that little shit." Linus noted, with a bit too much passion.

"Pot, kettle, black.

"Fuck you, fat man."

"He is a bit of a diva, but dude, hate is a strong word for some asshole you don't even know. You need to go to your safe place?" Rose asked.

I laughed. Linus fumed. Lucy presented like a French bulldog in heat.

"Oh…I see. Lucy has the hots for the little shit. Jealous much?" I asked.

"Fuck that noise. Why I want a wee little fellow?" Lucy drew her hands in close together illustrating Linus' penis size.

Linus presented a solitary digit salute. "My wee dick get plenty of hot ass."

"Don't you worry your little self, Linus. When…" [There was a clear emphasis on "when"] "… I get some…it's going to be with a God."

"Holding out for Tom Brady?" I asked, jokingly.

"Nah, I want a real man. LeBron James," Lucy whispered, passionately.

I tried for a moment to get my head out around the physics of Lucy's fantasy relationship. The image was disturbing, and I had to pee. The bathroom below the pool had been closed off in preparation for the hurricane. I made my way back to our condo, jumping behind Cantore long enough to give his bald head rabbit ears on live television. I crack myself up. He was less amused. Cantore was sans his normal crew. He had a small, professional-looking camera handheld by, what I assume was, his female companion. She stood close as he was depending on the camera microphone for sound. It appeared he was vacationing in Belize and got lucky with the timing of the hurricane.

While we still had Internet, I got caught up on the news, stock market, and the hurricane. Not a bit of good news to be found. The storm was a bitch of biblical portions. The island is barely above sea level and a few hundred meters wide and was sure to be covered by water. Major cities were rocked with riots, masked men and women hurling rocks and swinging batons at everything in their path with no visible purpose other than to create anarchy and chaos. Some carried signs encouraging the president to gift Atlanta to the Black Panthers as a sovereign nation. Others threatened civil war should he try. I guess Liberia was not an option or one that was not conveniently located and economically suitable. The California and New York congressional delegation had joined the Black Caucus in encouraging the president to do so. Oil prices had breached their 200-day moving average and gas was back above $4 a gallon...if you could find it. Energy, transport, and coal company stock prices were skyrocketing, while retailers and banks were plummeting. Silicon Valley companies were suffering, as well, while steadfastly supporting the Black Panthers in their move to secure Atlanta in their politically correct cause de jour. Notably absent from the riots were any sign of the Panthers.

Time had gotten away from me. I peeked outside. The sky had darkened, and the wind had strengthened considerably. Cantore stood just below our balcony, framing his impromptu live shot. The light from his camera helped illuminate my crew still slamming drinks in the relative safety, shielded from the wind by the pool bar. It had yet to start raining.

I stepped on the balcony, accidently slamming the sliding glass door behind me. Cantore shot me a dirty look as if I, standing on my own balcony, was somehow the intruder in this scenario. "Fuck you, Cantore," I yelled. "You bald-headed prima donna. Stephanie Abrams was too good for your little bitch ass." He walked off camera, waving his hands and yelling unintelligently. I tried the door. It would not budge.

The wind further stiffened as the first of countless rain bands came through. I was stuck on the balcony.

I waved from the balcony and yelled at my crew. The rain had drove them inside the bar. The bartender had left a solitary shutter open on the leeward side. I jumped up and down. I took off my shirt and used it as a signal flag, pretty much doing shirtless jumping jacks. Not the best look for a man of my age and physical condition. I had forgotten Cantore. He had not forgotten me. A bright light blinded me. I looked down, shielding my eyes from the camera's light and saw Cantore staring back at me with an evil grin, his female companion's camera directed to the crazy fat man doing shirtless jumping jacks from his balcony in the midst of a hurricane. Cantore's revenge was sweet.

I walked back to the sliding glass door seeking shelter from the rain and Cantore's prying eyes. Pressed against the glass were several small, black faces with bewildered looks. I motioned for them to let me in. Hambone slid the door open.

"What you be jumping around half-naked in the storm for, Mr. Zeke? You scare my chilrin half crazy. You be drinking too much for your own safety," Hambone lectured.

Pot, kettle, black came to mind. I held my tongue and flipped on the light.

"Mister Zeke, this here be my lovely bride."

Hambone's wife, to my genuine surprise, was a lovely, well put together, young woman with normal size breasts, despite her current occupation. Contrary to Hambone in almost every conceivable manner, she possessed a full set of very white teeth. If this in any way sounds racist, I have failed to properly describe the appearance, hygiene, and dialect of Hambone. She greeted me warmly.

"Thank you, Mister Ezekiel, for inviting us into your lovely home."

I nodded. She continued, introducing me to her mother, two aunts, five small children ages one through seven, and two older daughters from Hambone's previous wives. A puddle had formed at my feet. In my shock, I had forgotten I was shirtless and soaked. I excused myself to grab some dry clothes.

My crew from the bar made their way back to the condo during a short break in the weather. On the perimeter of a hurricane, the nasty weather comes in bands. Rose, Brad, Sue, Ruth, Linus, and Lucy, along with Hambone's extended family, would be riding the storm out in our condo. Jaws and Waldo claimed their space on the master bed, making a soggy and sandy imprint. It was going to be a bit crowded.

Thunder rolled across the windows. Rain fell upwards from the Earth in large sheets, banging off the windows in a menacing voice. The lights flashed and died.

"Somebody should check on Cantore?" Lucy asked. It wasn't a statement.

We all laughed. Lucy sighed.

Light filtered in the windows from the exterior lightning dancing off frightened faces and fashioning ghoulish ogres on the walls. The condo had its own generator to power the water and sewer plants as well as the common areas. Hambone's wife lit a candle and placed it on the breakfast bar. A baby squealed. Conversation became more and more difficult as the angry wind bellowed and howled, as if disemboweled unjustly at the hands of a tyrannical lord. Yard debris recoiled off the sliding glass doors, resonating throughout the room in mounting volume.

Seagulls and frigate birds began to crash into the windows, testing the limits of the hurricane rating.

The carcasses assembled in a growing macabre funeral pile outside the door in the relative cover of the balcony. Later in the storm, even fish found their way onto our balcony, some still alive and gulping frantically in the wind-driven rain and sea spray.

The sour smell of fear was amplified in the cramped, humid space. We huddled quietly into the night, Hambone's family praying and fingering their magic beads. The rest of us took our comfort from warm rum and burning herb, both strategies only giving a modicum of comfort. Around midnight, the storm subsided. I pushed apart the impromptu burial mound to step outside onto the balcony. The view was both somehow majestic and horrific. Every tree was either fallen or stripped of its vegetation. Curtains from several condos billowed gently into the night. Several feet of still water had replaced the courtyard, lapping quietly into the first-floor condos. I looked skyward and could see the stars, billions of them, against a black, still, clear sky. I looked out and I could see the treacherous eastern eyewall closing in on us. Dark, dangerous swirls signaled a few more hours of sheer terror.

Washington, D.C.; July 2018: *In a predawn raid today, the Justice Department served warrants on nineteen GOP Congressmen, including the Speaker of the House and the Senate Majority Leader along with most of the remaining party leadership. The Attorney General said the indictments were sealed and the Representatives and Senators would be held at Guantanamo Bay due to the nature and severity of their heinous crimes and the danger to the Republic.*

New Senate Majority Leader Chuck Schumer wasted no time in introducing legislation authorizing O'Grady's climate change payments to the Green Fund and the transfer of control of the U.S. armed forces to the UN. Schumer also called for a special election in ten days for the seats vacated by the traitors.

CNN applauded the move, calling the arrested lawmakers racists and Nazi's, and not entitled to protection under the law due to their beliefs.

In related news, AGN was briefly shut down due to protesters calling AGN a fascist organization and throwing menstrual blood-filled balloons at AGN arriving staff members. The police called it a peaceful protest and refused to intervene.

Alongside Global News

CHAPTER THIRTEEN

At some point, terror subsides. A peculiar acceptance takes hold. One becomes deaf and blind to the fury of the storm. Awe replaces dread at the storm's majesty... it's symmetry. A life so much greater than yourself... than all of mankind. Despite centuries of achievement, mankind can do nothing to stop the storm, and the storm can, on its choosing, wipe us off the face of the planet we call our own. We are but the fleas on the dog's ass. Insignificant, irrelevant, nothing but a pesky virus to the universe.

With the deliberate passage of time, one by one we fell into a restless slumber. By daylight, the wind still howled but with less anguish. The bulk of the sea water had returned to its rightful home. Odorous muck filled the pool along with most of the first-floor condos. A 35-foot catamaran precariously crowned the pool bar looking every bit fit to sail despite its ungainly perch. Every out structure, every tree, was impaired.

Hambone's wife wept. For a moment I thought to comfort her. She and her family were safe. How very American of me, I thought. Many of her friends likely died. All the locals had lost much of everything which was little of nothing. It would be months before water and power were restored to the island. The expats, us included, could just leave. She, her friends, and family would have to stay and suffer to rebuild their impoverished island.

I pulled a chair onto the balcony. It was breezy, and even a little chilly, but the air was uniquely fresh and the sky peculiarly vibrant, like a photo-shopped picture, the colors too intense to be true. Hambone's daughter brought me a bottled water and pulled up a chair beside me. She was coal black like her dad. Shoeless, she was dressed in a simple, loose, white cotton dress that did little to hide she was no little girl. Her hair was shorn tightly. Her skin flawless and her eyes...her eyes were large, round and incongruously, the color of the sea.

"Thank you," she said.

I scoffed. "For what?"

"You saved my family, Mister Ezekiel. You are a hero."

"No," I replied. "I did nothing of the sort. I opened a door to my home that is located on your island. It was literally the least I could do and not be an evil bastard. Besides, I am sure you could have found shelter with friends."

"Yes, Mister Ezekiel. I could have stayed with my boyfriend." She paused, choking back disappointment, "But he would not allow my family."

"Your boyfriend...he a local boy?"

"No, sir. He is a Yankee, like you," She said proudly.

"I am no damn Yankee."

She looked confused. "Florida is in Canada?"

I ignored her question. Those of us raised in the South cringe at being called a Yankee.

"Just how old are you?" I immediately pictured an old, perverted, rich, white guy as her boyfriend, a la McAfee.

"Nineteen."

"This boyfriend of yours. How old is he?"

She giggled. "Mister Ezekiel, you sound like my dad. He promised to come by after the storm to pick me up. I would like very much for you to meet him."

"And I would very much like to meet him." I suddenly realized I did not know her name.

"Dianne." She extended her hand, recognizing my predicament. "A pleasure to make your acquaintance."

We Americans have earned our ugly American reputation. We take and rarely give. We treat natives as foreigners in their own country. We rarely bother to learn any of their language other than to ask for food, beer, liquor, directions, and ass. We plunder their countries until they have nothing left to give. We get drunk, puke in their pools, piss in their streets, and impregnate their young women. It's like we are malevolent Gods wringing out all that is good before discarding the remains unceremoniously into the sewer. I had just met Dianne, but a shared suffering brings people together. Yeah, I wanted to meet her Yankee boyfriend. No American, ugly or not, was going to abuse Hambone's daughter on my watch.

Dogs wandered the sand-filled courtyard, ducking in and out of first floor units through smashed-in doors and windows seeking the edible flotsam of the storm. The clay tiles had been ripped from the roof and were littered about the courtyard. The concrete block walls of the building stood naked, the stucco having been sand-blasted from their surface. Piers from the dock stood like ghostly sentinels stripped of their planking. The cast-off planking was driven at odd angles into the building or drifting out to sea. A few of the condo maintenance men began surveying the damage but shortly just sat, defeated, and stared into the vast piles of debris. Most of the balconies were heavy with people, awestruck and silent. Hundreds of locals joined the tourists and owners gauging the damage that must have been inflicted on their own meager shelters and businesses. I was heartened to see so many of the expat community and tourists recognized the urgency of the storm and opened their condos to locals. Maybe there was hope for humankind after all.

By early afternoon, the remnants of the storm passed. The muck dried quickly, turning the pool and yard into a giant debris-filled beach. Makeshift grills filled the courtyard surrounded by improvised seating fashioned from the plentiful storm debris. The agreeable smell of grilling fish soon filled the air. With the electricity out, everyone was cooking anything that would spoil. There was a peculiar sense of carnival. Even the locals seemed festive. Perhaps celebration of their personal survival was the theme, the thought of future suffering on the difficult road to recovery not yet salient.

A neighbor motioned me down. He was the charter captain for a 25-foot fishing boat called "Nut Shot." "I have plenty of fish. Bring your people down and join me for lunch. Otherwise it will just go to the dogs."

We sat on makeshift stools and wordlessly ate red snapper and grouper. Another family brought us bowls of Belizean rice in exchange for a few grilled fish. Linus brought down a case of lukewarm beer. The dogs were well fed from the animal carcasses that had piled up in front of all the windward condos. It would stink soon enough.

Dianne appeared on the balcony, smiling broadly and waving at me. She motioned for me to come up. Beside her loomed a familiar face: tall, black, and angry. Khalid Muhammad was at her side.

Muhammad leaned over the balcony, scowling in my direction. Our eyes met, and a puzzled look crossed his face. We had never met. I would expect I was below his radar. Another no name cracker. He stared intently. I sat frozen with indecision. I mean, the guy didn't know me from Adam's house cat. I had befriended his girlfriend's family during a storm. That should count for something. Just go shake the man's hand and he will leave, I thought.

Hobo spit out a wayward fish bone into the fire of the makeshift grill. "You have a short memory, Ezekiel."

Hobo wasn't there even a moment ago. And I had not uttered a word out loud. But I was not surprised. Hobo found a way to be at my side any time there was trouble in my life. Whether he was the source of said trouble or just accompanied it was a matter of some debate.

"You are right about this one, Hobo. His stupid runs deep." Added Deuce, winking his scared socket in my direction.

Tarbaby laughed and continued eating. Fish smiled. Linus stood and stretched as if preparing to run the 400-meter hurdles, which, for him would have been a pole-vaulting competition. Hobo turned to Aja. "Where is their boat?" He pointed towards Muhammad.

"At the Boca Bacular Chico, just north of here; between Belize and Mexico," Aja replied.

"What are you guys? The Short Bus X-men or something?" Like Hobo, none of the Breakfast Rum Club members were here even moments before.

They ignored me and continued talking among themselves. I looked to Rose for some level of explanation, or, at least a modicum of moral support. Rose shrugged and went back to eating her lupper. Sue fished a joint from her bra and lit it. Brad pulled out a warm beer, handing it to Tarbaby to open with his tooth. Tarbaby opened the beer and gulped it down in two large gulps.

"Mister Ezekiel!" Dianne called out, "Come up and meet Bob." It felt like more an order than a request.

"Bob? Who the hell is Bob?" I mumbled. Her boyfriend was no doubt Khalid Muhammad.

Hobo turned to Hambone. "Your daughter's boyfriend is the leader of the New Black Panthers? You are such a disappointment."

Hambone shrugged. "She is my princess. He buys her nice things."

"Don't have much of a choice, Ezekiel. We need the disc. The Panthers have it or know where it is. Go up and get acquainted…" He pointed up to the balcony and smiled "…with Bob."

"Don't I have a say in this?" It was supposed to be a statement but came out more like a question. "Isn't this the man who wants me dead?"

"No," Hobo deadpanned.

"That makes me feel infinitely better."

"You are not special to…Bob. He wants all you crackers dead. He does, however, work for the man whose singular life's purpose it is to see you destroyed." Hobo took another bite of grilled snapper.

I looked at him, perplexed. Hobo continued to chew, pausing to thank the cook for his generous meal. He continued, "You recover the disc and we get to go home."

"I am home."

"I'll rephrase. Get the disc and you and your kind get to survive extinction."

"My kind? Now that is just racist. And I am still not seeing the upside."

"Geez," Rose said, standing. "I'll go get the damn disc if it will shut you two losers up."

"Sit down, Rose. It's not like the disc is in their back pocket. This mission requires finesse, not muscle."

"Up my alley, then," Lucy stood. "I am the damn queen of finesse."

"Not like you have had any sex for years...much less up your alley." Linus inelegantly added.

Rose raised her free hand and added, "Testify, sister."

Hobo studied Lucy for a minute as if formulating a diabolical plan involving a circus clown, a three-legged dog, and a female midget. I could almost see the wheels in his head spinning. I was all for any plan that did not include me getting killed. Heroism was for dead people.

"No. It won't work," Hobo shook his head and muttered.

"Let's not just throw the idea out wholesale. Let's brainstorm it and maybe we can fine tune it."

Dianne called out from the balcony again. This time with urgency. I expect she sensed Bob was not a patient man.

"You're up, Ezekiel." Hobo pointed toward the balcony.

"You're up? No words of advice or encouragement?"

"Don't get killed."

I looked at Rose.

"Don't screw up."

"Redundant much? Seriously...That all you got?"

"No worries. We will catch up with you at Boca Bacular Chico."

"Where?"

"Where they are taking you."

"Told you. Stupid runs deep," Deuce contributed.

Aja nodded in agreement.

"Great pep talk, Vince. And how?" I waved at the adjacent destruction.

Hobo pointed to the catamaran sitting atop the pool bar. "Giddy up, cowboy. Your destiny awaits." He pointed to the balcony.

It wasn't just Khalid. It was his entire posse. Eight angry looking men dressed in black with combat boots, black beret, and a malevolent-looking machete clipped to their belts.

"Halloween?" I asked. I frequently utilized humor as a tool to avoid shitting my britches.

Khalid scowled. He was silhouetted against the sky on the balcony. He didn't like me. But, then again, he did not like any white person. I was just hoping to be an average vile white man, not one of particular interest that warranted an excruciating death.

"Ezekiel, this is my fiancé, Bob." I noticed Dianne had dropped the Mister. "Bob, my Dad's best friend, Ezekiel."

An overnight battlefield promotion. Then again, guessing Hambone's friend list was not extensive. I extended my hand. He vaguely nodded and turned to leave. Whew, I thought, dodged a big one. Home free.

Seeing Khalid turn to leave, Deuce yelled out from below, sounding curiously like me; "You suck ass, Muhammad."

Khalid turned to me, "What did you say, cracker?"

"Hold that thought." I turned, looking over the balcony. "You suck ass. That is your grand plan? I want to trade my Short Bus X-men in for a new batch. Your guys superpowers are acting stupid, getting drunk, and being bat-shit crazy. I want that inexplicably hot blue chick and the hairy dude with claws on my team."

Khalid pushed by me to see who I was talking to.

Me, he had yet to recognize. Hobo, on the other hand, was someone not easily forgotten. I don't think he connected the dots, but he suspected something was afoul. He roughly grabbed my arm and pushed me toward his dark minions. "You, white boy...can come wid us."

"Thanks, Deuce," I yelled over my shoulder. "Don't let Rose sing at my funeral."

I was shoved in the back of one of four mules. We headed north toward the Boca Bacular Chico. It would be a slow journey as the road was washed out and filled with debris. I was praying my Short Bus X-men could get the cat off the pool bar in time and come up with a marginally better plan than the one demonstrated to date. I prayed hard. Khalid cursed. Dianne sobbed as we drove off heading north without her.

Washington, D.C.; July 2018: *President O'Grady signed into law a new tax bill, effectively doubling the federal income tax marginal rate to seventy percent on households making more than five hundred thousand dollars per year. Dramatic reductions in tax receipts along with increased spending have raised the national debt to just north of one hundred trillion dollars. Senator Schumer applauded the move saying, "It is time the rich finally pay their fair share." A separate bill excluded all federal employees and union members from federal taxes for reasons of National Security. O'Grady proudly noted accomplishing, under his brief term, "...less than fifty percent of Americans paying any Federal tax." The President pointed to a poll stating more than half of Americans thought his tax bill was fair.*

Gabriel Foster, a spokesperson for the ALT Right organization "Fair Tax", called the O'Grady Tax plan "{expletive deleted} nuts and the stupid {expletive deleted} poll self-evident."

CHAPTER FOURTEEN

The mules were powerful and agile yet still no match for the debris-filled road that, on its best day, was little more than a washed-out path heading north. The going was deliberate. Snails flew by, flipping us off with slimy digits. We had been over an hour and covered less than a mile. Up ahead, seven large palm trees crisscrossed the road, flanking a mostly intact fisherman's ramshackle hut. The occupant waved and smiled from his front porch, rightfully offering no apology for blocking the road.

Khalid's evil minions, armed with machetes, dismounted the mules and began to inexpertly hack away at the trees. These were city evil minions. I thought pulling the downed trees out of the way with mules a much more effective and efficient strategy. I remained silent on my thoughts. Time was on my side.

Muhammad marched back to my mule, relieving my appointed evil minion of his sentry duties. Khalid shoved him out of the driver's seat instructing him to join the others in the clearing effort. The ruling elite simply replaced the rich in the Marxist pecking order. He cranked the mule and pulled it into a rare shaded spot. A pack of dogs circled a large sink hole growling and snarling at a hefty crocodile swimming at the bottom.

"Who the hell are you, old man?"

"Ezekiel Foster." I extended my hand, "Khalid Muhammad," I dropped the Bob deception.

He did not take the offered hand. I had decided to play this straight up. This guy was a lot of things, but I didn't think crazy nor stupid was high on his list of character traits. Perhaps I could reason with him, I thought. After all, he was getting played by Smith and I doubted he would buy into the whole sole survivor son of man bullshit Hobo was pedaling.

Khalid's brow furrowed, and his eyes narrowed. "Who the fuck is that scrawny ginger you hanging about with?"

"Hobo?" I laughed. "That, my friend, is a damn fine question."

"I ain't your friend, cracker."

"Why you hating on us white folks, dude?"

"'Cause you people enslaved my people."

"My people? I am offended. Kind of racist, don't you think?"

Khalid sat up straighter and bowed out his chest. "A man of color can't be racist," He quoted the standard party line. Based on his posture, I don't think he really believed what he was saying.

"Well, that is just all kinds of stupid. I didn't take you for a moron."

He drew his hand back to backhand me but did not.

162

I continued. "You attended school at Furman, right? Full ride...got an advanced degree in African studies. Graduated damn near the top of your class. Bet that made your mama proud." It was a statement, not a question. Knowledge is a powerful weapon. As such, the Internet was a very potent armament.

"I'm from the streets of Atlanta, cracker."

I laughed. "Okay, Tupac..."

"You dumb, cracker. Tupac was from Harlem, not Atlanta."

"Whatever generic gangster you need to tell your minions, then." Current rap culture was not my strong point. An intimate knowledge of Khalid's past, however, was. Know your enemy. Thanks, Mr. Tzu. "Your dad was a successful orthodontist in Gwinnet County. The rich part of Atlanta. You attended private schools all your life. Hell, your dad made his fortune straightening little rich white kid's teeth. Until college, you attended school in predominantly rich white folk schools. The only street you from is paved in gold and littered with dead presidents. How did that African studies degree work out looking for a job, though?"

Our institutions of higher learning keep cranking out overpriced, useless degree programs, piling up student debt, while millions of highly paid, high tech, and even low tech jobs go unclaimed for want of qualified applicants. Recent graduates are compelled to accept menial call center and retail jobs facing mountains of debt. It is an unworkable system even without the debt variable. Brought to you by Bernie Sanders for President because Socialism works, damn it. But I do digress. Back to the regularly scheduled story.

"Fuck you, cracker. You don't know shit."

"Damn, you are full of misguided hate, son." He did slap me this time, but his angle was bad, and his hand slid off my face onto the mule's chassis. He winced in pain. I subdued a smile.

"I ain't your son, bitch. Call me by my given name."

"Okay, Otis, or, should I call you Mr. Nixon?" Privacy was a thing of the past with the Internet. Otis changed his name about the turn of the millennium. Khalid Muhammad seemed a more bad ass name for the son of an orthodontist.

"Fuck you, cracker. You people enslaved us and brought us here as slaves and, until this day, you oppress the black man."

I smiled. "That was sexist as hell. I think at a minimum, us crackers are equal opportunity oppressors." He shot me a look filled with hate. There is a smart-ass that lives inside me that will one day get me killed. "Okay. Slavery bad, we all can agree. Whitey done some real bad shit. So, on behalf of my great, great, great, great grandpas, I am truly sorry to your great, great, great, great, grandparents."

"Your apology don't mean shit."

"Understood. That said, a point of fact or two, if I might. Your own people enslaved you. European slave traders bought slaves from the docks of Africa that had been enslaved by other African tribes. Pretty rare the white dudes actually trekked their lily white asses inland and captured slaves on their own. Your ancestor lost a tribal war and his punishment was to get sold into slavery by another African."

"Bullshit."

"Exactly. Don't let the truth color your opinion. Secondly, as bad as it was for your ancestors, and I am not for a minute discounting their suffering, you came out the winner."

"How so, cracker?"

"Well, you for one, Khalid, are rich as hell, thanks

to crooked little teeth of rich white folks. But even the poorest among the black community are so much wealthier than many of their distant cousins back in Africa. Sometimes, it turns out, the winners are the losers. The poverty level in your Mother Land is astronomical. And I don't mean the 'I can't afford the new iPhone' kind of poverty. I'm talking dirt floors, no windows, rats are yummy as shit, kind of poverty."

I continued, "Oppression? No doubt your more recent ancestors faced a wall of bigotry, hate, and oppression. You...not so much. Not to say there is not the redneck Negro hater out there 'cause I'd put my money on them still existing. But hell, look at you. You hate me 'cause I am white. That is the very definition of racist. By the way, you ever notice we had a black president?" I whispered black. "The U.S. population is only thirteen percent black. That means a whole lot of us crackers voted for a black man."

"You vote for him?"

"Oh hell no."

"'Cause he black." Muhammad said, more as statement not a question.

"Oh hell no. 'Cause he is a damn Marxist and a puppet of your good buddy, Smith."

"Don't change nothing. Whitey keep the black man down. Always with a boot on the black man's throat."

"Excellent visual. And I don't totally disagree with you. Economic chains are as strong as those made of iron."

He looked at me, puzzled, like I was agreeing with him. "But it is your politicians and your leaders that enslave you now. Not us run of the mill, pickup-driving, flag-waving, gun-toting, crackers. Keeping the poor dependent on the government tit instead of encouraging you to stand on your own. 'Cause if you did, black Americans would succeed on their own merit and would not require the corrupt politicians and race-baiters anymore. When will you learn? The Panthers participate in this dangerous, false narrative. Young black boys, even middle-class ones, grow up believing the deck is stacked against them. Why even try? Sometime that man with his hand out helping you up is just holding you down. Take your boy Smith for instance."

The mention of Smith brought Muhammad back to Hobo. "Who the fuck is scrawny ginger?"

"Asked and answered, I call him Hobo."

"That don't answer shit."

"I don't really know shit and what I do know you would not believe."

"Lay it on me."

"Okay. He, Hobo, is some kind of supernatural being, a God if you will, from ancient times. The story goes he helped create this world and, in time of trouble, wanders the planet disguised as a vagrant. His real name is Viracocha."

Khalid's eyes narrowed before breaking out in a toothy smile. "Shit, cracker. You are fucking crazy."

"Perhaps." He had a legitimate point.

"What Smith, in your demented fairy tale, want with scrawny ginger?"

"Again, you won't believe me."

"Truth. But I still want to hear your bullshit. You make me laugh, fat cracker."

"Like Hobo, scrawny ginger, if you will, Smith is a supernatural being. Difference being, Smith plays for the opposing team."

"What other team?" Muhammad asked.

"You know, good and evil, God and Satan, Patriots and Raiders."

Muhammad cracked a sliver of a smile, revealing his perfect teeth again. "You truly one bat-shit crazy old man."

"I have long since embraced the crazy, Muhammad. I know my story sounds ridiculous, trust me, I hear it, too, and, more importantly, I have lived it. Suspend disbelief for a moment.

"What has Smith done for you?"

"You don't read the papers, cracker. He yielded Atlanta to me."

Progress, I thought. Muhammad had dropped "fat" from my name. Then again, maybe I had lost a few pounds. Silver linings and all. "Just gave it to you like, voila, for nothing."

"Not for nothing."

"So, what did you do for him?"

"I took care of a little problem."

"Yeah, I saw that." I discreetly chuckled, remembering the chaotic scene. People died. None the less, nut shots were always amusing, more so when delivered by children to grown men. "Got your ass kicked pretty good by a bunch of kindergarteners on the pool deck in the process. What else?"

"I got him a shiny gold disc."

Now I was making some progress. "So, let me understand what you are saying…in exchange for knocking off a Jewish guy that was blackmailing Smith and a gold…disc you say, he gives you the largest city in the south?"

"Atlanta is the birthright of my people."

"You even hear yourself? I am not the target audience for your bullshit."

"It was a big ass gold disc," he argued.

I put my hands a few inches apart. He nodded.

"Hell yeah. Got to be worth billions."

"And here I thought exaggerating size was a white man's disorder."

Khalid scoffed and smiled.

"You have any arithmetic classes in that African studies program? Let's say that gold disc of yours weighs five pounds. Gold is worth $1,250 an ounce or so. Five times sixteen, carry the one, times $1,250 an ounce...I really need a calculator, but somewhere around a hundred grand. Atlanta real estate going that cheap? Hell man, double it to ten pounds...two hundred grand."

Khalid pulled out his latest model iPhone and did the math. He quietly slid the iPhone back into his pocket. His face registered puzzlement. I guessed my math was pretty close.

"Alternative scenario. Maybe Smith is playing another game and, instead of being a partner, you are a rich white man's mark."

"Ain't just Smith. O'Grady. You might've heard of him, you dumb-ass cracker. He is your damn president. Obama too, cracker, the Secretary General of the UN. And Congresswoman Quisha gave us the money and land to build the New Black Panthers Consulate in Jacksonville."

"She the chunky black congresswoman with the flashy cowboy hats?"

"No, cracker." Khalid smiled, "She the fat one with crazy wigs riding around in Air Force One with Obama." Even Khalid couldn't avoid a chuckle. "Like, what does all the powerful people have to gain by giving me Atlanta?" Khalid asked.

I stole a line from Hobo. "You are still playing checkers while George is playing 3-D chess. You, Obama, O'Grady, and the wig lady are all just pieces on his board. It was George's idea, to have the Panthers sign a mutual defense treaty with the Brotherhood of Islam?"

He smiled. "Yeah. That got the media talking about us and the corrupt, fat, old, rich, white guys paying attention."

"You mean the politicians?" I sought unnecessary clarification.

"Pay attention, fat cracker."

Damn. I put those pounds back on. Dark cloud.

Khalid continued, "But that was just a propaganda stunt. Everybody know that was an empty treaty. We don't even like those self-riotous, rag-headed, camel fuckers."

"I see what you mean now. People of color can't be racist."

A puzzled look crossed Khalid's face.

I could not afford a tangential argument. I moved on. "You for a minute think that all us crackers in Atlanta just going get up and leave the city for your taking?"

"So, what I have to shoot a few crackers. What they gonna do?"

"Uhhh...shoot back. Revolt. Start a war which, according to your public relations stunt, would require the Brotherhood to come to your aid."

"That ain't gonna happen."

"You are right. It is not. Neither Gepetto nor Pinocchio can really give you Atlanta. You've gotta be smarter than that. All Smith wants to do is destabilize the oil market, sending oil prices through the roof. This will drive up the value of coal and transportation stocks. Which, if you read the papers, you would know he has been buying up in droves." I was banking on his suburban Atlanta private education that he would get the reference.

Khalid's minions finished clearing the palm trees. The old man's shack remained in the narrow path blocking our way. Four of the mules each took the two exposed corners of the shack, effectively ripping the old man's shack apart with him still inside.

"Way to stand up for the oppressed, asshole."

Khalid lifted his hand and struck. This time it was not a glancing blow. I let the blood trickle down my cheek and smiled. "You might want to reexamine what you really stand for. And, if you work hard enough, maybe one day you can become a real boy, too."

CHAPTER FIFTEEN

It was after dark before we arrived at Boca Bacular Chico. We made camp close to the ocean, in the open, on top of a jagged coral bluff that extended into the fabled cut. The mosquitos, sand gnats, and other UFO's lustily attacked every inch of exposed skin artfully dodging all efforts to thwart their violence. Body orifices seemed their beloved targets. The ground was hard and the night humid. Even so, everyone crowded the fires for at least the illusion of protection from the winged tormentors.

"Snakes like the fire too, you know," I taunted, foolishly.

"Fuck you, racist cracker. You think 'cause I am black I am scared of snakes?"

"Hell, I am scared of snakes."

"Bet you think I can't swim, you fucking cracker racist."

"Well can you?"

"Fuck you, fat cracker."

I preferred racist to fat cracker. Fat was just a little too close to the truth and smarted a bit. "I'll take that as a no."

"You know that Hobo fellow using you, as well."

"Yes."

"So how is that different than Smith using me?" Muhammad asked.

Progress, I thought. "I play for the Patriots. You play for the Raiders."

"What would you have me do?"

"Think for yourself. Look that gift horse in the mouth."

"The hell you say?"

We had generational as well as cultural differences that impeded clear communication. "Know that Smith has his own self-interest at heart and his self-interest is not good for anyone but, well...himself."

"I ain't turning down Atlanta. That would be a betrayal to my people."

"You ain't Moses and you ain't getting Atlanta, dude. And a lot of people, including yours, will suffer mightily if you try."

Khalid thought for a moment. "Can't do it."

"Then give me the disc." It was worth a shot. You will never get what you don't ask for.

"I ain't gonna give you no damn disc. It is worth billions."

"Khalid, to the right person, the disc is truly priceless. Take it to a Rick at Pawn Stars and he will give you $200,000, tops. The Old Man...even less."

"The hell you say?"

"Not a fan of Pawn Stars?" It was rhetorical. "How about I buy it?"

"You got cash stuffed up your asshole?"

"No, but I got a condo just down the road. It was worth close to a million before the hurricane. Still worth half that. You kinda sweet on Hambone's girl Dianne, aren't you?" I didn't wait for the answer. "Be a nice gift to her. She looked kind of pissed when you left her standing on the side of the road." I lied a little. She looked very pissed.

"Ain't no peace of ass worth Atlanta."

"Testify." I raised my hands in the air. "But you are not getting Atlanta."

"Why you want the disc? If it just worth $200,000, why you offering me five hundred large."

"The disc currently has utility. The condo does not."

"The hell you say?"

In lieu of an economics lesson, I decided to stay with the truth, crazy as it was. "You are not going to believe this story, either."

"Another one of your bat-shit crazy stories?"

"Yup, a doozy. The disc is a key."

"Key to what?"

"A door, a gate, if you will, that provides a shortcut to another universe."

"You mean, a wormhole."

"Damn, you took something other than African studies at Furman?" His nostrils flared. I needed to watch my sarcasm. The smart-ass always wanted to come out and play at inopportune times. I stowed the smart-ass and continued; "Exactly, a wormhole."

"Why you want to go to another universe?"

"Not me so much but Hobo and maybe Smith. It is home for them."

"Why they want you to go?"

"Hobo thinks I have something his people want. Now Smith, on the other hand, is determined no part of me makes it through the wormhole."

"Not following."

"You are abreast of current events, I assume?" I doubted it, but smart-ass self safely stowed, I continued. "Did you see where an amateur astronomer found what he thinks to be another planet in our universe?"

He nodded yes.

"It is called Planet X, among other names, and it's on a course to come close to our planet."

"Good thing it is just close."

"It's massive. Think hand grenades and nuclear bombs, not darts. It is an extinction event."

"So, that disc gets you off this planet." Khalid pointed at the ground with one hand while swatting at insects with the other.

"That it does."

"Why you?"

"Told you. 'Cause I am special."

He frowned, sizing me up. I am not an impressive physical specimen. "No, why you?"

I guess this was his line. "You know the story of Noah and his ark?"

"I don't buy that shit from the Christian Bible."

"Dude, a derivative of that story is in several hundred ancient texts. Do you know the story or not?"

"Course I do. Mama took me to church."

I considered it progress; he admitted both to going to church and having a mother. I flashed to him younger, all dressed up in short britches, suspenders, and a bow tie carrying a bible. I grinned broadly.

"What you got to smile about, cracker?"

I smartly stowed the mental image and the smile and continued. "Hobo is convinced that I am the only living person that has pure DNA from Noah's Ark and, consequently, all the way back to Adam and Eve."

"Now that is some crazy ass shit. You a drunk, fat

ass cracker. I am supposed to believe you are..." He searched for an appropriate word but couldn't find it.

"I know, right?"

∞∞∞∞

Low tide was just after first light. Khalid and his minions led me down a ragged path, leading to an obscured opening in the bluff, accessible only at low tide. Crouched, we walked inside. It was a giant limestone cenote with a small roof opening covered by dense vegetation blocking all but the most stalwart light. The flashlight illuminated the walls decorated with Mayan art. Giant men painted with odd helmets and, what could only be described as flying machines, towered over the Mayan natives. A stack of bones stood on a ledge just above the high tide mark. Two small speed boats with trip outdoor motors were moored to the ledge. A narrow path led around the perimeter of the cenote.

Muhammad walked to the stack of bones, clumsily pushing them aside to grab a heavy object wrapped in tobacco leaves. Possibly I had misjudged its weight and subsequent value. He tossed it into the cenote. "It's yours if you can get it."

"You know I can swim, right?"

He scoffed. "Swim yeah, but how long can the fat man hold his breath?"

"You may have a point." These cenotes were notoriously deep. "You know, this might just screw up your deal with Smith?"

"I didn't give you shit. Lost it, far as he will ever know. And I get the girl, right?"

I shrugged. "Maybe. What you need to deliver is a grand romantic gesture." I suggested. "May I suggest the movies of John Hughes for some pointers."

"Who the hell is…"

I put an imaginary boom box on my shoulder as a context clue. Muhammad scowled trying not to smile. He knew the movie.

"Like a million-dollar condo?" He and the minions swam up to the boats and climbed aboard.

"Damn. Did not see that coming." I mumbled.

The engines roared to life, echoing thunderously off the walls of the cenote. The boats maneuvered out the entrance to the cave and sped off west, toward the Bahia de Chetumal leading to Mexico.

I jumped into the water and placed my head down, cupping my hands above my eyes to catch some air bubbles. The water was still and clear. I could not see the bottom.

∞∞∞∞

At first it was just a low rumble, a sound echoing off the walls of the cenote. I was left without a flashlight and only a bit of indirect sunlight illuminated the space. After a few moments, I recognized the words.

"Ezekiel."

"Zeke."

"You drunken dumb-ass, where are you?"

Sadly, "the dumb-ass" voice sounded like my loving wife. Hopefully she was using cruelty as a subterfuge for fear of losing me. A man can dream.

I didn't know how much time had gone by, but the entrance to the cave was about half-filled with water. I walked outside the entrance and motioned for my would-be rescuers, the Short Bus X-men, to join me. Dianne, Brad, and Sue had come along for the ride. Dianne, for obvious reasons, none of which included aiding in my rescue effort. I assumed Brad and Sue just wanted to be entertained. I would soon discover their motives to be more esoteric. They anchored in the channel and swam to the entrance.

Diane was the first to speak, "Where is Bob?"

I shrugged. "I think you will see him again shortly." A cracker can dream, as well.

After her eyes adjusted to the dim light, Sue proclaimed, "Holy shit." She snatched a flashlight from Hambone, directing its light to the cenote's walls. "This is so fucking cool."

Hobo eyeballed me, grinned broadly, and said, "I see you are alive."

"Perceptive, ass clown." He withheld his typical lecture regarding his disdain of foul language and sarcasm. I falsely considered the absence of the lecture to be progress.

"Disc, man, the disc. You get it?"

"Sorta." I pointed to the water. "That bitch is deep."

Both Hobo and Deuce simultaneously dove in. After what seemed like an eternity, Hobo surfaced with the disc in hand. Deuce surfaced shortly thereafter with a breast plate that shimmered golden in the dim light of the cenote, reflecting tiny dots of light off the walls like a Studio 54 disco ball.

Sue, inspired, broke out in a sad rendition of dance fever. "Staying alive...staying alive. Uh, uh, uh, uh staying alive."

I thought that good advice. My challenged Short Bus X-men huddled in the corner, speaking in hushed tones. Meanwhile, Sue stopped dancing and started studying the cenote drawings. Her flashlight illuminated massive curved walls covered in what appeared to be Mayan glyphs.

"Well, that one is clearly a large dude with a boner." Rose noted.

Lucy pointed to another. "And a lactating mom."

"Gross," Rose gagged. Rose found little uncultured, but the entirety of childbirth grossed her out.

Linus found what appeared to be an orgy. "Getting busy with it."

Lucy noted it was a bunch of big dudes holding down a chick. "I think the word you are searching for is gang rape."

"That's two words, sugar," I foolishly interjected. My inner smart-ass is willful and reckless.

"What in heaven's name is wrong with you?" Lucy asked.

I ignored the question. Even if the question wasn't rhetorical, we did not have adequate time for the unabridged list of my faults. Instead, I pointed out the spacemen and their ships. "I wish we could understand their language." Clearly the glyphs told a story.

Diane took the flashlight and, after only a cursory inspection of the walls declared, "Yo. Really old people. These are emoji's. You know…like on your cell phone."

"I never use those things. My eyes are too bad. I can't tell if the emoji is waving or flicking you off. I'd hate to mess it up and accidentally send a friendly wave to the wrong person."

Dianne frowned and shook her head. "Just look. Start here." She pointed to my spaceman high on the wall. "Some space cowboys came here and crashed in a flying contraption. They were really all big dudes with rather large penises, poor eyesight, or massive egos." She moved the flashlight down and then across the cenote's walls. "The spacemen showed the natives new technology in agriculture, building, mathematics, and astronomy. The spacemen took native girls as wives. The Mayan men were jealous. Fights started breaking out among the spacemen over how they treated the natives." She paused and turned the flashlight to an adjacent wall. "A big planet appeared in the eastern sky. It grew larger each night. The tides changed, the weather got squirrely...earthquakes and tidal waves became frequent. The spacemen left. The community starved and disbanded. There is more but it is below the tide line."

"You study Mayan glyphs?" I asked.

"Duh. Mayan." She pointed at herself with both thumbs "and this." Dianne held her cell phone. "Emojis. Not that complicated."

In the South, many of us claimed to be part Cherokee, descendants of a princess from a pride warrior tribe. Few us are. In Belize, Maya was their Cherokee. Diane was not. I motioned toward the cenote opening. There was only about a foot left before the opening was submerged.

"Let's giddy up," I suggested.

Deuce tossed the gold breast plate back in the water. "What the hell, dude?"

Deuce shrugged. "Was of no value to us."

Genuinely puzzled, Sue said, "Speak for yourself, Cyclops."

We swam back to the cat. It was a small boat and pretty crowded. Hobo set sail to Belize City. Without diesel for the engine, it would take us a day to get there. There was no food and, of greater importance, no booze on the boat.

Deuce had the helm. The remainder of The Breakfast Rum Club, aka my Short Bus X-men, and my crew were lounging about napping and complaining about the lack of booze. Hobo smiled at me. "You done good, Ezekiel. I am proud of you. I thought maybe you could pull it off."

"Thought?"

"It wasn't certain," Hobo deadpanned.

"So, fifty-fifty chance?"

"More like seventy-thirty."

"I am glad you had at least seventy percent confidence in me." Not great odds with my life on the line, but I would take the spread.

Hobo scoffed, "No, thirty."

"Ouch."

Hobo shrugged. "Hey, I was wrong. We got the disc."

"We?"

"I didn't see your fat butt diving 200 feet for it."

"And I didn't see your scrawny ass doing hand to hand combat with ten armed panthers to steal it away from them."

Hobo arched his eyebrows. "That how it went down?"

"No. Khalid gave the disc to me."

"You mean, he threw it in a deep hole for you."

"A difference without distinction."

"You need to borrow a Webster."

I shrugged. You really can't argue with crazy. "What is the plan?"

"We get this tub back to the mainland and charter a plane to Peru. Take a train to the gate and pass through."

"Who is we?"

He paused. I think I saw his eyes water a bit. "Just me and you."

Washington, D.C.; July 2018: *Black-clad and hooded members of the anti-fascist group "Antifa" staged a national protest across several major cities today, calling for the removal of all monuments to "racist, sexist, fascist, rapey, misogynist, rude, uneducated, historical figures." Statues of Jefferson, Washington, Reagan, and Bush were targeted and vandalized in several major cities. Hundreds of counter protesters were pummeled with sticks, rocks, and tear gas by masked Antifa members and were later arrested at several local hospitals for disturbing the peace. The George Smith group, "Shout Them Down" (STD) funded the First Amendment rally today with a $2 million-dollar charitable grant.*

In other news, Antifa news approvers have joined every major news outlet, including Alongside Global, in a concerted effort to combat fake news and eliminate Russian influence on our political system. The Smith Group, STD, will be supplying the heroic patriots after the requisite indoctrination at Facebook and Twitter.

Addison Foster, the spokesperson for the Fascist group "Truth Matters", called the "news approvers" "...a serious threat to the First Amendment." Foster was forcibly removed from the news conference by members of Antifa and transported to a local mental institution for evaluation.

Alongside Global News

CHAPTER SIXTEEN

At some point, I laid down on the netting, alone. Sleep did not come, but the time passed at a remarkable pace. The moon and stars traversed the sky, skirting in and out of formations of clouds, punctuated by brilliant flashes of meteorites, as if on a time lapse. Soon, dawn broke, and I could make out the mainland coast. Hobo, shirtless, was sitting beside me drinking coffee. He had his favorite mug in hand. It read "Coffee makes me poop." Hobo took the entire "don't judge a book by its cover" to a new level.

"You just need my DNA, right?" I asked.

Hobo slurped his coffee. "We want you."

"Not the question."

"My mission is to return with you. But yes, to answer your question, we can make do with your DNA." He slurped his coffee again. I expected the cup was empty and he was using it as prop to buy himself time. "Don't you want to live, Ezekiel?"

"Not where I am the freak."

Hobo chuckled and raised his mug in mock salute. "You get used to it."

"I am not going if you can manage with just my DNA."

Hobo pulled out a pocket knife from his denim shorts. He had magic pockets. "Give me your finger."

I started to hand him my hand. He smiled and plucked a couple hairs from my beard. "This will do the trick."

"Ouch, asshole."

"You rather I take the finger?"

I ignored the question. "Why is it again only you and I can go through the gate? Looks like a big ass gate."

"For one, Ezekiel...supplies: sea coal and quicksilver. The very reason we ever came to your planet to begin with. Passing matter through the hole creates a disturbance. Pass too much through and the Earth will literally shake apart at its seams."

"So, a little coal is more important than getting your friends home?"

"It's more complicated than that, Ezekiel. Animated objects..."

"You mean people, Hobo. Living and breathing people. Don't dehumanize them by calling them objects so you might sleep better with your decision."

Hobo continued, "Animated beings: dogs, Watchers, Cherubs, and people. Don't be so narrow-minded that you think you are the only intelligent species on the planet. Animated beings, as I was saying, create a thousand times more disturbance per KG than inanimate objects. Just me going through the gate with the DNA will trigger a massive earthquake off

Peru's coast. We could end it all now for your planet and take the whole team through. Don't think it wasn't discussed. Unfortunately, we are the Patriots, remember…not the Raiders."

"You and a follicle of my hair?"

Hobo smiled. "Your DNA is priceless but don't get too big for your britches. We also collected DNA from over a million other beings."

"I don't get it."

"It is your planet's story. Your true history. Not the fairy tales you teach your kids."

I smiled, "Hobo's Ark."

Hobo nodded, "And you are my Noah." He lifted the strand of my hair.

"So, what is wrong with my sisters?" I asked. Had three of them with the same DNA, I thought. Why can't at least one of them go through?

Hobo smiled, a rare, mischievous grin, pointing toward Ruth. "You want the complete list or the Reader's Digest version?"

"Given time constraints, I'll take the Reader's Digest version."

Hobo's smile faded.

"She ain't all that bad." I said, not sure if I was trying to convince Hobo or myself. She was feral as hell. The last couple years with Ruth living with us had not been awesome. But somewhere under her wild exterior, I knew, she at least meant to do no harm.

He chuckled. "No, your sisters are good women. Some more…some a little less. They are just not your sisters."

"Look, asshole, don't even try to disparage my mom's reputation."

Hobo scoffed. Took another imaginary sip of coffee and continued, "The woman you call your mother is an honorable woman. I would never utter a reproachful word about her or your birth mother."

"What the hell are you saying?"

"First off, language. Secondly, self-evident." He took another phantom sip.

"Bullshit."

"Got any baby pics of little Ezekiel?"

"My parents were dirt poor, Hobo. You know that. Photographs were expensive."

"Plenty pictures of the girls, now, aren't there?"

He had a point. Rose had teased me about being adopted when she first met my mom. Mom pulled out the picture albums, like all moms do, to embarrass their sons in front of their new girlfriends. There was a stark absence of pictures of adorable little Baby Zeke. Mom had dodged Rose's inquiry. And I really did not favor anyone in my family. "So, who do you suggest are my birth parents?"

"You have met your father."

"Darth Vader, I presume." I made a meager attempt to imitate Darth Vader's heavy breathing.

He looked puzzled and pseudo-sipped his coffee. Pop culture was not in Hobo's wheelhouse. "No," he shook his head from side to side. "Jonas."

"Jonas!" I almost screamed. Jonas was well-known to me. He was a Christian missionary that was certifiably bat-shit crazy. The man eventually drowned himself in a bath tub at a mental hospital. Doesn't get much crazier than that.

"And my mom?" I asked.

"One of the Peruvian villagers."

I was a bit dumbfounded. "I don't get it. They all died." Jonas was a missionary at a remote village in Peru. It was alleged the village women bashed in the heads of all the men and children in their sleep subsequent to drowning themselves in the Lake. Lovely story Jonas shared when I first met him, and I pissed my pants in front of my dream girl. We, my budding dream girl and I, did not survive the incident as I fantasized.

"They did. Save one." He pointed at me. "Your mother placed you in a reed basket and pushed you down the lake, out of harm's way."

I was stunned into silence. Like most kids, I had, on occasion, considered the prospect of being adopted. But to be a product of that horrific tragedy…I just could not get my head around it. "So, you are saying I am the product of a crazed missionary and a Peruvian villager that reenacted a scene from the Bible to save my ass."

Hobo nodded.

"And you, I assume it was you, saw fit to place me with my dirt-poor parents in the middle of bum fuck nowhere South Georgia?"

"What better place to hide a priceless treasure but in a peasant's shack?"

"And my Dad, you might recall, he was a dick?"

"You judge to harshly, Ezekiel. Your Dad was a mortal man with limited resources. I placed an enormous burden on his shoulder."

"So, he knew who…what I was?"

"Mas o menos. It would have been too much of a cognitive leap for him to truly understand. Your Dad was a religious man, so we used a language he could understand."

"You told him I was the second coming of Christ?"

Hobo laughed and sipped his coffee. "Don't flatter yourself, Ezekiel. We told your parents you were a prophet. And there would be powerful evil forces searching for you to destroy you. Pretty heavy load for a high school dropout son of a sharecropper. He saw you as you were: soft and weak. Jonas had spoiled you. Your brief time with me had not helped. You were such an adorable toddler before you grew up into a cynical drunk."

"Ouch."

Hobo continued, "He knew you needed to be hard and strong. Your Dad sought, in the crude methods he knew, to toughen you up. Smith and his gang have been trying to find and kill you since you were born, Ezekiel. Your stepdad wasn't perfect, but he kept you alive. You should be thankful to him and not so bitter. You were an emotional and financial burden on your family and you put them in harm's way. I kinda see that as behavior worthy of praise. Darn near heroic, don't you think?"

I was bitter. I blamed my Dad for anything and everything that was bad in my life. From the demons that tore at my soul to striking out in little league... Dad's fault. I accused him of stealing my childhood and carried a deep resentment of him throughout my life. Mom had tried, no, Mom had begged, that I forgive him. "It's all he knew to do." She would say. I never listened to her great disappointment. And she never revealed the truth about me. "I guess this makes me the dick in this story?"

"Your word, not mine." Hobo smiled. I think he was kind of enjoying this. Hobo continued, "You know, none of this, even your death, stops Planet X from coming."

"I get that."

"And the chaos before the end will be brutal. Total anarchy. You will see the worst of your kind."

"There is worse?"

Hobo nodded.

"I got the Breakfast Rum Club, my own personal X-men." I added, under my breath, "as challenged as they may be."

He shrugged. "Their duty is over, but they will surely watch over you out of a peculiar sense of loyalty. Even so, they can't save themselves, much less you, Ezekiel, from this threat."

"I got it." I looked over at Rose and sighed. Jaws' massive head was in her lap. There was no separating those two. We both adored the little shit. Jaws was Rose's only child. This was not going to be easy, but even so, I knew what Rose would have me do. "How about Jaws?" I asked Hobo. "Can he go through with you?"

Hobo smiled broadly and slurped his coffee. "King Yudisthira demanded passage of his dog to the gatekeeper. And, like the King, I had as soon go to hell as enter a place that did not allow Jaws. I'll slim him down a few kilograms before we get to the gate."

I shrugged, vaguely remembering Hobo's dog story. "Yeah...good luck with that."

Hobo hugged me, kissed me on the cheek, and handed me his favorite coffee mug. "To remember me by."

I took a sip of the warm elixir as we pulled up to the Oar House. Hobo deftly leapt out of the boat when we were still a couple feet off the dock. He looked back at Jaws and whistled, patting his thigh. Jaws uncharacteristically hurdled the watery void to the deck, following Hobo. Rose came to my side. Without words, I knew she understood and, more importantly, agreed. A rare, solitary tear fell down her check. Jaws turned and sat, looking back at us. He howled a long, mournful note before turning and regaining Hobo's side. Hobo never looked back. I yelled after him, "Good luck with your God quest. I hope he..."

Lucy interrupted me, "She."

I finished my sentence, "...doesn't disappoint you."

"You know she is not a fairy tale, right?" Lucy asked, as I watched Hobo disappear down the dock.

"Wonder Woman?"

"That would be a comic book hero."

"Well, I am pretty damn certain Cinderella and Joan of Arc are fairy tales? Or hell, maybe I got that wrong, as well." My entire belief system about who I was and my place in the universe had been shattered.

"One out of two."

"You mean, the carriage did turn back into a pumpkin?"

Lucy ignored me. "No. God, Ezekiel, God. She is not a fairy tale. Mankind has just been looking for her in a misguided direction for a few thousand years. What you considered Gods were simply advanced civilizations. Your people mistook God for men in shiny armor, bearing trinkets, and performing magic tricks."

"And smallpox blankets."

Lucy smiled and shrugged, otherwise ignoring my sarcasm, "But she exists. You are evidence of her existence. Hobo will find her."

"Him." Linus interrupted.

"Asshole." Lucy retorted. "I need a drink."

The Breakfast Rum Club expertly tied the boat to the dock. We got off and secured supplies; rum, water, cigarettes, ganja, and crackers. There was no fuel to be had.

Ruth came up to me with rare tears in her eyes. "Good-bye, step-brother." I assessed she had been eavesdropping on my conversation with Hobo.

"Where the hell are you going?"

"I need to see my kids, my sisters, and Mom."

I nodded. We hugged. "Give them all my love." I would never see them again, perhaps never speak to them again. It was an overpowering thought. I had so many questions to ask. So many apologies to offer. Ruth walked down the dock, empty-handed, and likely with very little in her pockets. I hoped she would find a way to get home. "For what it is worth…" I yelled after her, "…tell Mom I forgive him."

Deuce whirled his hand in the air and we jumped aboard. Hambone and Tarbaby pushed the boat off the dock. Then they used long poles to stick us out of the creek into the sea. We sailed in solitude back to San Pedro, each caught up in our own dark thoughts. In spite of the resupply, no one drank or ate. The wind was not favorable. We did not reach San Pedro until mid-morning the next day.

Lima, Peru; July 2018: *THE USGS reported an earthquake with a magnitude of 8.8 just seventy-five miles off the coast of Lima. The resultant fifteen-foot tidal wave triggered considerable coastal property damage but no loss of life. The USGS praised Peru's Geophysical Institute for correctly forecasting the quake and evacuating the coastline. The Institute's leading scientist, Dr. Emma Grace, credited the forecast to an unnamed third party.*
Alongside Global News

CHAPTER SEVENTEEN

I gave Diane the keys to the condo after we grabbed our passports and packed a couple bags.

"This is yours now." I waved at the condo, a little worse for wear but, mostly intact. The bottom floor units were toast. And I expected it might be months before the power was restored. The condo's maintenance team had found fuel and had the generator running. So at least there was water and sewage. More than most of the island had going for it.

She looked confused. I explained, "Khalid...Bob bought the condo for you and your family."

"Where will you go?"

"Sue and Brad have an extra room. We will stay with them for a spell."

"To hell, you say!" yelled Sue.

"I got booze and killer weed."

Sue smiled, "To hell, you say!" Same words, different meaning.

We said good-bye to Hambone, Dianne, and extended family. The rest of us headed south, toward Lucy and Linus's place. Brad and Sue lived just a little further down the beach.

After a few minutes of dodging debris, Linus suggested we build a raft for our supplies and walk in the ocean. We stopped under the relative shade of a mangled palm with tin-roofing wedged between its trunk and a small, partially capsized fishing boat. Given the immense selection of debris, it was relatively quick work to fashion a raft for the supplies and our bags. We headed south, making good time in the shallow sea, dodging flotsam by navigating out some fifty yards or so from shore.

The midgets' house was simply gone. Not even a trace of the foundation remained. A small pile of graffiti balanced perilously in the sand marked where their bedroom once sat. Everything had washed out to sea. "How many bedrooms you have, Sue?" I asked.

"Two, and killer weed or not, I have dibs on the master." Sue noted.

"You mean we, hon?" Brad inserted, more as a question than a statement.

Sue scoffed.

"Hey, they are little. We can make room in the guest bedroom with us."

"Fuck you, fat man." Linus responded, his sense of humor further muted by the current scene.

"Or not."

Surprisingly, Sue and Brad's house was still intact. The housing previously attached to them had simply evaporated. Their townhouse was now a single-family unit, located on a little peninsula. The inside was covered with a couple inches of sand but otherwise, the house seemed undamaged. We left our supplies outside in the shade of cluster of twisted mangroves and went about making the house habitable for the evening.

Sue whistled, signaling a break after we had cleaned out the master, living area, and kitchen. Sand had lodged the guest bedroom door shut. Brad cracked the fridge and brought us all out warm beers. We sat in the mangrove shade while Sue uncharacteristically walked back inside to tackle the guest room alone.

I chugged my beer and went to help Sue. We were guests, after all. There was a large pile of sand still blocking the door and she was one small pile of girl. I got there just as she cracked the door open. There was little sand inside the room and, inexplicably, the room appeared just as they left it. An odd assortment of supplies lay neatly on the bed: Duct tape, plastic sheeting, lime, shovel, hatchet, and zip ties.

Linus walked up to the guest room door and peeked in. "Well, now," He observed. "That is a tiny bit disturbing."

I looked at Linus, "Really? You have to quit throwing me softballs."

"Fuck you, fat man."

For the first time in two days, I suddenly remembered I hadn't eaten and was pretty damned hungry. I ignored the insult and the disturbing inventory. "Let's find something to eat," I said. "We will come back to this."

Sue took the opportunity to put considerable distance between us and made herself busy searching the cabinets for food. The inventory was not impressive, but it did include Cheetos.

"Dibs on the Cheetos. Never underestimate the curative powers of Cheetos and beer." I grabbed them and another warm beer from the fridge. Suitable nourishment in hand, I made my way out to the shade of the mangroves. Linus and Lucy joined me with a half loaf of moldy bread and full jar of peanut butter.

Mid-chew, Linus asked, "What you think gives with Sue's Dexter kit?

"I dunno. May she is not over Brad laying pipe to Tarbaby's whore."

Once the sun set, it was dark. Sounds like a no brainer, but there is dark, and then there is the total absence of light. This was that. No shadows, no nothing. The only sound was the waves gently lapping on the shore. Not even a dog was barking. The heat was oppressive in the guest room. The solitary window let in precious breeze and the small room was well-heated by five warm and smelly bodies. Linus insisted on shutting the door; "Dexter kit and all." Seemed like he was being a tad paranoid.

I was fidgety but made an effort to lie still and not disturb the others. I finally abandoned all pretense of sleep, got up, and stumbled outside to sit on the porch to confront my dark thoughts in fresher air. There was no moon. The only light was from countless years past. Observing starlight proved time travel. You are witnessing an event that occurred light years before observed. With no light pollution, the sky was remarkable; every inch crowded with stars stacked upon stars. I could make out Sirius and could not help but wonder if Hobo made it home. I searched the sky for signs of Planet X but could only see Venus and Mercury. Soon, Hobo claimed, Planet X would be all too evident by the naked eye. Eventually, the Planet, seven times the size of Earth, would fill over a third of the sky. The moon, infinitely smaller, pushed the ocean around. I could only imagine the chaos the gravity of Planet X would do to our planet. I was not planning on witnessing that chaos. But then again, man plans... God laughs.

My eyes were heavy, and my thoughts turned to earthly subjects. I needed to talk to Mom, but all cell and internet service remained down. What would she say to me? She had kept a secret from me for over fifty years. And, of more immediate concern, what the hell was up with Sue? I puzzled over legitimate purpose to such an illegitimate collection of items. Eventually I dozed and was awakened by the warm light of the rising sun.

"Later dudes, we are out." Linus proclaimed, strolling passed my makeshift bed. "Too small, too weird."

"Again with the softballs. Every now and then, throw me some high heat to keep it challenging."

"Fuck you, fat man."

Linus and Lucy headed back toward where their house once stood. They carried nothing but a single bottled water each.

"Hasta luego, pendejos." Linus waved without looking back.

Brussels, European Union; August 2018: *Secretary Obama announced the United Nations contingency plan today to protect our planet in the unlikely event Planet X were to continue on a near collision course with Earth. The $25 trillion planetary dollar project will be led by the Brotherhood of Islam Caliphate. The BOI plans to construct a craft capable of intercepting and landing on Planet X, placing a nuclear bomb at its core, and exploding the planet into manageable size pieces. Critics questioned the choice of the emerging nation of BOI which has no current space program. Obama shot back at the critics reminding them the "Arabs invented Algebra <dramatic pause>. Suggesting <dramatic pause, smirk> men of color <dramatic pause> incapable of solving <dramatic pause, smirk> a problem <dramatic pause> of this nature <dramatic pause, smirk> is false, hurtful, and, most importantly, disturbingly <dramatic pause, smirk> racist."*

A BOI spokesperson responded to a reporter who had called the plan naïve and "Hollywood derivative" by schooling the reporter, "There is simply no reason to reinvent the wheel. Bruce Willis already has developed a fool-proof plan."

According to an STD poll, "One hundred and ten percent of world citizens believe the Willis plan to be fool-proof and support the BOI." A second STD poll said ninety percent of world citizens agreed anyone who disagrees is racist.

Alongside Global News

CHAPTER EIGHTEEN

We spent the days fishing and gathering coconuts and fuel for a cooking fire. Sue's home, like most on the island, had a rain water cistern that was fortunately full, thanks to the storm. We boiled our water and grilled our fish over the open flame. At night, we sat around the fire, drinking warm rum until we crawled to bed and passed out, nervously waiting for news in whatever form it might come.

After a few weeks, we made our way back to the condo to check on Diane and grab a few more of our belongings. Our path took us by The Peanuts pairing's campsite. There was no sign of them, but their considerable progress was evident. There was large, single-room shelter adjacent to the stacked stone graffiti where their home once stood. I called out for them but continued walking north after hearing no reply. It really wasn't safe to nose around someone's camp. Water and food were scarce resources and people had taken to some harsh tactics to protect what they had and take what they did not.

Before we got out of ear shot, Linus called after us. "Want a cold beer?"

I looked at Rose before turning. "That little shit said cold."

Rose smiled and nodded. I took one and, indeed, it was cold. "How the hell, man?" I asked

He smiled, "Let me show you around."

Linus had fashioned an expansive shelter with a tin roof, supported by large beams constructed of fallen palm trees for the main housing. Over the tin he had placed a thick layer of plastic bottles, flip-flops, and other flotsam. An additional thick layer of vegetation covered the debris and was held down by a large blue tarp. "Insulation," he explained. The walls were covered on all sides with mosquito-netting and a tarp that could be rolled down in inclement weather. The wood floor was about two feet off the sand. Linus had salvaged the remains of several docks. The floor, although a bit rustic in appearance, was finished in a manner suitable for a multi-million-dollar beach home. In between the supporting vertical beams hung a series of hammocks. A series of LED lights surrounded the platform affixed to the beams. A solitary naked bulb also hung from the center of the shelter. In the back corner sat a small apartment refrigerator. I walked over to pay my respects.

"Ice remains a luxury but at least we have cold beer." Linus opened the refrigerator and got us all another beer.

At each corner of the roof was a cistern elevated to the edge of the metal roof. Linus had fashioned logs to act as gutters. The cisterns were connected to a larger plastic barrel by a pipe. This cistern contained alternating layers of charcoal and sand with, what looked like, several layers of mosquito-netting at the bottom to filter the sand from the water. The remains of a rusty bicycle were attached to a pump on the cistern. A hose led to an area off to the side curtained off for a shower with salvaged wood paneling. The hose dumped into a large, clear bucket exposed to the sun.

"Lots of free building material if you don't mind digging through the debris."

"Yeah, but some of your stuff looks brand new."

"Ahhh. Let me show you." Linus motioned for us to follow. The entire campsite complex was crisscrossed with paths outlined in conch shells. The area outside the shells had been recently raked free of debris. Along the sea front, Linus had constructed a two-foot high sea wall out of salvaged planks and backfilled with Sargasso grass and covered with sand. The decomposing grass made a mild rotten egg smell. Linus was attempting to insert order in a chaotic world.

At the back of his shelter were two large shipping containers standing face to face, supported off the ground with concrete block. On the top of both shelters was a series of scavenged solar panels. The shelter closest to the living quarter had the front cut out and placed on hinges to act as an awning. It was currently open. Inside, a couple dozen batteries rescued from the numerous golf carts on the island were connected in parallel with 6-gauge cable. Off to the side was a series of windmills made from scavenged outdoor ceiling fans. These were connected to the shipping container via a pulley system. Extension cords fed into the living area. Propped up on a counter was a group of halved coconuts, connected via colorful wires.

"See." I pointed the coconuts out to Rose. "And I

thought they were shooting for a Robinson Crusoe vibe."

Lucy joined us, pointed at the coconut display and said, "No, more of a Gilligan's Island theme. Always fancied myself as a Ginger."

"Long-legged, well-bosomed redhead? Nailed it!" Not even close. "The Professor and Gilligan, I presume," I said, pointing to Deuce and Tarbaby walking out of the jungle, both carrying large armfuls of firewood.

Linus's encampment was all in all pretty impressive. The Breakfast Rum Club's appearance explained a bit of their progress. Linus continued his tour. The second shipping container was locked with an impressive looking padlock. Graffiti on the front explained the dire consequences of anyone attempting to break in. Inside explained a lot. In the front of the container was one of the Panther's mules, of which I assumed, they had retrieved from up north. Behind it, the container was packed with new construction materials, beer, and rum.

"I see you have the essentials."

Linus explained "The container was washed up on the beach when we came back.

"Whose is it?" I asked, as a stupid question. Property rights were suspended. Possession was now ten-tenths of the law.

"Clearly a gift from God. Who else packs mosquito netting, tarps, lumber, and tools with beer and rum?"

I shook my head in agreement. There really was no other logical explanation. So, like our ancestors had done for millennia, we attributed the inexplicable to God.

The tour continued. The cooking area was just north of the shelter. A triangular tarp hung in the remains of two palm trees with the opposing side fastened back to the shelter. A salvaged, rigid iron fence lay across a U-shaped, coral-lined pit. Firewood was stacked neatly behind the pit under the tarp. A semi-circle made of palm logs lay a few feet away from the fire pit. Another pit was dug just outside the cooking area. It was partially filled with empty bottles.

"Repurpose, recycle, reuse is the rule of the day." Linus chuckled. "And, for once in my lifetime, it makes sense."

Linus handed me another cold beer. "I hope you have a brewery."

Linus laughed. "No, but Lola's is intact, and the storeroom is full of beer and liquor." He tipped his beer and pointed toward Tarbaby. "And I have infinite faith Tarbaby will have the still running soon."

"No doubt." I was certain his faith in Tarbaby was well-placed. The whole necessity is the mother of invention thing. With Tarbaby, liquor was an essential.

The final stop on the tour took us about a hundred feet south. Given the prevailing wind was from the north, this made perfect sense. Screened behind a low wall made of salvaged wainscoting was a trench cut five to six feet deep in the sand. The trench was lined with tree branches to support the sand from caving in. Atop the trench sat two vertical stout palm logs low to the ground with horizontal planks forming a low but suitable deck. A polished mahogany toilet seat sat on top. A water spigot with a hose was conveniently attached to one of the logs. A bucket of sand with a small shovel was adjacent to seat. Its purpose seemed self-evident. Next to the active toilet was a second hole. The expedient source of the sand bucket and future toilet, I surmised. The walls were decorated with shells and the small, make-shift table held flowers. A mirror, framed artfully with driftwood, was affixed to the paneling. An inoperative, elaborate crystal chandelier was attached to a cable strung between the trees. The crystal caught the sunlight, creating dancing rainbow fairies on the bathroom walls. Strings of multi-colored Christmas LEDs framed the interior and twisted themselves into the supporting trees.

"Nice touch." I pointed to the flowers. Seems you thought of everything, little man...except normal-sized guests."

"Feel free to shit in the jungle, fat man."

Rose and Lucy joined us inside the small, outdoor water closet. Rose was duly impressed with the facility. There was nothing odd at all about four people standing in a small, outdoor shitter on the beach drinking cold beer.

We said our good-byes and made our way north, toward our condo, cold beers in hand.

"I could get used to this," I told Rose, proving Einstein's theory once again.

She offered a warm smile.

We made good time on the beach, as much of it had been cleared. Many stretches of the beach were now cleaner than ever. Necessity was the mother of many things. The debris had value. Even the seaweed could be used as fuel or burnt, and the ashes spread on campsites to discourage bugs.

CHAPTER NINETEEN

Rose knocked on the screen door. "That's new," I noted. Without air conditioning, the ocean breeze was the only way to stay cool. Someone had taken the time to do a really good job with adding the screen door. A large, black figure soon silhouetted the door.

"Fuck me."

"What?" Rose asked.

"Hello, Zeke," Muhammad said. "Welcome to my house." Khalid opened the screen door, making a large, sweeping motion with his well-muscled arm for us to follow him inside.

I had never gotten around to exactly telling Rose I gave Muhammad our house in exchange for the gold disc. She assumed we were just letting Hambone's family stay there as we had other options.

"You got some splaining to do," Rose seethed.

I smiled. Task at hand, I thought. Muhammad smiled and extended his hand in welcome. Dianne gave us both a warm hug. Hambone nodded from the couch. Come sit, Muhammad indicated with his hand, gesturing towards the deck. It was infinitely cooler in the breeze.

"What brought you back to our little slice of unairconditioned paradise?"

Diane came out and sat in Muhammad's lap. She was a beautiful young woman, but I expect, given Khalid's charisma and position, beautiful young women threw themselves at him as a matter of course.

"Self-evident." He opened his arms wide, gesturing toward the princess in his lap.

Diane smiled, kissed him on the cheek, and went inside. "You guys are like a weird Ozzie and Harriet."

"Who?" Muhammad asked.

"More like a weird Ozzy and Sharon," Rose observed.

"Who?'

"Lead singer for Black Sabbath."

"Oh. You mean the crazy dude that ate the vulture on stage."

Rose nodded. "Bat...close enough."

Muhammad laughed. "I could be a rock star." He continued, "You have no worries, Zeke, from the Panthers. I made it all good wit' them."

"You out?" I asked,

"That I am, man." He looked over at me and smiled. "Look at us. Khalid Muhammad and Ezekiel making peace on the mountain top."

I scoffed. He continued, "You were right. Smith never intended to go through with giving us Atlanta."

"Yeah, that silly old Constitution tends to get in the way of most would be dictators."

Rose added, "For now."

"But really. Not buying it. There has to be more for a guy like you to give up the spotlight...the power."

Muhammad pointed to the sky. "The end is coming, you know."

"So, you are a believer now? "

"Kind of out of the bag now. The whole world knows about Planet X. Hell, man, you can see it with the naked eye. The governments are putting some bullshit spin out about having it under control. 'Gotta plan if, on the outside chance, it gets too close.'"

"Yeah, I bet they do. The whole bend over kiss your ass good-bye plan."

Muhammad smiled flashing his perfect teeth and nodded yes. "They need something to help the children sleep at night. Bunch of those end of the world placard guys marching about with crazy eyes and shit. TV evangelist shouting 'repent, I told you so, mother fuckers. Send me your damn money.' Tree-huggers blaming pollution and climate change. People scared enough. Shit gonna happen. No sense terrorizing the damn kids."

"Yeah," I nodded with my brow wrinkled. "Terror is a bad thing."

Muhammad nodded in agreement, totally missing the irony.

"Kind of funny, really."

"Everyone. Man, woman, and child, on the planet gonna die and that shit funny to you, cracker?"

"Says the man on the balcony who has indeed killed innocent people."

His nose flared.

I backtracked. "Funny was a bad word choice. Not amusing. Queer." Muhammad frowned like I had insulted homosexuals. I started to point out his religion, not mine, tossed homosexuals off rooftops. But I was getting off on dangerous track.

"Peculiar…nah…inexplicable…yes, it is inexplicable."

"Inexplicable? Hell, man, I can explain death. Pop a cap in a man's ass, he bleeds out. His heart stops beating, and he stops breathing. Lights out. End of story."

"Pop a cap? You people still say that shit?"

"That is racist, cracker."

"So, its racist I comment on the use of your outdated, colloquial phrase but overlook the act of murder described. This is why the world is going to shit. Words matter more than actions. Damn participation trophy generation is a waste."

Muhammad pointed to the sky. "Slow your roll. Ain't none of that matter, Ezekiel. There is a big ass rock on a collision course with us sitting right here. That is why all this…ain't none of it matter."

I nodded and stepped off my high horse. "We are all going to die. We accept, even embrace, a well-timed death. Part of the beauty of life is its very fragility. But something about a near simultaneous death, an extinction event, is not acceptable. It is downright terrifying."

"Speaking of killer rocks…" He turned up his long empty bottle, pretending to take a swig. "Why you not go with scrawny ginger? You got the golden ticket, man, and you just say, 'nah, I'm good?' Something seriously the fuck matter with you."

Rose nodded her agreement. "You want the entire list?"

I shrugged.

"Ain't you a little bit curious what another world looks like? But wait, there's more…you get to live, brother."

"Think of it as Vegas. Awesome place to visit, but really don't want to live there."

"But you would be alive, Ezekiel. Lots of brothers

happy to be on death row instead of getting the needle. And the row ain't no five star. You just ain't making good sense."

"I would be the freak, Khalid…you know, the gay, black republican of Fox News."

Muhammad laughed.

"Nah, even worse…I would be the gay, black, republican with a back brace in South Georgia public school in the '60s."

Khalid "You mean Democrat."

I shook my head no. History was elastic. Rewritten, torn down, and forgotten to suit the fanciful whimsies of the masses.

"Since you staying, think…" he took another swig from the empty bottle "…scrawny ginger might find room through that gate for me and my girl?"

I shook my head no.

"'Cause I'm black." He smiled.

"Yeah, that card expired. Hobo, scrawny ginger, took a bunch of raw materials and Jaws back through with him."

"Raw materials?"

"Quicksilver and coal," I explained.

"Quicksilver?"

"Yeah… mercury. It is the only metal that remains liquid at room temperature. Used for superconductors."

He looked puzzled.

"What, no physics classes in your Masters of African Studies?"

He ignored the slight. "Coal? That seems like a low-tech fuel source for an advanced culture."

"Not sure what gives. I don't think it is for fuel. Hobo explained there is no carbon on their planet. They have mined mercury and coal from other planets for a, well…long ass time."

I finished my beer as we sat in relative silence. You got to know when to hold them, know when to fold them…so Charlie claims. Shut up when you have won the argument. Seems I had won. Rose got up to pack. Diane helped. They made quick work out of it. I rose to leave, saluting Khalid with an empty beer bottle.

"Ezekiel."

I turned.

"There is something else."

Had I counted my chickens hastily?

"There is someone else on the island. A woman."

"Yes."

"She works for Smith. A money launderer and internet security whizz."

"Yes." Now I was interested.

"George knows you are here and who you are. She will be coming for you."

Rose turned and looked at me; "We're bunking with Linus."

I nodded in agreement.

Washington, D.C.; November 2018: *Explosions rocked Capitol Hill in the predawn hours this morning, igniting a massive fire, and destroying much of both the Senate and House Chambers. Capitol Police have three members of the white supremacist organization, The GOP, in custody. FBI Agents are currently rounding up an undisclosed number of subversive Republicans throughout the nation. No reports yet on injuries, but it is expected to be minimal, given the hour of the terrorist attack.*

The White House has secured the nearby Mandarin Oriental Hotel to serve as both a meeting place for both Houses of Congress and to serve as temporary housing for legislators to ensure their safety. The President's own armed Antifa will serve as security.

STD Global Truth

CHAPTER TWENTY

We spent the days fishing, gathering firewood, and drinking beer in the shade. Linus' inventory of beer proved to be a great asset. Beer was paper currency; cold beer was gold. He had traded beer for a couple more full-sized refrigerators, an icemaker, a massive bag of rice, weed, a satellite dish, and a projector TV. He strung together several bedsheets to make a giant screen along the edge of jungle. After sunset, dozens of our new neighbors sat on the beach and watched TV with us. At first, we watched a lot of news. All in all, that was just depressing as hell. More and more we watched movies.

Linus traded three warm beers for one cold one. An hour of battery charging cost a six pack or a handle of Rum. Fuel remained incredibly scarce. A gallon of gas or diesel was the golden ticket and meant all you could drink. Eventually, he placed a placard out front explaining his price structure. We were getting richer by the hour. Rose pitched in with Lucy as bar keep on busy nights. Deuce and Tarbaby were security. Our security team was paid in rum and marijuana and were often horizontal by midnight.

Deuce used the mule to drag another shipping container to our beach. We needed more space to hold our riches. "You seem to have unlocked the magic success formula," I said to Linus.

He smiled, "Any endeavor that ignores the frailties of human nature is destined to fail."

I looked around at the growing complex and the abundance we had in a scarce environment.

"But you haven't failed."

"Damn straight." Linus said. "When you witness humanity from my angle, those frailties are thoroughly apparent."

Tarbaby fashioned additional bathroom accommodations for public use of more suitable height. Linus worked on upgrading the electrical grid. Rose and Lucy organized the supplies and upgraded the prices on the menu based on need. Adam and his unseen hand were at work. I drank beer and worked on my tan in the shade.

Months passed. The routine changed little. Khalid and Diane walked down and hung out frequently. Hambone spent most nights with the Breakfast Rum Club, drinking 'til they all passed out on the beach; Deuce being the only one that ever slept in a hammock. Planet X was clearly visible now in the evening sky. It would not be long before the planet's gravity started to influence our weather and the tides. We were on a coral island, pretty much at sea level. I could do the math.

The news channels were disturbing. Main stream news

blamed the problem on Republicans and their policies ignoring climate change. Al Gore, Leo DeCrappio, and all the other carbon footprint preachers were doing "I told you so" circuits in their private jets. The crowd had taken to throwing objects at the screen/bedsheets. Lucy ultimately banned all news channels by blocking them on the satellite receiver. We started watching movies exclusively. The older the better. No politics.

There was still a sense of denial among the islanders. We had all grown accustomed to living the rustic lifestyle. Actually, more than that. Rustic suited us. We became reacquainted with each other. The virtual world no longer existed. Hell, pretty much anything off this planet did not exist to us. But, one night it all changed. AMC was playing a movie from the late 1950's, "On the Beach." I should have known better.

It is a post-apocalyptic Kubrick flick about a small group of survivors in Australia and an American sub after a nuclear holocaust. A Debby downer movie, for sure. One of those train wrecks you don't want to watch but can't help yourself. Spoiler alert. Pretty much everyone commits suicide. As the show's credits start to roll, everyone started filtering out. Deuce stood up: "Don't leave, folks. Zeke has lined up a special showing of "The Day After Next.""

Nothing was the same after that night. Business remained good, but there was a sense of hopelessness, sadness, and desperation. What was just recently a happy island community of castaway drunks turned into a community of often violent, hateful drunks.

Deuce and Tarbaby were busy most nights breaking up fights. Linus called for last call at ten. We started posting watches at night. Lucy updated the price list. Ten rounds of ammo for a cold beer. Functional automatic weapons earned a lifetime drinking bracelet.

It was the night of the first murder that put an exclamation point on our lives. Deuce summarily executed the perpetrator without trial or jury in front of the drunken crowd. Major buzzkill. He buried both the deceased in the public toilet. Lucy declared the bar closed 'til further notice. We cleared the remaining drunks and sat around the fire. It was pretty light out thanks to a full moon and Planet X appearing now almost the size of the moon in the sky. You could still see and smell the blood in the sand.

"Anarchy is coming before that big ass mother gets us," Deuce said, pointing to Planet X. "I can hold it off for a while, but it won't be pretty."

We all nodded in agreement. There was nothing pretty about watching a man be choked to death and tossed into a pit full of shit and piss.

"You still want to dive The Big Ass Hole?"

We nodded.

Linus declared, "Road trip."

Deuce and Tarbaby went off into the night to secure suitable transportation and equipment.

Washington, D.C.; December 2018: *With barely a quorum, and just hours before breaking for the Winter People's Break, both legislative Houses of Congress abdicated their duties and voted unanimously to transfer all legislative power delineated in the US Constitution to the Office of the Supreme President. Armed, black clad Antifa guards applauded wildly at the passage of the bill before escorting the legislators to waiting black SUVs outside the hotel.*

A recent STD poll shows one hundred and ten percent of Americans favor a single branch of government under the leadership of the Supreme President O'Grady.

In related news, the former presidential candidate Clinton has publicly denounced all claims to the presidency stating delusion and confusion due to an overuse of "Chardonnay." Clinton has been moved to a beachfront property in Cuba for reeducation and rest.

STD Global Truth

CHAPTER TWENTY-ONE

Linus traded his compound straight up for a crewed, sixty-foot luxury cat, monikered the "Salty Swallow." The owners, a newlywed gay couple, had leased the boat from a travel service in Mexico that specialized in gay weddings. The crew fled back to Mexico before the storm. As noted, possession was currently ten-tenths of the law.

None of us were coming back to San Pedro. The large cat would provide ample room for us and terminal supplies. We spent the morning loading the cat with provisions from the shipping containers; beer, marijuana, rum, tarps, hammocks, mosquito-netting, rice, automatic weapons, and more beer. Linus dumped into the sea the leftover weapons and ammo. Muhammad loudly protested. Linus sent him home with a consolation prize of rice and beer. The cat was otherwise well-stocked as one might expect with sex

216

toys, Halloween costumes, diving and fishing gear, and a full tank of diesel. Linus drove a hard bargain and he was a wealthy man by current standards. The cat owner tossed in the dildos and costumes to seal the deal.

There was a largely uninhabited island, Half Moon Caye, just a few miles from the Hole that was familiar to us. Its lack of inhabitants was a large draw. None of us knew how the island fared in the storm, or if it even existed anymore. It was still a risk worth taking as the cat was large enough to live aboard if it came to that. And the Caribbean, at least, was lousy with uninhabited cayes.

Belize is a small, independent nation. Mexico, its closest neighbor with resources, was also hammered by the hurricane. The States were self-absorbed, trying to prevent a second civil war. Britain was an ocean away. Planet X loomed in the night sky. Paper money would never again hold value in this country. No one was coming to help. And if they did, what difference would it matter.

We filled the dingy with diesel from our stores. The cat had a wind-powered generator that could produce a couple thousand watts, but we had really gotten spoiled having cold beer and ice in our rum drinks. Strip away the luxuries in life and it is remarkable the simple things we have always taken for granted that we discover are the most important. We would not use the diesel engine, except to supplement the windmill for power generation. The fuel would likely last over a month, giving our diminutive professor time to invent and construct a power source on Half Moon Caye.

Linus and Lucy claimed the master stateroom with its king-sized bed and full-size tub. The irony did not go unnoticed but, then again, it was their boat. Rose and I shared a queen bed. The state room was luxurious compared to the previous catamaran and included a small writing table, a closet, and to my great relief, a near full-size shower with a separate shitter. I still had PTSD from the hurt locker. There were four similar staterooms and the crew quarters. It was a big cat. Deuce and Tarbaby shared a cabin. The other cabins were filled with supplies.

Slowly, the giant cat moved through the water. I think even Ruth could have swam Indian laps around the cat. We were barely making five knots, and, at this pace, it would take us three days to reach Half Moon Caye. No one complained. The boat was comfortable enough at night inside, and during the day, we lounged on the netting or under the tarp. The generator was running as needed to keep the beer cold and run the icemaker. We kept the AC and diesel engine off to conserve precious fuel. Deuce chose the shortest route, which meant abandoning the safety and calm water we would've had inside the reef. The first day, the ocean was calm and the breeze gentle and cool.

The birds followed us, silhouetted by the setting sun, flashing shades of gold and orange onto the sea. "We're stopping for the night, right?" I asked Deuce. There was no moon or Planet X visible as of yet and soon it would be pitch dark. Charts had little value after the storm and, even at five knots, hitting a random reef or sandbar would have dire consequences.

"And drift?"

"Duh...anchor, dude."

"Do me a favor, Zeke, and see if there is 1,200 feet of anchor line stowed in the anchor compartment. I might have missed it when I looked."

"You don't have to be a dick."

"And you don't have to be an idiot."

"It's my nature."

Rose and Lucy acted as our stewards. After dark, it was our tradition to switch from beer to rum. Lucy cracked open a rare bottle of dark Myers rum, instead of the local brew, to celebrate our new beginning. I thought, a short lived one and laughed silently at my inappropriate pun.

Planet X appeared on the horizon, giving us more light than that of a full moon. Linus pointed to the planet. "There is simply no one that can deny that bitch now."

"Khalid says the government has a plan."

We all laughed.

"How much time we got, Deuce?" I asked.

He looked thoughtfully up at the planet rocketing towards Earth's orbit and smiled. "Depends."

"Always...but on what?" Adult diaper jokes don't get old until you are wearing them.

"Well for one, there is shit worse than dying. I have seen it. You wait for that thing to kill you..." Deuce pointed up to the planet, "...and you will likely see it, as well."

"That's nice, Doctor K."

"Just truth-telling."

"And for two?"

"Where you stay. Close to the ocean, you going to go up front. That thing going to mess with the tides big time. Weather going to get crazy, as well. Hurricanes, tornadoes, floods. Bottom line, if you are in low ground, you got a low number."

"And three?"

"Anarchy. You got shit; food, water, medicine, hot women, beer, but ain't got shit to protect it with...you got a low number. Disaster brings out the worst and best in people. And it ain't the best that gang butt rape you, eat your dog, and screw your bitch while drinking your beer."

"Lovely imagery."

"Truth-telling, Ezekiel. You want I paint you a flowery fairy-tale?"

I knew this. We all did. Deuce was just vocalizing what we tried to deny. The anarchy was why we left San Pedro. We were well-armed, but I had seen enough zombie movies to know that eventually we would succumb to the superior numbers of the mob. Necessity is a determined mother.

We were running lights out. There had been reports of pirates patrolling the sea in search of easy marks. Deuce ordered Linus to toss his joint overboard. An environmentalist at heart, Linus flipped it expertly inside his mouth, extinguishing the flame without wasting the resource. A speed boat was silhouetted on the horizon.

"We see it. He sure as hell can see us." Deuce pointed up at the mast. "Time to break out the firepower and hide the women."

Rose looked incensed. "That ain't happening," she mumbled as she disappeared below deck.

Thanks to Linus' island arm trade enterprise, we were well-stocked with weapons; three M-4 semis, two M-16s full-automatic, one AK-47, and the piece de résistance...a browning 30-caliber machine gun. This was in addition to a dozen 9-mm side arms and two tactical 12-gauge shotguns. The crew cabin was located in the center of the boat and was filled with extra ammo and surrounded by cases of beer. The Salty Swallow would not succumb to the same fate as the Lusitania.

Rose returned with, no shock, the 30-caliber and a can of ammo. Deuce snatched the Browning from her. "Rose, that weapon weighs more than you do soaking wet." He pulled a 9-mm from his waistband and handed it to Rose. Seething, Rose expertly chambered a round.

I wasn't horribly concerned if the speedboat saw us and had ill-intent as we were well-armed and prepared for most scenarios. Deuce had proven himself a dangerous adversary to anyone that ever crossed him...or me, for that matter. He was a man that hated violence but did not shrink from it. Rose ran to violence like a moth to light. My only fear of her is that she overestimated her abilities. Sure, she was a better shot than me, but that was at a stationary target that was not shooting back. It was yet to be seen how she would react under fire. Lucy and Linus were untested, as well. Although small in stature, Linus was fierce at heart. He would die a thousand deaths before he let Lucy fall into enemy hands.

The Salty Swallow was slow and not very maneuverable. That was our great weakness. The speedboat appeared to not notice us but just as it cleared the horizon, the speedboat extinguished its running light.

"Que es no bueno," Deuce muttered. "Linus, you have the helm."

Linus dragged a case of beer under the ship's wheel to stand on. Deuce pulled a set of night vision binoculars out and followed the progress of the speedboat. I may have mentioned Linus' arm trade enterprise being successful. The boat had circled behind us and was running slow to avoid a visible wake. "How dumb does he think we are? I got one eye and can make out the bastard at the wheel."

"What is your grand plan, Captain?"

Rose said, "We blow that bitch out of the water." She had re-secured the 30-caliber.

"Give me that." Deuce shook his head. Over the next hour, the boat slowly closed the gap until it was about 400 meters back. Abruptly, the speedboat switched on a series of bright, blinding, flashing lights and accelerated toward us. The unmistaken sound of trip props churning the water could be heard even as Deuce let out a short burst from the Browning, taking out the speedboat's lights. Immediately, the speedboat slowed.

"Don't think he saw that coming." Rose took the M-16 and climbed up to the top deck. She lay prone on the deck. Deuce asked, "She a pretty good shot?"

"Better than me." He grabbed an M-16 and handed me an M-4.

"Let's join her."

It was a bit of a Mexican standoff. The speedboat kept its distance directly behind us. "What's the plan, Captain?"

Rose spoke up. "As soon as we get a shot at the outboards, we will take them out on my mark."

"What the hell, Rambo?" I asked.

"Shut up, Ezekiel. And prepare to execute on my mark."

"What? We don't get a countdown? You know, shoot on three...two, one..."

"Rookie mistake. You get a one-second window and you want to count off for three seconds? Be ready to fire, on my mark, no countdown."

None of the rifles had night scopes but Planet X had risen high in the sky, illuminating the sea like a cloudy day. The boat pulled closer, but it's aft remained hidden and, consequently, the outboards.

"Patience," Deuce advised. My arms began shaking. "Linus. Turn fifteen degrees to port, on my mark."

"Port?" Linus pointed to his right.

Deuce pointed in the opposite direction. "Why didn't you just say left?" Linus asked.

"Get ready." A moment passed. Deuce whispered, "Mark."

Linus continued straight. "Turn now, asshole." Linus scoffed, mumbled a vulgarity, and turned to the right.

The boat's outboards slowly came into view. "Ready, mark!" Rose whispered. Almost simultaneously, three shots were fired. Then a fourth, as Rose shot my target to ensure I had not missed. I had. The speedboat was dead in the water.

"You missed," Rose smiled.

"You counted down. Threw me off."

Linus let out a yell, "Wahoo. Pirates of the mother fucking Caribbean. Dead men tell no tales. What I'm talking about."

Deuce picked up the glasses to survey the speedboat. Linus had not corrected his course and we were circling back toward it. We were less than 200 yards out. Tarbaby jumped down and grabbed the wheel to correct course when we heard an all too familiar voice; "What the hell, bitches? You shot out my motors." Sue stood and waved. Deuce raised his rifle, taking center mass aim. I lowered his rifle with my arm. No one else was visible aboard.

"We ain't picking her up."

I nodded. "And we ain't blasting a hole through her skull."

"I was aiming center mass."

Sue yelled across the void, "Why y'all acting so weird, running without your lights. We thought you might be pirates."

"In a cat?"

Deuce's weapon remained aimed at Sue, "They all gonna die a slow, ugly death. I'd be doing them a solid."

I nodded. "Some truth in that, but no."

We started putting distance between us. Sue continued pleading her case, but it was becoming more and more difficult to make out what she was saying. Once we were over 300 yards out, two men clad all in black popped out over the side and started firing. The sea was relatively calm, but the shooters were inexperienced, and all the rounds traveled above our heads. A few rounds found the sail, punching .223-inch symmetrical holes in the sheet, but not causing any real damage. Deuce had grabbed the Browning and he let out a long burst just below the speedboat's water line. The shooters ducked reflexively, as though the fiber-glass would give them any cover.

"Punched a few holes for them. Should limit their suffering a bit."

"Mighty Christian of you, Deuce." He let out another long burst over their boat to keep their heads down as we passed 400 yards out. "That should do it,"

Sleep did not come, in spite of the alcohol and the drugs. The adrenaline had yet to wear off and the morning sun broke the horizon, unaware and indifferent of our planet's pending doom. The next two days were uneventful. We spotted a few boats, but none made an effort to intercept ours. Deuce taught the midgets how to sail. Tarbaby fished and drank rum with varying degrees of success. Rose and I worked on our tans in the shade of the newly-punctuated sail.

Near dark on our third day, Deuce cupped his hands around his mouth and called out, "Land, ho." His flair for nautical returned.

Our moods had continued to darken. Half Moon Caye was on the horizon. We would be there within a couple hours. Deuce climbed the mast and surveyed the island through his binoculars. He planned to circle the island before anchoring inside the shallow bay protected by the reef.

The Caye's dock was gone, no doubt a casualty of the storm. No lights or fires or any sign of life emanated from the island. "We will anchor out here tonight,"

Deuce declared. We were about a half-mile offshore. "And keep watch to daylight." We all spent the night outside, sensitive to every sound, every wisp of air, or change in pressure. If there was someone on the island, they might be desperate for supplies. Certainly, we had supplies to share, and we would. They did not know that. Desperate men are driven to desperate actions.

The next morning, Deuce fired up the engines and we circled the island under power as close as we dared. The charts would be useless, given the strength of the recent hurricane. The island appeared deserted. Still, Deuce had us anchor offshore for a second night. This night, he and Tarbaby swam ashore. The moon was down, but Planet X gave off plenty of light. They returned at sunrise, giving the all clear.

"If there is someone alive on the island, they are doing a great job at hiding." We sailed onto a beach close to a campsite Deuce had selected and began unloading. The few structures on the island had been destroyed, along with much of the vegetation. An old brick lighthouse, long since in ruins lay exposed on the southern beach near an intact foundation of an old shack. This was our campsite.

By late afternoon, we had a rudimentary shelter built. Linus went off to scavenge, hoping to find material to make drinking water and electricity. We continued improving the shelter 'til dark thirty. Linus brought back a few solar panels and a litter of kittens on the back of a functioning golf cart. He had found a garage that contained several others, along with spare parts and batteries. The roof had collapsed, and several trees blocked the remaining carts, but he was hopeful we could recover the batteries.

"What the hell?" Rose asked. She was not a cat lady.

Linus shrugged.

"Kittens. Seriously, man." Lucy was displeased, as well. The kittens were only a few weeks old and the mother was not with them. It would be difficult to keep them alive. Watching them slowly starve to death would be a disquieting analog for our current quandary.

"I got this." Linus split a coconut with a machete, soaked the milk from its core with the tail of his shirt, and hand fed the kittens.

Rose turned away, mumbling to Lucy, "Your man is just one pussy away from being the crazy cat lady."

"My man?" Lucy responded.

At dark, we started a large fire at the campsite and returned quietly to the relative safety of the cat. Deuce let the outgoing tide drift us offshore about a hundred yards. Tarbaby stayed on shore. Deuce slipped into the water and swam ashore to join him after ordering us to keep someone on watch on the cat. He was elevating this Captain thing. It was a long night and we were exhausted. We were woken by Deuce climbing on board shortly after daylight.

"Should court martial the lot of you."

"Aye, aye, Captain," I replied. "See you didn't get eaten by any cannibalistic clowns."

Over the next several weeks, we continued to make improvements to the shelter. There was less debris to harvest, but Linus channeled his inner Robinson Crusoe. Soon we had a drinking water reservoir and a modest source of electricity. Below the shelter, we stacked bricks from the old lighthouse and coral a couple feet thick with gun portals spaced evenly apart. Deuce used iron from the old lighthouse to build a crow's nest in between two of the remaining palms close by. Eventually, we knew we would have to defend our position. Deuce searched the island several times over and found no signs of life. Never the less, he strictly enforced black out rules at night, forbidding campfires after dark, or lights if we had the sides folded up. The catamaran came with a sat phone, but the owners had kept that in San Pedro. Deuce smashed the marine radio. Pirates were a thing and no sense advertising our whereabouts.

Rightly concerned about the finite supply of alcoholic beverages and lack of an available supply chain, Tarbaby was consumed with constructing a still. Linus had salvaged several large plastic barrels for cisterns and one metal one. He surrendered the metal one to Tarbaby for the still. Tarbaby found copper pipe in one of the caretakers wrecked shacks and used our campfire to forge the pipes in the cylindrical shape required. After a couple days, Tarbaby had a leaky, yet functioning, still. Linus thanked him for the desalination plant. Tarbaby scoffed and went out in search of enough coconuts to turn into mash. In order to comply with the blackout rule, Tarbaby dug a large pit, centering the still at the bottom with superfluous precision. Using the sand from the dig site, Tarbaby further cloaked the bottom two-thirds of the still. The contraption, all in all, looked pretty ominous, and I appreciated the extra layer of protection the still's placement and camouflage would provide on the inevitable explosion. To ward off evil spirits and the implausible revenuer, Tarbaby hung the colorful dildos from the Salty Swallow like deviant wind chimes along the perimeter of the still. It would certainly give any would be intruder pause.

The heavy-lifting complete, we returned to our routine of early morning beach scavenging, which proved fruitful, keeping Tarbaby in fresh coconuts and fuel for the still and Linus in construction supplies. Our collection of left-footed sandals was also impressive. Linus had yet to find a suitable purpose for the orphan sandals, yet insisted we collect and store them. We rotated, completing the minimal household chores, but for the days the shitter needed repositioning. No one person should shoulder that duty.

After chores, it was beer drinking and fishing by day and rum drinking by night, listening to the AM radio Linus recovered off the cat. We overlook the Earth is round. Standing on the beach, we could only see about three miles off the horizon on a perfectly clear day. Most radio signals, consequently, shot off into outer space, advertising our whereabouts and folly to the universe. The atmosphere bounces a portion of the signals back to Earth, according to the frequency, some better than others. Unfortunately, due to airwave clutter, most of the signals get garbled. In the early 1940's, the FCC had the foresight to predict the need for a reliable, worldwide mass communication method. The FCC worked with other countries to clear certain frequencies. These Clear Channel stations, on a good night, could be heard for tens of thousands of miles away.

"Only ninety-nine murders committed in Chicago over the weekend," the WGN radio announcer proudly reported. "This is the first weekend this year the city has experienced less than triple-digit homicides."

Rose scoffed. "Yeah, I think Chicagoans regularly call that kind of body count Tuesday. And that was even before the killer planet showed itself."

The shadows from the trees grew long as the sky bloomed shades of pink. The breeze stiffened gently, rocking the hammocks.

"Where is everyone?" Rose asked, sipping on a rum and mango drink. It was almost dusk and by now our crew was normally back at our camp.

I took another long pull of White Widow from Linus' secret stash. "I dunno," I answered, exhaling. "Deuce went to move the Swallow to deeper water earlier."

Over the last few days, the sea had receded from the island by some one hundred meters, exposing more of the reef, along with several wrecks. "Should have been back by now."

Rose got up from the hammock and lowered the seaward canvas, blocking our light from escaping. She tuned the radio station until she found music. The news was just too damn depressing and the talking pundits' wild speculation was infuriating.

"Bagpipe music?" I asked. "Didn't know you were a fan."

"Not coming from the radio."

Wearing a plaid kilt, Deuce drew the canvas aside and somberly marched into the shelter, playing a haunting version of Danny Boy on the pipes. Rose snapped the radio off.

"What the hell, man?" I asked, struggling to sit upright in the hammock.

Deuce, without pausing from his recital, replied, "Some gifts are better left unwrapped, some doors unopened, some paths untraveled."

Lucy stumbled inside on stilts, wearing a blond wig and bright red lipstick. She kissed Rose full on the lips, placing a red wig onto Rose's head. Painted in clown face, complete with bright red nose, Linus rode a unicycle into the room, making practiced laps around its perimeter. A little girl with orange curls asked me for a light. A stone Cherub hovered inches from my face and raised a chubby finger to his lips. Bagpipes sang. The pigeon spoke. The train rumbled. It began to snow. I lost consciousness.

∞∞∞∞∞

I turned to Rose lying beside me on the beach. "Where do you suppose the right feet are?" Strange, the things that seem important after a few beers and a purposely confined brain.

"What the hell are you talking about, Zeke?" Rose did not deign to lift the hat from her face to reply.

"You know. Every day we find dozens of flip-flops. We must have a thousand. And every one of them is a left-footed shoe. Doesn't that seem peculiar?"

From beneath the hat, a bored voice responded, "Very."

Rose was exceptionally crotchety. We had listened to the Cubs sweep the Yankee's in the Series the afternoon before. Never you mind the riot afterward that killed a couple thousand. The evening was a bit hazy. I thought, silently to myself, trying to occupy my brain by deciphering the mystery of the left shoe. But nothing came to mind. Slowly, despite my efforts, the darkness crept in.

"Rose?"

"Yes, Zeke."

"I am ready to dive the Hole."

Rose pulled her hat off, setting it beside her in the sand. She propped up on her elbows and faced me while a rare, solitary tear gently drifting down her cheek.

Paris, France; December 2018: *The Italian peninsula was rocked yesterday by a series of earthquakes and volcanic eruptions. Eye witness reports state the city of Florence was swallowed by the Earth in a fiery explosion. No one is independently reporting from anywhere inside Tuscany to confirm the story, but the USGS reported an earthquake centered in the old city of Florence registered a shocking 9.1 on their scale. Further south, concurrent with the earthquake, Mt. Vesuvius erupted. The lava flow is currently at the outskirts of Pompeii and is threatening to reach Naples.*
STD Global Truth

CHAPTER TWENTY-TWO

We set sail early the next morning for the Big Ass Blue Hole. We never vocalized our intentions, but I think we both understood. Even Deuce suspected our intent and approved. The midgets, they were clueless. Linus spent his days making improvements to the shelter and his nights making plans to improve the shelter. It was his coping mechanism and he was blind to anything else around him. Lucy swore off clothing. In spite of her diminutive stature, without the benefit of razors, she was not mistaken as a prepubescent girl. She decorated her hair with tropical flowers. Lucy recruited Tarbaby to garnish her body with island tats, crudely drawn with a sewing needle and colored with dye produced from a seashell. Rum consumption steadied his hand and her body was soon covered with elaborate tattoos depicting the glyphs from the cenote.

There is blue, like in a Crayola box, then there is blue, like in the Caribbean; well, several shades of blue, that are outside description. One must witness the color to understand its beauty. The indescribable blues were punctuated with white as the wind was brisk and we made good time out to The Hole. We spoke little but held each other tight, much more than we had in some time. I missed this.

Deuce sailed through a shallow cut in The Hole and anchored off a sandy shelf, just inside the reef. The water on the inside is dark blue in contrast with the light blue hues on the outside. There is little color to the actual water. The color we sense is a result of the nature and angle of light in the sky, reflecting off the sea bottom. The Hole was over 300-feet deep; consequently, little light reflected off its bottom. Bottle-nosed dolphins circled the boat. The dolphins jumped and frolicked, as if welcoming us to their world.

"First time for everything," I said, as I geared up for the dive. The water was warm at the surface, but I pulled on a short wetsuit to protect from the cooler water at depth. No reason to be uncomfortable. Lucy and Linus were joining us. They were inexperienced divers, but there was little to lose at this point, and Deuce did not object, other than to warn the Peanuts pairing not to follow us too deep. Deuce and Tarbaby were staying on board to protect the boat. Pirates were a thing.

I turned to Lucy and Linus as they waddled to the swim platform on the Swallow. Dive gear is awkward enough for full-sized humans above water and they were not full-sized humans. Lucy smiled. Linus flipped me off, then gestured oddly with his hands bent at right angles. It was an oddly familiar tic not previously demonstrated by Linus.

Linus pointed to Lucy, "Don't forget your contacts."

"You know, dude, I have known you for spell. It's about time you dropped the bullshit and tell me your real names. Not buying into the coincidental Peanuts pairing monikers."

Linus grinned, reaching his hand out to shake; "Hi, I am Sam." He turned to Lucy, "And this is my big sister, Lucy."

"Wait a minute..." It was a disconcerting deja vu moment for an assortment of reasons. I was too ruffled to even comment on the irony of "big" as an adjective describing Lucy. "You are not my old neighbors' kids... are you?"

"You really aren't very good at math."

"You married your sister?" I knew they were freaks, but this was a bridge too far and I did suck at calendar math...algebra...geometry...calculus...trig...okay,   I sucked at math.

Lucy scowled. "Gross. You are one bowl full of stupid. Ain't no wee penis dude gonna tap this fine ass." She attempted to turn and demonstrate the fineness of her ass. Given the bulky dive gear, the effort was an epic fail.

"That is your line? The size of your brother's penis, not the familial relationship?" I asked.

Without further explanation, Lucy and Sam giant-stepped into the ocean. Shaking our heads in confusion, Rose and I followed, making our descent to about eighty feet. Diving the Blue Hole is a bucket list dive for almost any diver on the planet, but like having sex for the first time, isn't all that you dreamed of. It was a hole. No pun intended. The cave structure was impressive, along with its stalactites, but the Hole's walls were devoid of the color one comes to expect on a Caribbean dive.

We motioned for Linus and Lucy to surface after about twenty minutes, in part for their safety, but mostly, we just wanted the Hole to ourselves. Lucy's tattooed body was covered in giant goose mountains. She had forgone a wetsuit, remaining loyal to the nudist creed. We dove deeper. My depth gauge registered 130 feet. I still had a thousand pounds of air. Rose, I knew, a much more efficient diver, would have had more. We stayed in the main Hole with blue sky above us, not venturing far into any of the hundreds of caverns within. Sharks, hammerheads, bulls, blacktips, and reef, circled on our perimeter, above and below us. Majestic rays flew beneath us, disturbing huge schools of blue tangs, jacks, and snappers. A massive Jewfish hovered close to the wall.

We swam around aimlessly. We were much too deep for our normal atmospheric air mixture, having drifted to 140 feet and were both a little bit giddy from the onslaught of nitrogen narcosis or, as Cousteau called it, "the rapture of the deep. Not an unpleasant sensation, but a dangerous condition. I squinted to make out my pressure gauge. It registered 500 pounds which was close to the safety limit for a dive this deep. We would need a ten minute or so safety stop on our ascent to avoid a serious case of the bends. And, with no access to a decompression chamber, a painful death. I motioned for Rose to ascend. She took out her regulator and smiled, shaking her head no. I took my mouthpiece out and kissed Rose softly on the lips. It was delightful.

We swam deeper.

Je suis

Acknowledgements

I love Florida. Sandy beaches, blue skies, warm weather, afternoon thunderstorms, tree-ripened citrus fruit, and a seemingly infinite supply of bat-shit crazy people. I am not the most imaginative writer; I just take notes and listen to the voices in my neighbors' heads. Thank you, my fellow Floridians, for the boundless supply of quirky characters and story ideas.

Writing a novel, even a bad one, is soul-sucking. No one deserves more credit for this work than my smoking hot wife Jennifer (self-high-five) for both her patience with a very crotchety old man and for her editing skills.

Everyone used to thank God. Unfortunately, He/She/It has fallen out of favor in the last decade or so with the in-crowd. For me, I must acknowledge God in completing this work and inspiration in writing this and the other Ezekiel novels. I say fuck a lot and challenge the traditional view of God. Doesn't mean I am not a believer. I am...just a warped one.

In addition to The Good Book (the Bible), the writings of Mark Dewayne Combs, *End the Beginning*, was helpful in researching alternate creation stories and the hopefully fictional Planet X. And thanks to Joshua Mark, Dogs in the Ancient World, for the story of King Yudisthira and his dog.

Visit my web page at DMaloneMcMillan.com for links to Ezekiel a Novel and Belizean Pedicure.

CPSIA information can be obtained
at www.ICGtesting.com
Printed in the USA
LVOW13s0406160318

570073LV00005B/9/P